KINDRED SPIRITS

FAMILY BY CHOICE

BLOOD RELATIONS
BROTHERS IN ARMS
KINDRED SPIRITS

PRAISE FOR THE *FAMILY BY CHOICE* SERIES

"The writing was great, and the characterization, especially of Alex, was spot on. It's been a long time since I encountered a character who I liked so much. (...) I loved this. If you like dark fiction, supernatural, and a good dose of action, then try out this series. You will not be disappointed."

I Heart Reading book reviews

"Alex is a great character. He's complicated, and has many different layers. The story was good, and the writing was spot on the entire time. I was drawn into this book from the first page, and enjoyed it very much."

Forever Book Lover reviews

"Caroline Fréchette is one of my favourite fantasy writers in the National Capital Region. (...) If you are a fan of fantasy I would definitely encourage you to pick up both of these books. The story has a great pace and the strong writing makes them an easy read. As well, Alex Winters is a very interesting character."

Alejandro Bustos, *Apartment 613*

"While I find this series to be a quick read, it is also an incredibly good read. (...) I highly recommend it for your summer reading list."

Geeky Godmother reviews

KINDRED SPIRITS

A FAMILY BY CHOICE NOVEL

BY CAROLINE FRECHETTE

Renaissance

Cover art by Franck Formantin.
Cover design by Caroline Fréchette.
Interior design by Natasha Brousseau.

Edited by Kyle Bentley, Marjolaine Lafrenière, Sanja Valentina Cimesa, and L.P. Vallée.

Legal deposit, Library and Archives Canada, October 2014.

ISBN 978-0-9936575-4-2

1. Winters, Alex (fictitious character) – Fiction. 2. Superpowers – Fiction. 3. Mafia – Fiction. I. Title. II. Family by Choice (Series).

Renaissance Press

http://renaissancebookpress.com

info@renaissancebookpress.com

To Joelle and Manue –

this one wouldn't be the same without
the adventure we shared.

I sigh and pull the pillow from over my head. It's the third time they've called me in under ten minutes. Whoever it is, looks like they're not going to give up. I reach for the cell on my night table, expecting to see one of the idiots that work for me on the caller ID, and I sit up, my heart jumping to my throat, when I see it's Luke. He's never called me this late since I've known him, not once.

"Hello?"

"Alex? It's Luke."

"I know. What's wrong?"

"It's Naomi. She's disappeared."

I frown at this, but nevertheless, I relax a bit. Naomi can take care of herself, and she's been known to go out all night. Since she's more a protector for the kids than one of the patrons of Luke's house, she can ignore the curfew.

"Are you sure? Maybe she just went out."

"I'm sure. She did go out. With Liz. Now Liz is back, and she says Naomi's been taken."

"Taken? What do you mean?"

There's silence for a little while.

"Well... I think it's your kind of business, and we probably shouldn't talk about it over the phone. Do you think...?"

"Yeah, I'm on my way."

I hang up and pick up the suit I was wearing today, putting it back on. I glance at the clock as I button my shirt. Looks like I won't be getting any sleep tonight, but if someone's made off with Naomi, this is serious, and it can't wait. It's possible I'm paranoid, but I give Russell a call just to make sure. He doesn't answer, which does nothing to make me feel better. I decide not to bother with a waistcoat and tie, and call Jimmy as I finish getting dressed. Jimmy's phone rings three times before he picks up, and, when he does, I hear the Sex Pistols roaring in my ear so loud I have to pull the phone away from my head. I hear some shouting over the music, and, when it's finally turned down, I place the phone back against my ear.

"Jimmy?"

"Hey, boss. What's up? It's pretty late."

"Luke just called me. Someone's taken Naomi."

"Let me guess. You need a ride?"

"Yeah. How soon can you be here?"

"Well, I was kind of in the middle of something."

"It's important."

He sighs audibly. What is up with him? He doesn't usually question me when I ask him for something, and he certainly isn't in the habit of giving me attitude.

"Fine. I'll be there in half an hour."

"See you then."

I hang up as I head out to the hall. The light's still on; looks like Tom can't sleep again. I find him in the kitchen, sitting at the table, his feet on the chair so that he's hugging his legs and leaning his head on his knees, staring at a bowl of Froot Loops. My stomach rumbles, and cereal suddenly sounds great, so I get a bowl and open the fridge door to get the milk. I stare for a few seconds, looking for the carton, but it's not in there.

"It's next to the TV."

I look up at Tom, blinking, and see the milk carton next to the TV, in the living room. I let out a sigh, trying not to sound too annoyed.

"I thought we agreed you weren't gonna do that anymore."

He looks up from his cereal, staring at me absently, like I interrupted an important train of thought.

"Huh?"

"Reading my thoughts."

"Oh. That. Sorry. Sometimes, it's hard to tell the difference."

I sit in front of him, and pour myself a bowl of Froot Loops. He hasn't touched his, and the cereal is so soaked it's twice its original size, and what milk remains has turned that funny orange-pink color. He's still just staring at it, though. As I start eating, I notice he hasn't even got a spoon.

"You know, those are for eating."

He shrugs.

"I wasn't hungry."

"Then why the cereal?"

"I just like to watch the milk color."

"Can't sleep again?"

Tom never sleeps much. At least, it's been that way since he moved in with me. Can't really say I blame him; he'd spent the last five years of his life under heavy sedation, so I figure he's sick of sleep now. He's still way too thin, but at least his cheeks aren't caved in, and he can walk on his own now.

He shakes his head.

"No. I don't like my room. I think I should have the small one back. Your old room won't let me sleep."

"Why not?"

"It's full of your old memories. They're kind of like rotten food you forgot under your bed, you know? You get used to the smell, but once in a while it creeps up on you, and then it makes you sick all over again."

"So, what, my memories stink?"

"Well, if they didn't, why'd you move to the guest room?"

I stare at my cereal. About a month after he moved in, I gave him my old room and moved into the guest room. It just made more sense that way; I couldn't bring myself to sleep in the bed I shared with Lori anymore, and I couldn't really sleep in the living room forever.

"I didn't. They don't. I just... didn't like the bed anymore."

"Why don't you change it? I mean, I've seen the money you bring in, you can afford it."

I glare at my cereal. I'm suddenly not that hungry anymore.

"I haven't gotten around to it."

He raises his eyebrows at me.

"Like you haven't gotten around to the room at the end of the hall? I mean, there's a whole room there that we could be using."

I take a deep breath. I don't like getting mad around Tom. At the same time, he should know not to push my buttons. I know that he knows what I'm thinking, so he knows what that room means to me. It's all full of Nicolas's stuff. It's been over a year, and I haven't been able to bring myself to walk in there. How could he even suggest I get rid of that stuff?

I put my spoon down and stand. Tom sighs, but he doesn't look at me.

"I'm sorry. It's just... I know you don't wanna talk about it, but it's always on your mind, so I can't help thinking about it too, and I think maybe it would help..."

I start walking away. The last thing I need is a therapy session from a sixteen-year-old kid.

"I gotta go."

He says something else, but I can't hear him. I don't care how long I'll have to wait outside. I can't be in here anymore.

MAY 17TH, 1:22 AM

I check my cell phone, and sigh. He's taking longer than he should. He's probably at Erik's house again.
I don't understand what he does there all the time. I start
the next track, putting the ear bud back in my ear. Jimmy
has been taking longer and longer to arrive, so I've started
to learn Italian to kill time. I'm not great yet, but I get
by, and it makes Mister Lupino happy.

He finally pulls over and steps out of the car. I see him
get out his keys, but I slip in the passenger seat. He rolls
his eyes, sits back down on the driver's side, and shakes
his head.

"Come on, man. You gotta get more practice, or you're
gonna fail your test. Again. It's like three times now."

"It's only twice. And if you didn't make me do it with
a standard, I would have passed. I'm not in the mood.
Can't you just shut up and drive?"

He sighs, but starts the car anyway.

7

"Look, as long as I'm the taxi driver here, I get to tell you when you're being lazy."

I shake my head. Things have been a bit tense between Jimmy and me lately. Lupino's about to retire, and I still haven't decided whether I'm continuing this business or not. He knows I'm still debating, and he just doesn't understand what's making me hesitate. He was born to do this. Not me.

We're quiet until we get to the house. It looks good now: Luke's put up a sign and everything. He registered it as an official charity a while back, and he's been getting decent funding, pulling more kids off the streets, getting them into rehab, and all that.

Jimmy doesn't turn off the motor; he just leans across to speak to me through the open door.

"I'm gonna go get a beer while you're here, ok? Just give me a call when you're done."

I nod, and he drives away. He's not comfortable going inside the house, even though he left the brothel years ago. It doesn't look the same at all anymore: Luke's completely renovated everything because of the fire.

The only light on is in Luke's office, on the third floor, so I make my way there. I have to walk past my old room, right next to his door, and I'm glad the door's closed. I have to admit I've avoided coming back here, too.

Luke is sitting at his desk, and, when I walk in, my legs turn to jelly because, for a second, I think I'm seeing a ghost. The girl sitting in front of him has the same slumped posture, the same bleach-blonde hair, but when she turns around to look at me, I can see it's only Liz with a stupid new hairdo, not Lori. It's never Lori. It won't ever be again. I let out a deep sigh and clear my throat, in part because I have to be assertive and I can't do that if I'm emotional, but also because I'm about to bite her head off for looking like Lori, and she doesn't deserve that. She doesn't look like she could handle it, either; her eyes are red, and her mascara is running.

I nod at them. "All right. What's going on?"

Liz looks at Luke, and he nods at her to start speaking.

"Well, Naomi and me, we went, like, clubbing, right? So anyway, she meets these guys, and they're all, like, into her, except they look, like, real fishy, right? They ask her to come out back with them, and she's like, yeah, sure, and I tell her they look like, weird, and she says, I can handle myself, so anyway, I let her go, and I follow her, and when they get outside, they go in, like, this alley, right? And then they just turn on her and attack her, and she does, like, her screaming thing, except, like, it doesn't work, and they just take her. They just took her, Alex! In a car! And they drove off!"

She stares at me, and I lift a finger to stop her if she's about to start talking again. I have to take a minute to sort this all out, and to separate all the words she just squeezed into those 10 seconds before asking an intelligible question.

"So, when you say she did her 'screaming thing,' you mean she tried using her power?"

Naomi is special, just like me, which is why I know she can handle herself. Where I can make fire just by thinking about it, she has this supersonic scream thing that can break glass, even knock out some people. Liz nods emphatically.

"Yeah! Except, it didn't work! Like, not even on me!"

"Hmm."

I take the empty seat next to her, and I sigh. If she wasn't able to use her power, then that means she was up against supers, people sent specifically to get her, probably a null.

I take out my phone and try calling Russell again. Still no answer. This time, I'm really worried. I dial Julie's number. It rings, and rings, and rings so long I'm sure I'm going to get voice mail, but the voice that finally answers sounds way too tired to be recorded.

"What is it?"

"Julie? It's Alex."

"I don't care if you're the friggin' Pope. It's the middle of the night. I was having a real good dream about having sex with Colin Farrell, and you interrupted."

For a moment, I just sit there with my mouth hanging open. That was way too much information.

"It's important. And kinda urgent."

"Then make it quick."

"Naomi's missing."

"And you want me to what, find her? Bring her back? Whatever it is, it'll wait until morning."

"No. Well. The point is... I think she was specifically targeted."

"So?"

"By supers. To be more precise, a null."

There's silence at the other end of the line, and for those few seconds, I savor the moment. She's so unpredictable, it's not often I have the upper hand in our conversations.

"Are you sure?"

"Yeah. Almost completely sure."

"Have you called Russell?"

"I have. He's not picking up."

She curses, and there's some rustling on the other end of the line.

"Fine. Do you have a safe place to go?"

I try to think.

"Not at this hour, but I do live with Tom. I'm pretty sure I can get advance notice if things are about to move."

"Fine. I'm going to meet you at your place tomorrow morning. For now, I want you to call me if there is any change, anything at all, all right?"

"Sure. Same to you."

I hang up and look at Luke. He frowns, so I know I don't look as neutral as I think I do, and he nods at Liz.

"Go get some sleep. I have to talk to Alex."

She looks at me, all wide-eyed and panicked.

"But what about Naomi?"

I sigh. "I'm looking into it. Don't worry, I'll do everything in my power. Now do as Luke says."

She nods, looking a bit haunted, and I can't look at her as she walks away. I hate to see that kind of look on girls. Luke watches her go, and then turns a serious face on me, watching me over the rim of his glasses.

"What's going on?"

I sigh. I feel so tired, suddenly, and I know it has nothing to do with the late hour.

"You remember GenEx, that organization that did experiments on people with super powers, the place where I was held when I disappeared?"

He nods, gravely. "You think this is them?"

"It sure looks that way. At least, if it is, they're not going to come after you guys. Naomi was the only one of interest here."

Luke lets out a deep breath, sounding every bit as tired as I feel.

"Be careful, Alex. I don't like that you get into situations like this."

I stand. Luke is one of the only people in this world to have seen me show weakness, except maybe Lori, but that doesn't mean I like him to think I'm helpless. I pick up the phone, and answer him as I dial Jimmy's cell phone, making it clear that the discussion is over.

"I don't either. But there's not much I can do about it if they won't leave me alone."

Nicolas grabs my ponytail again, yanking it. It doesn't even hurt a bit; I guess it's the happy smile and gurgling that make it painless. I bring him over to the kitchen, where Lori is taking lasagna out of the oven. It smells delicious, and she looks great, wearing only a nightshirt that reaches the middle of her thighs. It should embarrass me that she's dressed like that in front of Mister Lupino but for some reason, it doesn't. It must be because she looks so happy. Besides, he doesn't seem bothered. I hand him Nicolas and sit down in front of him, across the table. He says a couple things in Italian to my son, and then he smiles at me.

"They're here."

I frown a bit at him. What he's saying doesn't make any sense.

"What?"

Lori serves us each a plate of lasagna, putting them down on the table. She runs her hand through my hair,

14

leaning her hip on my arm. She bends over to kiss my forehead.

"Wake up, Alex. They're here."

I frown at her. Who are they talking about? What's going on here? When I look back at Mister Lupino, I see Tom standing behind him, and everything falls into place. Nicolas, Lori and Lupino disappear, and, for a short moment, it hurts to not see them, because I know that at least two of them are gone forever. But now that Tom's here, I know that something's wrong, and what they've been saying finally makes sense.

They're here. I gotta wake up.

I sit up and throw my blankets aside, almost falling flat on my face in my effort to get out of bed running. I scramble to the hall, and I'm halfway to Nicolas' room when I remember that he's not there, and he doesn't need me to rescue him. I thought I'd get used to it after all this time, but I guess I just can't. I wonder if I ever will.

Tom's standing in the doorway to the master bedroom, his eyes wide. He sees he finally has my attention, and whispers.

"They're right outside, in the hall! They have a null with them, but he's not strong enough to block me."

GenEx. They're here already. I thought I would have more time. I was right to think Tom would feel them coming, but I guess I should have given some thought to what I would actually do when they got here. I turn around

15

to give Tom some instructions, to figure out what to do, when suddenly, my front door literally explodes. I jump on Tom to cover him from the blast, and as I do, something hits me in the back of the head.

MAY 17TH, 7:06 AM

"Hey! Wake up! You all right?"

Someone is shaking me awake. I look around when I come to, but the first thing I see, the only thing, is my condo up in flames. I stand as quickly as I can manage, which feels both too fast and really slow and sluggish at the same time. I hold out my hands, extinguishing the fire with my mind. I don't really need the gesture, but I find it helps me concentrate when I'm not angry enough. There must be more fire than I thought, because it takes a hell of a lot out of me, and I'm almost falling back down by the time I'm done. Someone catches me again. This time, I take the time to look at him, because he's taller than me, so it can't be Tom.

It's some older guy I don't know. Wait. I do know him. He's my neighbor from across the hall. What the hell is he doing here?

"What are you doing here, man? Where's Tom?"

"Well, there was... an explosion. It took out my front door. And Tom, that's your friend, right? The one who lives with you? I think he went downstairs, with some girl."

I blink, and then I run out into the hall. I stumble a bit, but it doesn't matter; I can't slow down. They can't have Tom. If they have him, we're all dead.

I make it to the stairs before I trip and fall flat on my face, and then I have to seriously reconsider this idea. I'm not gonna be much use if I break my neck. I sit at the top of the flight of stairs, my head in my hands, and my neighbor is suddenly there again. I squint at him. I seem to remember something about him being a lawyer. Possibly a prosecutor, actually. Wasn't I supposed to stay away from him?

"Hey! Are you all right? Maybe you should take a break! You don't look too good. And... you're in your underwear."

I look down at myself. Looks like he's right. I sigh. I seem to get crappier at helping people as I get older. What's wrong with me? I get up and head over to my condo. I walk into my room, grab the suit I wore yesterday, and put it on as quick as I can, again, neglecting the waistcoat and tie, going for expediency rather than style. While I'm dressing, my phone rings again, and I see that it's Julie's number on the caller ID, so I pick up.

"Yeah?"

"Oh, you're all right. Good. I'm downstairs with Tom. They're gone, but they're gonna be back. Hurry up."

18

"Fine. I'll grab a few things and be down."

"I'd make it quick if I were you. I can hear sirens, so the fire department's on its way."

I curse as I hang up the phone. Fire department means cops, and that means uncomfortable questions, and an excuse for them to interrogate me, which I really don't need. I know I'm cited in at least a half a dozen case files, and, now that I'm over eighteen, I could get in serious trouble over all of this.

I grab my phone, my keys, and my smokes, and I'm about to run outside, when I stop and look at the door to Nicolas' room. I'm not going to be back here for a while, and who knows what they're gonna touch that I don't want them to?

I step into the room quietly. It's is exactly the way I left it, save for the thin coating of dust that now covers everything. Seeing it again brings back this rush of feeling, like the first time I came home without him, the sudden realization of a fact I've known for over a year now.

I reach into his crib and grab his bunny. That was the first thing he ever held in his arms. I'm starting to hear the sirens myself, so it pulls me out of my thoughts as I stuff the bunny into my coat. I take a deep breath; this isn't the time for this. I manage to drag myself out the door and kick my brain back into functioning mode.

My neighbor blocks my way as I get to the hall. I start, and take a step back. I didn't think much of him being there at first, just a neighbor being, well, neighborly, but now, he's starting to seriously bug the crap out of me.

"What do you want?"

"I need to talk to you. It's important."

"Well, tough. I'm kind of in a hurry, in case you haven't noticed."

I try to duck past him, but he blocks my way again.

"Look, I saw what you did. The men who caused this explosion... I think they're after me too. Please, can we talk?"

I sigh, and look him up and down. He doesn't seem like much. Maybe he's just paranoid. I mean, his home did blow up too. Could be coincidence. Then again, maybe not.

"Fine. Gimme your number, I'll try and call you. But right now, I really gotta go."

He seems relieved, and hands me a business card. I pocket it without looking at it, and head to the staircase.

As soon as I've reached the bottom of the stairs, I try to make myself scarce, which is hard because there's a crowd of onlookers, some of whom are just staring at me. I look around, and then a hand grabs my upper arm and I feel myself being pulled apart in all sorts of different directions. The next thing I know, I'm sitting in the passenger's side of Julie's car, and she's in the driver's seat, and I feel like I'm gonna puke. It's a good thing I didn't have a chance to eat breakfast yet. I still have to put my head between my knees not to lose what little there is in my stomach right now.

"Ugh. Don't do that."

She shrugs. "I had no choice. The cops were right around the corner, and you look wicked conspicuous with all that soot on your face."

I take deep breaths to banish the nausea. One of the back doors opens, and I can see Tom coming in, the conventional way, to sit on the back seat. I looked up too quickly and I gag for a few seconds before placing my head between my knees again. I'm not sure, but I think I can hear Julie snigger. I say nothing, though, 'cause I'm as likely to puke on her as I am to win my point. She starts the car.

"So, where to?"

I sigh, sit up, and try to think and keep my stomach contents down at the same time, which is every bit as hard as it sounds. Let's see. I need a place that has no direct link to Julie, or me. Someone that has enough room to hide us, and isn't one of my closest friends. I try to refrain from groaning when I know I have just the place; it's not an idea that's particularly pleasing, but it's good. I pick up my cell phone to give him a call, and as I dial, I glance at Julie.

"Do you know how to get to Old Town? I think I have an idea."

MAY 17ᵀᴴ, 9:04 AM

Jimmy's car is in the driveway when we park at Erik's place, and I find myself staring at it. Is he sleeping over here every day now? I consider giving him a call, since I couldn't reach Erik, but I decide against it. We're already here, anyway. Might as well knock. Tom and Julie get out of the car, and look at the house suspiciously. I think Julie even seems grossed out, and I can't really blame her. As usual, the landscaping hasn't been done in ages, everything is growing wild, and the house is in serious need of a new coat of paint, if there ever was one to begin with; the wood finish is so bare and damaged it's peeling off the frame. The windows are all painted black, like they always were.

"Who the hell do you know that lives here, anyway?"

I look at the house. How do I begin to explain Erik?

"It's complicated. He's a friend of Jimmy's."

I look at Jimmy's car again. I'm having doubts. What if I'm interrupting something I really don't want to walk in on? I shake my head. I'm just imagining things. Aren't I?

I walk to the front door. There's no doorbell I can see, only what looks like a hole covered in ancient duct tape, so I give the door a hard knock, then light a cigarette. Whatever it is they do all night, it's likely that neither of them is up. Jimmy doesn't believe in starting the day before noon, and Erik, well, he's a vampire. I knock again halfway through my smoke. Tom doesn't say anything, staring at the ground and folding his arms over his chest, but Julie looks up.

"Are you sure there's someone in there? I mean, I know some hoboes that wouldn't want to live here."

"Yeah, I'm sure. They're probably just still asleep."

I knock again, but there's still no answer. I decide to try the door, and, unsurprisingly, it's not locked. I suppose that people like Erik and Jimmy don't have a lot to fear.

I walk in, gesturing for Julie and Tom to follow me. She does, looking around at the house and making a face at the horrendous 70s decor, but Tom hesitates a bit. Does he look pale?

"You ok?"

He nods. His clothes are too big, because he's so thin, and it makes him look even sicker. He looks around nervously.

"Your friend Jimmy's here. And your other friend, too."

I look inside again. He's probably hearing them think. I guess it can't be easy to know what goes on inside the head of guys like these.

I give him a smile and punch his arm lightly. "Hey, come on, don't worry about it, ok? They're weird, but they're ok. We're people they like, they won't hurt us."

He looks at me sideways. "You're people they like. We're just people you like. Trust me. To them, there's a difference."

I don't really know what to say to that, and he doesn't add anything else before walking in, so I just follow him and look inside. I see someone moving on the stairs, and I get there quick before Jimmy or Erik has time to do something permanent to people they might not recognize. As I get to the bottom of the staircase, I can see it's Jimmy standing there, his face still puffy with sleep, his hair in disarray, and, most importantly he's completely naked. I've never seen him naked; I've crashed at his place once or twice, and I've never even seen him without a shirt. I know he's had a fucked up life, and so have I, but still, what I'm seeing right now is sickening. He's covered in scars. Some of them are from old stabbings or shoot-ings, I can tell the difference, but most of them... He's got a lot of burn marks. One side of his chest is so mangled I could swear someone poured acid all over him. Even with all that, I have to admit what gets me most is the naked-ness. I stare at him, my mouth hanging open, so shocked that it's a while before I notice he's holding a brick in his right hand. He rubs his eyes and squints at me.

"Alex? What are you doing here?"

I give myself a shake, and look at my companions. Tom is sitting in the living room, on one of the brown leather couches, but Julie has come to stand next to me and is staring at Jimmy, eyebrows raised, and with an appreciative smirk on her face. Trust her to look past the scars and see only the muscle, or whatever it is she's staring at. I try to put her out of my mind to be able to answer Jimmy as straightforwardly as possible.

"Uh, some stuff happened. We need a place to stay. What's with the brick?"

He looks at the brick in his hand.

"Oh, that? Well, I thought you were intruders."

"... don't you have a gun?"

He grins. "Well, yeah. But this is a lot more fun."

I imagine him beating someone to death with a brick naked and somehow, the nakedness is much more disturbing than the violence. I guess I'm getting used to Jimmy.

"Wanna... maybe... put some pants on?"

He looks down at himself like he didn't realize he was naked, and then he laughs.

"Huh. Right."

He just turns around and walks up the stairs, leaving his brick behind, but I think I see a little embarrassment in his expression. I scratch the back of my head, and look at Julie, who's watching Jimmy's ass disappear in the hall upstairs. She grins at me.

"Your friend is pretty hot."

I raise an eyebrow at her, and just walk past her to the living room. How can she be thinking like that at a time like this? She joins me. I slump on the leather couch opposite the one Tom has picked, and she sits next to me. I retrieve my silver cigarette case, and grab a smoke from it. When I snap it shut, I notice my neighbor's card stuck to it. I was right; he is a prosecutor. He said something about the GenEx guys being after him. Was he lying just so he could talk to me? Maybe, but there must be better ways, especially for someone whose job it is to be good with words.

"You should call him."

I look up when I hear Tom's voice; he's looking at the card. Of course, he's been listening to me think for... well, since I met him. He was bound to have an opinion on the matter.

"I should? Why?"

He gives me a look that's halfway between puzzled and annoyed.

"Come on. We live next to the guy. You're not the only person whose thoughts I hear, you know."

"That doesn't tell me anything."

"Just call him. It's relevant."

"Fine."

I take my cell phone, but just as I'm about to dial, it rings. I almost think it's my neighbor, 'cause the coincidence would be too awesome, but it's Lupino's number on the caller ID, so I pick up.

"Hello?"

"Alex? Are you all right?"

"Uh... I'm fine."

"I just heard about the explosion. You are not hurt?"

Shit. I should have called him. Now he's all worried.

"I'm fine. I should have called you, I was just... preoccupied."

"Tell me what happened."

I rub my forehead and sigh.

"I really want to, and I will, except now's not a really good time, Mister Lupino. Could I call you back later?"

There's silence on the other end of the line. I know he respects me enough to give me my space when I ask for it, which is not often, but I also know him well enough to realize how much it kills him to do so.

"Very well. I will be expecting your call."

"Thank you."

I hang up, and I have to light another cigarette. I'm about to call the guy again when I hear footsteps coming down the stairs, and I look up to see Erik and Jimmy. They're dressed, though it seems to have been done in the dark and in a hurry. Neither of them is wearing socks, and I'm pretty sure Jimmy doesn't own the battered The Clash shirt he's wearing. Jimmy sits down, grabbing my cigarette case but not looking at me, and Erik gives me an annoyed look, putting his hands in his pockets.

"Why do you always come here when you're in trouble?"

I snort. "I resent that. I get in trouble a lot more often than I come here, I promise."

He has a small smirk, but I can tell he's not really amused.

"Real funny. But I mean it. Why am I your go-to safe house?"

"Cause, we don't hang out, so people can't tie me to you."

He sighs. "Well, I don't want you to just come barging in here whenever you have a problem. Especially with a bunch of strangers."

"Get used to it. Looks like we might need to be hiding here for a little while."

"You could have at least called, first."

"I did. Three times. You haven't activated your voice mail yet."

He grunts and pulls his phone out of his pocket. He seems to struggle with the lock button, and then just tosses the phone to Jimmy.

"I put it on vibrate again, and I don't know how. Fix it."

Jimmy just picks up the phone and starts fiddling with it, leaning back on the couch comfortably. I frown at him. Since when does he just do what anyone tells him without saying anything? I mean, he calls me boss, and I can't be that abrupt with him.

I have to turn my attention back to Erik, though, because he's still talking to me.

"Well, fine. At least introduce me to your friends, then."

I look around. I had almost forgotten about them. Julie's sitting next to me, grinning at me like she's having some sort of private joke at my expense. Tom's still on the other couch, but now Jimmy's next to him, punching buttons on Erik's phone. I reach into my inner jacket pocket and pull out my wallet while I motion with my chin to introduce everyone.

"This is Julie. And Tom. That's Erik. Jimmy, give Tom your phone."

Jimmy gives me a look, and then shrugs, pulling his phone out of his pocket and giving it to Tom. Tom takes the phone, and stands up, because obviously, he knows what I'm thinking before I have to say it, and he takes the money from my hand. I still explain it, though, for the sake of Julie, or maybe just to feel like the sound of my voice is still relevant.

"Why don't you order us some pizzas? I'm sure Erik has some yellow pages somewhere. I'm going to call our neighbor."

MAY 17TH, 3:47 PM

Julie parks the car in the lot, next to a mini-van. I've rarely seen so many mini-vans all in one place, but, then again, I don't come to the suburbs very often any-more. I look at the building when I get out of the car. The Burger City looks exactly the same as the last time I visited it, some five years ago. This is the exact place where I ate my first meal as a free man, after I escaped the house I had been raised in. It brings back memories, though they're not as unpleasant as I thought they were going to be. I'm not sure why I picked the Burger City in High Plains, but here we are. I guess it's the first place that came to mind that was far enough away from down-town that we shouldn't be seen by anyone important. No matter how good the reason, I can't be seen anywhere near a prosecutor.

Still, what if I run into someone from my past? Do the people who raised me still live around here?

Julie stops halfway to the front door, and calls out to me, pulling me out of my thoughts.

"Hey handsome! You coming?"

I nod and follow her in. Even if there was someone I used to know, I'm not the boy I was all those years ago, and I doubt anyone would recognize me. Still, I have a nervous look around the place when I walk in, but there's no one I know, just young families with their kids playing in the ancient slides of the family area. And, in a corner, my neighbor, who's fiddling with his iPhone while nursing a coffee. He hasn't noticed us. We're early, and I really expected to be here first, but that doesn't matter. I pull a twenty out of my pocket and hand it to Tom.

"Why don't you go get me a cheeseburger and meet me at the table?"

He nods and goes to the counter, while I go sit in front of my neighbor, at the small, two-person table he chose next to the bathrooms. He looks up from his phone when I sit, looking surprised.

"Oh! You're here already! I didn't expect you for some time."

"Well, I'm here. You said it was important, and could only be discussed in person, so here I am. Make it quick. This is a big enough waste of my time as it is."

He gives me a look like I've said something incredibly offensive, and I just stare at him. I meant every word of what I said. I don't like to be bothered, I have other things to deal with right now, and I hate it when strangers try to boss me around. He puts his phone down and picks up his coffee, sipping it, looking around himself in

32

a really paranoid and obvious manner. I roll my eyes. It's a good thing for him I'm not selling drugs or anything, because for someone who wants secrecy involved, his demeanor is just screaming 'I'm here! Look at me! I'm doing something suspicious!' When he's done inspecting the restaurant, he calms down some. I guess he's satisfied that the people watching their kids go up and down the slides are not some kind of spies. He clears his throat.

"Like I said, this is a delicate matter. Should we not go somewhere more... private?"

"What, like the bathroom? This is fine. Now go on and spill already."

He looks me up and down, and sighs in resignation.

"I suppose you've had your share of shady dealings in your young life; you should know."

I raise an eyebrow. "Look, dude, you're the one who wanted to meet, and I don't think insulting me is the way to gain my trust, is it?"

"I didn't think I was being insulting." He seems genuinely bewildered; I guess he must have really thought he was paying me a compliment.

I try to refrain from sighing. "Just say what you gotta say so we can go our separate ways already."

He looks offended again, and then he looks over my shoulder. I turn to see Tom and Julie getting to the table. Tom just stands, and looks at the two-seater awkwardly, but Julie squeezes in next to me, pushing me against the window. If she were a man, I would have punched her, but all I can do now is glare at her. She grins at me, pops a French fry in her mouth, and chews.

"Kinda close quarters you picked there, handsome."

I turn my face away. This is the closest I've been to a girl since Lori died, and the warmth of her body and the smell of her shampoo are making my stomach feel tight. She's oblivious to it, of course, since she hits on almost every guy she meets, but I'm not in the mood for her kind of crazy right now. Tom glances at the bench where our neighbor is sitting, and looks for another table while talking.

"Maybe it'd be better if we moved?"

Julie smirks. "I'm fine here, thanks."

Our neighbor rolls his eyes, and looks at Tom and Julie. "Who is this?"

I turn to Julie, still squeezed against me, and then at my neighbor again.

"Can we move? I'll explain."

He clicks his tongue, obviously annoyed, and stands up with his coffee and phone, following Tom to a nearby table that has enough room for four. Julie sighs, still smiling, and shrugs.

"Ah well. Too bad, it's nice and warm here."

34

She stands with her tray, and I take a couple seconds to compose myself before following her. Of course, Tom and our neighbor are sitting on the same side, which forces me to sit next to her again. At least this time there's enough room for her not to have an excuse to press herself against me. Tom picks up a double-decker from his tray then pushes the remaining fries, cola and cheeseburger over to me. My neighbor watches us, and then glares at me.

"Well? Who are they?"

"That's Tom, and this is Julie. They're friends. Tom lives with me."

He nods at them, polite but still cautious. "And I'm Antoine Dow. I do apologize, but I had told Mister Winters that this was to be a private conversation."

Julie shrugs, eating another fry. "We're private people."

He gives her a withering look, which only makes her laugh. I have to admit it's funny, so I chuckle a bit. I'm not completely sure why, but I enjoy picking on the guy. Must be his profession. After all, he makes a living putting people like me in jail.

"They're all right. They can hear what you have to say. First of all, Tom probably knows what it is already, and second, they're in the same trouble I m in. Or we're in, according to you."

For a minute, he looks like he's considering it, but seems no less annoyed. He shakes his head, looks at his phone again, and takes a sip of coffee before talking. I take advantage of the silence to eat. I can't be intimidated into talking first if there's food on the table, and, besides, he's the one that invited me here, he should do the talking.

"Very well, I suppose. I wished to talk about those men who caused the explosion."

I nod, sipping my cola, letting him go on. He looks around himself again, then at Tom and Julie, and then sighs, as if resigning himself to say something he hadn't meant to.

"I believe those men are after me, too."

He watches all of us in turn, as if gauging the effect. Tom doesn't react, because he hasn't learned to fake reactions to things he already knew about yet, and Julie only raises an eyebrow. I keep eating my cheeseburger. When I think he looks sufficiently distressed by our lack of reaction, I swallow my bite.

"What makes you think that?"

He recovers slightly from his dismay, but still looks a bit put out. "Well, they came after me yesterday."

I raise an eyebrow. "They attacked you?"

He shakes his head. "They came to talk to me. They made some vague threats. I was to come with them, or else. They made it sound like I didn't have much of a choice."

36

"But you didn't go with them."

"Evidently."

"What happened?"

"The police arrived. My mother got worried and called them."

I just stare at him. "Your... mother?"

"Yes. She was having dinner at my place last night, when they showed up. She's alone, so we visit each other relatively often."

I'm speechless. His mother? This guy's old, at least forty. And he still sees his mother? I look at Julie and Tom, but I can't tell what they're thinking. My mind goes to Luke, and Jimmy, and the kids... I don't think I know a single person that still has any sort of relationship with their parents. It takes me a while to get over it, long enough for Dow to get a confused look on his face.

"What?"

I shake my head.

"Nothing. So, uh, the cops came, and they just left?"

He nods, apparently happy to get back on subject.

"Yes, before the police could get there. My mother said they were on their way, and they said they'd be back."

"And what makes you think that those were the same guys?"

"I heard them in the hall, and saw them through the peephole in my door. One of them was with the man who came to see me last night."

"And what did they want with you?"

He gives me another look. He invited me here, so he should be the one to say it first. I hate when people make me talk about supernatural stuff.

"I said so. They wanted me to come with them."

"Why? They must have said. And you said that it had something to do with what you saw me do this morning."

"It does."

I sigh. He's not gonna say unless I make him.

"So... what can you do?"

His eyes go a bit wide, and he looks around in that paranoid fashion again.

"What do you mean?"

I roll my eyes.

"Oh, come on. Aren't we way past the point where we're playing games with each other here? I control fire. What can you do?"

He looks a bit pissed off, but then he sighs and looks resigned.

"I've... never discussed this with anyone else before."

I shrug, to show him I won't make fun of him.

"I have to discuss mine all the time. So. out with it, we won't judge you or anything."

He nods, and seems to gather his courage, so I wait. Julie's face turns into a mocking smile, but she has the good sense not to say anything while he's making up his mind. Tom finishes his burger, and waits, politely, like he doesn't know what's about to be said. Dow finally nods to himself, like he decides he's ready, and folds his hands on the table.

"I... have the ability to become invisible.'

I raise my eyebrows. I haven't met someone that could do that before. He sees my face and starts looking worried, so I give him a smile that I hope is reassuring.

"Pretty handy."

He looks relieved, like he thought, after all this, that we wouldn't believe him.

"Yes, it has been, on several occasions. What about... the two of you?"

He looks at Julie and Tom, and his voice is all hushed, like we're discussing state secrets, and I suppose that, to him, it's a pretty taboo subject. I've used my power as a tool for intimidation for too long to have any real understanding of the way he feels.

Julie shrugs.

"I teleport. And Tom, here, well he's a psychic. That's why he never looks surprised. He always knows what you're thinking."

Tom looks up at her, and then at Dow, like he got caught doing something wrong.

"Oh. Uh. Right. Well, I try."

Dow looks at him like he's seeing him for the first time, an expression on his face halfway between being intrigued and impressed. Then, he shakes his head.

"Well, I saw this morning that these men mean business. I cancelled all my appointments for the day, and I don't dare return home for the time being. What about you?"

"We've dealt with these people before. We can deal with them again. Tom here is our ace in the hole."

"What are you planning?"

I shrug.

"I dunno. Find them. Kick their asses. That's usually how I go about it."

He shakes his head like I said something immature and stupid.

"I suppose it would be, in your line of work. Perhaps I can offer you a more... level-headed style of doing things?"

I smile to myself. What, does he think we can just put a restraining order on these guys, and they'll be impressed?

"Oh? What are you suggesting, exactly?"

"That remains to be seen. What do we know about them?"

Julie jumps in, talking with her mouth full.

"I got a bunch of files on them at the office. I didn't have time to pass by, I thought I'd go today after visiting Alex, but then his place exploded and things got complicated."

Dow looks a bit impressed.

"What kind of files?"

Julie shrugs, and seems to think.

"All sorts of stuff. Research notes, stuff like that... I'm sure there's something in there we can use."

"Well, we have a place to start, then!"

Julie takes another fry from my tray.

"Fair enough, but I don't want to go back there alone."

I take out my phone.

"I'll call Jimmy. Hey, with him, and the four of us, we should be able to handle it, no?"

Julie stops the car in front of her office. I've only been here once or twice; it's in a small building in Old Town, so of course Jimmy's already here, smoking a cigarette, leaning by the door. He must have come straight from Erik's place, because he's still wearing that stupid The Clash t-shirt. He notices us and waves.

We all get out of the car. I see that Dow has gotten here too, and is waiting in his SUV. When he gets out of it to approach us, he eyes Jimmy suspiciously. He must have heard of him; there's very few people in this town who know anything about the underworld that haven't. We gather in front of the building, and Julie takes out her keys to unlock the door, peering through the window. Jimmy watches her, and nods at me.

"How come you're always getting in trouble?"

I shrug.

"Hey, when you can do what I can, you draw attention. You should know; you draw your fair share too, you know."

"Why'd you need me here, anyway? There's no one. I checked."

"Just in case."

He has a grin, and looks at my companions, then me.

"So, a bunch of superheroes need help from a guy like me, huh? I'm flattered."

I nudge him with my elbow.

"Don't let your head get too big."

"What, you mean, like, as big as yours?"

Julie rolls her eyes, and walks in.

"Settle down, boys. It doesn't look like we'll need you after all. Doesn't seem like anyone's been here."

We walk in after her, and she's right. The place is spotless. Well, it's dirty, but it's her kind of dirty, not like someone searched through it or anything. She goes to the desk and sits behind it, leaning down to retrieve something from under it. I relax, and lean on the wall. Dow seems tense, looking around constantly, but then he's not used to being in the situation we're in now, and, to me, he always seems tense. Tom, though, is fidgeting nervously, and he looks a bit green. He gets that way around Jimmy, but this time, it seems worse.

"You ok, Tom?"

He makes a face, and shrugs. "I don't know. I don't feel so good."

"What do you mean? Like you ate something bad?"

He shakes his head. He's still looking worried, and it's starting to make me nervous.

"No... it's not that kind of thing. It's more... like a feeling. A bad feeling. Like something's gonna happen."

I frown. He's never made predictions before, but, coming from that kid, I'd be willing to believe he can turn into a badger.

"Something bad how?"

"I don't know, exactly... just... I have this weird feeling. And I feel kind of... fuzzy."

Suddenly, he looks right at my eyes, alarmed. "I can't hear you."

This makes Julie look up sharply, frowning. "What do you mean?"

His eyes are wide, and he turns to look out the window.

"I can't hear your thoughts."

She stands, putting something in her pocket.

"I got what we came for. Let's go. Now."

I nod. As we turn to exit, the window suddenly shatters. I duck, pulling Tom down with me. I didn't hear anything. Jimmy crouches next to the window immediately, grabbing a gun out of his coat, looking at the street, and Julie ducks behind her desk. Dow stands around, fidgeting, apparently unsure of what to do.

"Get down, Dow!"

He stares at me for about a second, which is a second too long, because I hear something that sounds a bit like a muffled gunshot, and he goes down. I curse, and look at Tom.

"Do whatever you gotta do, but stay down, is that clear?"

He nods. I don't think I've ever seen him scared, and I've lived with him for almost a year now. Then again, he spent years at GenEx and he's never seen a null strong enough to cancel out his power. I get up, not standing, but crouching so I'm still under relative cover, and try to summon the fire. It doesn't come, of course. I half-crawl, half-walk to join Jimmy by the side of the window. He's not shooting, so I guess he hasn't found a target, and I take a look. There doesn't seem to be anything out there. Nothing I can see, anyway. I turn around to look at my companions. Dow is still lying on the floor, but there's no blood. Julie's hiding behind her desk, and she looks furious. I look back at Jimmy.

"See anything?"

He shakes his head. "Best check on your friend."

I turn to inspect Dow again. There's still no blood, which is reassuring. I look for a wound, but I can't find one, until I notice the small red dart embedded in his upper arm.

"They're using tranquilizer guns!"

I don't know if the others hear me or not, because Jimmy shouts at almost the same time. "I see something!"

He's looking toward the door, so I look, and see something moving, but it's way too fast for me to see what it is. The glass on the door shatters then, and something that looks like a tin can flies through it, rolling across the floor, releasing thick white smoke. I take a look around while I can still see the others, trying to assess the situation.

Julie's moving towards Tom, who seems a little lost without his power, and I decide to go for Dow under the cover of smoke. I run, crouching, but there's another shot, and what hits my leg hurts way too much to be a tranquilizer dart. I scream and fall on my knees. When I look, there's blood gushing from my thigh, and it hurts like hell. I've been shot before, in the gut, and I don't remember it hurting like that. The room is quickly filling with smoke, and soon the only person I can see is Jimmy. He's looking out the window, and he finally sees something, because he shoots his gun twice before some guy comes running at him so fast he seems to appear out of nowhere, grabbing his gun hand and tackling him to the floor. I try to stand

47

and help him, but, when I lean on my leg, it feels like it's tearing open all over again, and I stumble. Before I can even think about trying again, a huge guy steps through the broken window and grabs me by the back of the collar, then hurls me across the room. I crash over Julie's desk, hitting my side, and I can tell I've broken or at least cracked a couple of ribs; I recognize the pain.

I try to push myself up, which is impossibly painful because of the leg and the ribs. My eyes are starting to burn. I wheeze, trying to refrain from coughing, because, with everything else, the pain in my ribs might make me pass out. I can hear, more than see, the huge guy walking towards me, and I try to make the fire. Of course, my power still doesn't work, so I look frantically for anything on the desk I can use to defend myself. I hear more gunshots as my hand closes on a heavy metal three-hole punch. I can feel him right behind me and, before he grabs me again, I turn around, using the motion to put weight into the blow I strike right to his head. He stumbles back, leaning on the desk for support, I hit him again and again. Every time hurts, but if he gets his hands on me one last time, with the state I'm in and no powers, I'm done for, so I put all my desperation into my arm. It won't be enough, I know, but if I'm going down, it sure as hell won't be without a fight. I move to hit him again, and he grabs my forearm, lifting me up by it and yanking the punch out of my hand. I have time to get the satisfaction of seeing his face mangled and bloody where I hit him before he throws me to the ground and starts wailing on me.

My mouth tastes like blood, and I can feel I'm about to pass out when there's a loud popping sound, and a flash of light. It attracts the huge guy's attention, and he

48

turns to look over his shoulder to see. I try to hit him again, but I can barely lift my arm. The smoke suddenly clears like some kind of wind I can't feel pushed it away, and I can see a guy walking towards me. He looks weirdly familiar; it's as if I'm looking at Tom, but taller. bigger, meaner, and with a lot more scars. He raises his hands, glaring at the giant, and the huge guy grabs his head and moans, then just falls, crushing me with his weight. The pain in my ribs is finally too much to bear, and I pass out.

"Are you ok? Wake up!"

I feel my eyes still rolling in my head as I come to. It's like being on a roller coaster in a fog: I can't see really well, and I want to puke. My throat feels raw, my ribs hurt like hell, and I'm so dizzy I can't tell if I'm sitting or lying down. When my eyes focus, I see Julie's face right above mine, looking weirdly serious, even concerned. She seems to relax when I blink at her.

"Julie? What's going on?"

She sighs in relief and calls over her shoulder. "He's awake!"

We're somewhere I don't recognize. I'm lying on dirty concrete, in some kind of abandoned warehouse. I try to sit up, but it hurts so much that I have to accept the humiliation of having Julie help me up. She leans me on a crate, because I can't really hold my weight up. At least, the fog is starting to lift from my mind, and I can see that the others are mostly ok. Julie is apparently unhurt,

51

Dow only seems a bit confused, Jimmy's shirt is all bloody but it looks like someone else's blood, and Tom... well, there's two of him.

I rub my eyes and stare. Either I've got a really bad concussion, and possibly some brain damage, or there really are two of him. There's the one I know, sitting in a corner, hugging his knees, looking more insecure than I've ever seen him, and then, there's the one I thought I hallucinated before passing out. He is taller, and somehow older. He's filled up, for one; he's a lot more muscular than my Tom, and he has the quiet, confident, and disillusioned look of someone who's seen too much. Tom already has a bit of that look, but on the other Tom, it looks worse, and it's not helped by the fact that his face and arms are covered in battle scars. The other Tom nods at me when he sees me looking, and I turn to Julie.

"Am I hallucinating?"

She laughs. "No, don't worry. And you're not seeing double, either."

I rub my eyes again, and my left eye hurts like hell. I wonder how bad I look, and sigh. I'm kind of tired of getting my ass kicked.

"Well, is anyone going to explain what the hell's going on? Where are we? Who's Tom's evil twin?"

Julie chuckles again, but turns to Tom's double to let him answer.

"I'm Tom. I'm from the future."

I blink at him. It seems obvious, and doing what I can do, I'm more prone than others to believe all sorts of weird stuff, but I'm having a hard time swallowing this.

"You're shitting me."

Future Tom raises an eyebrow, and I can tell he's got even less of a sense of humor than his past self.

"I'm not. I'm from five years in your future. Well. In a future that I've come here to prevent, anyway.'

"I'm listening."

He nods, and motions with his chin towards Julie.

"I've given her a hard drive with files on it. There you will find all the information that you need to prevent it."

I frown. "Just so we're clear, what is it we're preventing? I mean, maybe you've all heard it, but I haven't."

He has a small, humorless smile; they have the same features, but there's almost nothing of the boy I know in that expression. What could have happened to change him so much?

"The next world war. Between different factions of supers. Needless to say, when I come from, there aren't that many normals left."

"What happened? Or will happen... or whatever?"

"At the point in time where you are, GenEx is rapidly reforming. They've struck a deal with the government, conducting research on supers to make a new breed of super soldiers. Six months from now, they are going to orchestrate a catastrophe that involves a group of supers. They're going to use that to push a registration law. It'll spread to other countries until it's a world-wide concern, all in a matter of a month or two."

"Ok, so what's so bad about that?"

He sighs, like I'm thick and I just don't get it, which I suppose is a bit true.

"War will erupt between the different factions of supers. Those who don't want to register. Those who do. The super-soldiers they'll have engineered to enforce the new law. And... well, those who think normals no longer have their place in the world."

He sighs, and folds his arms over his chest. Even his upper arms have scars.

"Where I come from right now... forty-five percent of the surface of the United States is an uninhabitable wasteland. I lead the last surviving group of normals, and the supers that protect them. There's only a few thousand of them left."

"What, the others have all gone?"

He looks at me, sad, and serious. "No. The others are all dead. Billions of people are dead where I come from.

When I come from. What happens in the next year must be changed, at any cost."

I try to listen, but suddenly I'm thinking of Nicolas. Why am I thinking of him? It's absurd. But the only thing on my mind is, in five years he'll be seven. Is he still alive in that future? Does he find me? Do I find him? Save him?

I have to stop thinking about it. Clear my head. I ask a question, 'cause talking usually helps.

"All right, so what do we need to do?"

"In the files that I've given you, I have put all the details of everything that happens in the chain of events over the next four years. I've traced everything down to here and now, this event. What happened today."

"But there must be something specific we need to do to change it all."

"It's already started. I prevented some of it today, by saving you."

"What do you mean?"

"Where I come from... when I come from, you're all dead."

That hits me like a brick in the guts. I knew I was going to die someday, probably sooner than later; I was pretty much prepared for it, but to know for sure... it's different, I guess. Again, I'm thinking about Nicolas.

He doesn't know who I am... but I wish I'd have seen him one more time before I died. What am I thinking? I'm not dead. I've got time. Maybe I should find him. Let him know I exist. Tell him...

"Focus, Alex."

"Huh?"

Future Tom is looking at me sternly. Which is weird, because present Tom just looks like he's going to puke. A couple years can really change someone. I should know.

"I'm here. I'm back."

I try to stand, and it doesn't hurt as much as it should. Then I realize that I'm not standing, I just felt like I was. What's going on? My head feels light, and things look like they're getting darker. Maybe the light is fading. Is it late? It must be late. I look down at myself. My fingers feel numb. I'm sitting in something wet. Is that blood? Is it mine? All of it? That can't be good. My pant leg is soaked through, and there's a red puddle around me. If I've lost all that blood...

"Alex?"

I look at Julie. She's calling my name, but I can't really understand what else she's saying. It's getting harder to see her, even. Everything gets dark, and I start feeling warm and comfortable.

MAY 17ᵀᴴ, 10:14 PM

It's dark when I wake up, and I don't recognize where I am. It's hard to see; only my right eye will open all the way, and I feel a bit disoriented, but it's not too long before I realize that it's a hospital bed I'm lying on, and I'm plugged to a couple of machines. I sit up, a little too abruptly, and I have to grit my teeth to prevent myself from moaning with the pain in my ribs.

"Settle down. You are all right."

I turn, and realize that Mister Lupino is here, with his hand on my arm, sitting in a chair by my side.

"Mister Lupino? What's happening? Where am I?"

"You are in the hospital. You were hurt today."

I look around. No one else is here. Is this a dream? I stare at Mister Lupino, and he frowns, concerned.

"Should I call the nurse?"

"No. No, I'm fine. I think. How did I get here?"

"Your friends brought you. You were unconscious."

There's a weird feeling in my heart like it's come to a complete stop, and is simultaneously beating really, really fast.

"They did?" I'm out of breath as I talk; my mouth is dry, and I'm sure I sound even worse than I think. "What did they tell the nurses? The doctor? I've got a gunshot wound. Why isn't this place crawling with cops?"

He has a small smile. "If you settle down, I will tell you."

I blink at him, and I'm ashamed to be treated like a child. If it was anyone other than him, I wouldn't tolerate it. Since it is him, I lie back down, and I wait as patiently as I can for him to tell me what's going on. He waits a bit, as if making sure that I'm good and obedient, then he gives a satisfied nod.

"You have a new friend, Antoine Dow?"

I feel like throwing up all over again. He knows I've been talking to the prosecutor. Does he think I'm betraying the family?

"He's just my neighbor. We only really met today. It's not about business."

He nods, and I feel so much better it makes my head hurt.

"I know. Your friend Jimmy told me."

58

"Jimmy?"

"He is the one who called me. To let me know where you were. I was a bit worried about you, you know.'

I stare at him. Jimmy called him? He must have been really worried about me. Like, thinking I would die worried about me. He hates Lupino, and he's never been ashamed to say it. To think he'd be capable of picking up the phone and calling him...

"Your friend made arrangements so you would not be bothered by the police."

"Huh? Jimmy? How?"

"No. Your new friend, Antoine. He is with the district attorney's office. He said you were in the witness protection program, and that he was handling your case."

Is he actually approving of me hanging out with a prosecutor? I don't know what to say.

"...oh."

His face loses some of its softness, and he looks at me seriously.

"Now, I would appreciate hearing from you what happened today. Jimmy told me some of it, and I saw that you had other friends with you, but I want to hear it from you."

I lick my lips. "Well... it's a bit... complicated."

He raises his eyebrows, and stays silent. I know what he's thinking; I hate when people just answer me that it's complicated, like that means something. So I go on.

"It's kind of... superpower business. Do you remember when I disappeared for a couple of weeks?"

"I most certainly do."

"The organization we thought we took down... well, it would seem that they're back."

He frowns at me. "And they are trying to take you again?"

"Either that, or kill me. The guys we fought today, the way they fought... they didn't seem too concerned with capturing us."

He nods, seriously, as if asking me to go on. I do.

"There are some things we need to do, and... I think I'm going to have to put the business aside for a little while. Again. I'm sorry."

Just as I'm saying it, I realize that it's true. Not only that, but it's kind of a relief. I know Jimmy can handle it if I leave it to him for a while, and it's a weight off my shoulders not to have to worry about it. And I know Mister Lupino's been talking about me leaving.

He shakes his head. "You have nothing to be sorry about. I understand completely. I only wish that you keep me informed. Not as your superior, of course... but as your friend. As someone who thinks of you as a son. Will you do that?"

I look at him. His face is full of concern. Not disappointment, or scorn. Just... he's worried about me. My throat feels too tight to answer, so I just nod at him. He smiles, and pats my forearm.

"Good. Do not keep an old man in the dark. You know how I feel about that."

"I... I promise, Mister Lupino."

He stands. "Now, if you will promise to be still, I will go fetch your friends. They are still here. One of them, a pretty young lady, seems very concerned about you."

He has a wry smile, and his eyes twinkle as he says it. He does that every time he thinks I've met a girl. He started playing matchmaker with me about six months after Lori died. If only he knew Julie like I do, he would probably think about it twice. I'm not sure she's the kind of girl that settles down. But I don't want to disappoint him, so I don't say anything. He stops in the doorway before walking out.

"Good night, Alex. Be well. And please, do not forget to call me."

I nod, and he walks out, leaving me alone.

It does give me time to examine where I am. My clothes are nowhere to be seen, and I'm wearing one of them stupid hospital gowns that open at the back. I can't see any of my things anywhere, in fact. Not my cell phone, not my wallet. Not the silver cigarette case Lori gave me. Not the plush toy I picked up from Nicolas' room. My chest feels tight again, and my eyes burn. Shit, I'm not gonna cry, am I?

Julie walks in, with Tom, and it feels so absurdly good not to be alone with my thoughts anymore I want to hug them. Instead, I just nod, all stoic-like, and wait long enough to trust my voice not to betray me when I talk. She sits in the chair Mister Lupino was just in, yawning and stretching. I look toward the door, but I can't see him. I guess he must have gone home. When I'm sure my voice isn't going to quiver and make me seem like a wuss, I turn to Tom, and then Julie.

"Where's my stuff?"

She looks at me, an insolent, mocking grin on her face, and retrieves a small plastic bag from one of the huge pockets of her trench coat. I don't know why she wears that; it makes her look stupid. She throws the bag at me, still mocking me with her smile.

"Why? Can't sleep without your bunny? And you get all worked up when I call you kid. Hah!"

I glare at her for a second, but it's pointless. She doesn't understand. I gave up Nicolas around the time that I met her, so she never knew about him. She probably thinks this is something from my own childhood. To hell with her; she can think what she wants. Tom, on the other hand, is saying nothing, just looking at his fingernails. He understands, of course, because he always knows what I'm thinking. I feel weak, all of a sudden. Must be the blood loss. Yeah.

I check to make sure everything is there, not just the bunny. There's my wallet, my silver cigarette case. I reach out to run my fingers on the case, and I stop myself. Don't want to get emotional again. What's wrong with me, anyway? Better start thinking about business.

"So, uh, what's going on now? Where is Dow?"

Julie shrugs. "He's gone with your friend Jimmy to pick up some food. The hospital cafeteria is closed, and even if it wasn't, that stuff is vile."

My stomach growls. I hadn't even noticed I was hungry. "He better be picking something up for me, too. I'm starved."

She chuckles, and pulls out her cell phone. "I'll call him and make sure."

She starts dialing, and I turn to Tom. He still looks pale and anxious, though it's nowhere near as bad as it was in Julie's office, or in the warehouse.

"You ok?"

He shrugs, and pulls an empty chair next to the bed to sit on.

"I guess. I just... well, I didn't think there was a null that could best me. Guess they found one."

I nod. It must be terrifying for him. The GenEx labs were pretty bad, but for me, at least, it only lasted a couple weeks, and then I got out, and I managed to take everyone with me. And I could walk around, talk to people. For him... well, I can't imagine being tied to a bed, experimented on and kept under just enough sedation to be aware of how crappy your situation is for over five years.

I also know enough about body language to know he's not telling me everything. I try to think of a way to say it, but then I look at him, and I remember that he can hear what I'm thinking, so I just stare at him to make my point. He sighs and rolls his eyes.

"Yeah, it's real convenient for you that I can't turn this off. One moment it's all like, don't read my mind I want some privacy, and the next, well I don't know how to say something so I'm just gonna think it? Make up your damn mind."

I raise my eyebrows. If he's that sensitive, whatever is bothering him must be pretty bad. But I don't like other people prying about my personal stuff, so I understand if he doesn't want to talk about it. Julie's hanging up her phone, so I turn my focus to her.

"So what have you found out? Have you looked at the files that Future Tom gave you?"

"Well look who's all work and no play!"

I raise one of my eyebrows at her, but she only laughs. What does it take for this girl to take something seriously?

When she sees that I don't think it's funny, she rolls her eyes and sighs.

"No, we haven't had time to look into it yet, what with you bleeding to death and everything. Unless, you know, you wanted us to let you die in that warehouse so it didn't disrupt our schedule, 'cause that'll be handy to know, next time."

I shake my head, and take my cell phone out of the bag to look at the time.

"It's like four hours since the factory. All this time you've been just standing there?"

"Well, if you must know, we've been making arrangements for you being admitted here question-free, and making buying lists so everyone had everything they needed. Unless you don't mind walking out of here in your hospital gown."

That brings my hopes up.

"Am I walking out of here? Soon?"

She shrugs. "The doctor said you were all patched up. They want to keep you under observation overnight, but Antoine said it wasn't a good idea, that there might be people looking for you and he had to return you to protective custody. The doctors admitted there really wasn't anything else to do than let you rest and heal, so we thought we'd leave it up to you."

I sigh with relief. "Good. Good. So I can get out of here as soon as they're back?"

She grins. "You just won me twenty bucks. I said you wouldn't want to stay. Antoine wasn't so sure."

I pick up the silver case, and open it. I still have three cigarettes left; I'm gonna have to pick up more. I put one in my mouth and light it. The smoke feels great, and then I notice Tom and Julie are watching me funny.

"What?"

Julie rolls her eyes. "Dude, you can't smoke here."

"It's a private room. Who cares what I do?"

"Fine. Whatever. What's the plan once we get you out of here, anyway?"

I have to think about it. I look for something to tip my ash in, and I decide to use the bedpan that's on my bedside table.

"Well... we should go back to Erik's place, and see what the files are that Future Tom got us."

Julie takes the flash drive from her pocket and looks at it, and then something hits me.

"Wait. I don't think Erik has a computer. He's only got one of those old TVs that have knobs, and I think his most recent gaming system is like the first Playstation."

She shrugs. "Antoine is like this big shot prosecutor guy. I'm sure he's got a laptop or something."

"Good. Now, we just need to eat and get the hell out of here."

I finish my cigarette, and put it out in the bedpan. I sit up and slide myself over to the side of the bed. I grunt, because it hurts like hell, but I'm used to that kind of pain. All that remains is being able to walk all the way to a taxi.

MAY 18TH, 12:06 AM

Erik is waiting for us at the door to his house when we get there. He looks moody, and is still dressed exactly the way he was this morning, without socks. The taxi pulls over and I pay the driver. Only Tom came with me, because I'm ok with him hearing me groan in pain, since he already knows I feel it. I guess we got here before Julie, Dow and Jimmy, because they were in Dow's SUV, and the only car there is Jimmy's. I have to use the crutches they loaned me at the hospital to walk, because it's way too painful to lean on my leg, but at least I didn't need to take the wheelchair they insisted I should. There's no way I'm going around in a wheelchair.

Erik looks me up and down when we get there, and he raises his eyebrows. He grins, too; seeing me in pain seems to be cheering him up considerably.

"Well, I guess they weren't kidding. You got all your pieces? You sure you didn't leave bits of you in the cab, there? You need me to carry you?"

"Shut up."

He shrugs, and moves aside to let us through.

"Hey, you can't blame me for being concerned, what with your new style and all."

I roll my eyes. Maybe I should have sprung for a hotel, but at the time, it seemed a bit complicated. He is right about the style, though. I should have insisted on something specific. I look really dumb, with a stupid bright blue track suit. Julie was laughing at me so hard she was crying.

I limp my way inside, and to the couch, where I just crumble and put my crutches aside. I sigh with the relief of not being on my feet anymore, and light a cigarette. Erik leaves his door open, and comes to sprawl on the couch opposite me. Tom sits next to me, a little too close for comfort, leaning as far away from Erik as he can.

"So, apart from getting your ass kicked, what went on today? Jimmy didn't have time to tell me much."

I shrug, like there's nothing to it.

"Got a visit from a future version of Tom. He told us about this big world disaster that's about to happen. We're supposed to prevent it."

Erik raises his eyebrow. "Couldn't he do it himself, like in *Terminator*?"

I smirk and nudge Tom with my elbow. "I guess not. Couldn't you have tried harder?"

Tom just shoots me a look of anger and anxiety that completely kills the mood, and doesn't answer. I share a confused look with Erik, and he just shrugs.

"We're here!"

Julie walks in through the front door, followed by Jimmy and Dow. Dow's carrying a suitcase, and Julie has a brown paper bag that smells like French fries. She squeezes in next to me, pushing me against Tom. Jimmy sits next to Erik, and Dow goes to take the lone comfy chair, opening his suitcase and retrieving his laptop. I look at Julie, who's opening her bag and retrieving a double cheeseburger from it, and raise my eyebrow.

"More burgers? How many dinners do you need to eat in one evening?"

She looks offended, even though she takes a large bite just to answer me with her mouth full.

"Hey! Almost dying makes me hungry. Are you calling me fat?"

I shake my head, because I'm not sure what to answer, and I'm also still hungry even though we ate dinner like an hour ago. At least I have the excuse of the blood loss. I say nothing, because she's bound to make one of her stupid growing boy remarks. I turn my attention to Jimmy and Erik. They're sitting a bit closer than necessary, and talking in a low voice, I can't tell what about. As soon as he notices me looking, Jimmy nods in my direction.

"How's the leg? Made it here ok?"

"I'm here, aren't I?"

He nods, like what he just asked was relevant, and runs a hand through his hair. I can tell he's nervous, even though someone who didn't know him as well as I do never could. The silence is uncomfortable for both of us, so I say something just to be talking.

"So, you called Mister Lupino?"

He shrugs, and reaches in his pocket to grab a new pack of cigarettes. He takes a smoke from it, and tosses me the pack afterwards.

"Yeah. Well. I thought you were gonna die, and he might wanna know."

I nod at him. I need to talk to him about what Lupino said, and about the business, but I know it's neither the time nor the place.

"Thanks."

"Sure. So what do we do now?"

I look at Dow, who's fiddling on his computer. I can see he's got the flash drive plugged in, so I ask.

"Anything?"

He looks up, and looks surprised that we're talking to him.

"Hmm? Oh. There are tons of files here. I'm still looking through them. It looks like it might take a while. Perhaps you had better get some rest, and we can reconvene in the morning."

Tom lets out a relieved sigh, and stands.

"Good. I'm exhausted. Where can I go to sleep?"

Erik glances at me, and stands.

"I'll show you. Alex, you coming?"

I look at Jimmy. He's finished his cigarette, catches me looking at him, and gives me a small nod. I'm glad that even though I didn't see that thing with Erik coming, we still know each other enough to guess what the other is thinking. I look at Erik.

"Not yet. I've got a few things to take care of. Besides, I'd rather sleep on the couch."

He shrugs.

"Suit yourself."

He leaves, leading Tom up the stairs. I stand, helping myself with my stupid crutches, and make my way outside. Jimmy grabs the pack of smokes, and follows.

I have a hard time going down enough stairs so I can sit comfortably, but at least Jimmy knows not to help me. He waits for the considerable time it takes me to be settled, then sits next to me, offering me a cigarette, and lighting his own.

"This ain't about Erik, is it? 'Cause I don't make excuses."

I have a small smile, and shake my head. I don't know why, but I like it when Jimmy feels insecure; it reminds me that he's human, and he does have feelings beneath all the crazy.

"Nah, don't worry about it. It's your life. This is about the business."

He nods, still not looking at me. "Thought it might be."

We stay silent, smoking, for a little while, as I gather my thoughts and try to formulate what I'm going to say next.

"I might have to leave the business for a little while. While I take care of this... stuff."

This time, he looks at me.

"Figured you might. Glad to see you came to the conclusion yourself. You want me to take over for you while you're gone?"

"Yeah. The thing is... I don't know how long that'll be. Do you think you can handle it without me at all, for months at a time, if need be?"

He narrows his eyes at me. I wish I knew exactly what was going through his mind right now. I know he can handle it, he's been doing this longer and better than me, but I need to know he knows it too. Everything I discussed with Mister Lupino over a year ago has been coming back to me. What if I don't want to pursue this line of work? I have to know he can take over for me. I can trust him; I don't know that I can trust anyone else in this business. He'll make sure the kids aren't bothered, if I don't come back, and when Lupino retires.

He stares at me, finishing his smoke, and throws the butt out on Erik's awful lawn.

"Yeah, I can handle it. But you are coming back, aren't you?"

I shrug, and start to stretch, but I wince and stop in mid-motion, because it hurts my ribs. I hiss silently through my teeth and I bring my arms back down. When I turn to Jimmy, I expect his usual mocking grin, but his expression is dead serious. Almost grim. I sigh, and I gather up my courage to be perfectly honest with him.

"That's the plan, at least for now. But... it's possible I might not."

He keeps staring at me, and then he just leans his head in his hand and lets out a deep breath.

"I thought you might say that. I've kind of been suspecting it for a while. What would you do?"

I shrug. I never thought that far.

"Flip burgers, I guess."

"Oh, come on, man. You're better than that."

I smile at him.

"Well, maybe you know that, but all I know is, I can't exactly write "capo for the Lupino family" on a resume, now can I? And even if I could, I never even finished middle school. Who'd hire me?"

He chuckles and shakes his head. He understands where I'm coming from; he never even went to any kind of school, not even kindergarten. I used to send him texts, because it was more convenient than phone calls; he never replied, and he eventually got mad at me and told me to stop doing that, so I figured out he doesn't even know how to read. It's a good thing he loves what he does; I can't imagine him ever doing anything else.

I sigh. There is a more serious aspect to my request, though.

"Also, there is the very real possibility that I might not make it through this alive."

He looks at me.

"Ah, come on, man. You're like a superhero. You'll manage."

"You heard what Future Tom had to say. I was supposed to die today. In some alternate dimension, I'm dead, right now. I think."

And I never got to see Nicolas again. Why does it make my chest feel like that every time I think about it? I thought I'd moved on, by now.

"Well, in this one, you aren't. You're gonna be fine. You've got all that info stuff on the lawyer guy's computer, right? So don't worry about it."

I nod. The lawyer guy. I hate having to work with someone I just met. How do I know this guy can even be trusted? I shake my head. I can't start doing that now.

I clap Jimmy on the shoulder, and start the long and difficult process of standing.

"You're right. I'm gonna go have some rest, and start over in the morning. He'll have something useful by then. I mean, what's the use of coming back from the future without giving us anything we can use?"

MAY 18TH, 9:47 AM

I didn't think it was possible, but my ribs hurt even more when I wake up the next morning. Did it always hurt this much? I had them cracked quite a few times when I was young, and a couple more times since, but I don't remember it feeling like that. Is this what getting old feels like?

I'm disoriented at first, but I've been at Erik's place often enough to place it relatively quickly. There's snoring, and I can see Julie, lying on the couch opposite me, her hair loose, under a blanket that only covers her from the waist down. She's not wearing a shirt, only a bra, which is pink and black. Did she intend to show me this?

Her skin is smooth, and flawless. I've never seen anyone with so few scars. Even Lori had her share, but with Julie, her skin is completely unbroken. Even the hand I can see looks soft, lying across her perfectly toned stomach. Her other hand is under her head, supporting it, and I swear, even her armpit is perfect. She's such a sloppy dresser, with her ripped jeans and baggy t-shirts and ugly trench coat, I never imagined she could look like that under her clothes. She snorts, and shifts in her sleep. I look away, afraid that she's going to wake up and find me staring, but she's still asleep. Hating myself just a little, I reach for my crutches and try to stand, making as little noise as possible.

"Need some help?"

I start, which makes me lose my balance in the middle of getting up, and fall seated on the couch. I can't refrain from moaning, and if I could lean over, I would punch Dow for startling me like that. Now, though, I just glare at him, my teeth gritted, while Julie finally wakes up. He looks at me, confused.

"Didn't mean to startle you. Do you want some coffee? I found some in the kitchen. All he's got is a kettle and a French press, but I worked out how to make it. There's enough for a few more cups."

I nod, taking shallow breaths, trying to calm down and make the pain go away. Julie sits up, yawning, and I can see that she's wearing white underwear that doesn't match her bra. Her stomach is as flawless as the rest of her. I look away quick, though she doesn't seem to be embarrassed in the least, and I have the satisfaction of catching Dow staring too. I kick him in the ankle. He realizes what he's doing, blushing and heading to the kitchen. Julie calls out after him.

"I'll have one too!"

She reaches down to the floor and retrieves her black Iron Maiden t-shirt, pulling it over her head before putting on her jeans. She nods her chin in my direction.

"Feeling better?"

I nod, even though I'm really not. If anyone's going to know how crappy I feel, it certainly won't be her. She yawns again, combs her hair with her fingers, and pulls it into her usual ponytail.

"Good for you. I feel like shit. These couches are too old. You can feel all the springs in them. It's not a good sleeping place."

This makes me smile a bit. Having slept on the beds at GenEx myself, I know firsthand how uncomfortable they were. Since she lived there most of her life, I know she's used to much worse than Erik's couches.

Dow finally comes back in with a couple more cups of coffee, and puts them on the table between us before going to sit on the comfy chair he's apparently claimed as his own. There are notes and papers all around it so that he has to sit at a certain angle not to disturb anything.

"I couldn't find any sugar or milk, so I hope it's all right."

She shrugs, picking up her cup. "Coffee's coffee."

He nods and picks up a stack of papers on which he scribbled a bunch of notes. It makes no sense to me, I mean, why write on paper if you've got a computer, but whatever, to each his own, I guess. I pick up my mug, and breathe in the scent. The caffeine in the fumes jolts me just a little. At least he makes his coffee strong enough.

"So, found out anything?"

He makes a face after he sips his coffee, and shakes his head.

"Not really, unfortunately. Some of these documents are impossible to open, I guess they were done on programs that don't exist yet. Fortunately, there's a text document that is full of dates, and names, that might be really useful. It's like a full list of everything that will happen leading up to the beginning of the war, and everyone that is going to be enlisted and will have a significant role to play."

He doesn't seem too encouraged, though it seems to me like that ought to be useful. I take a sip and wait for him to go on, but he doesn't, so I prod him along.

"I feel a 'but' coming on."

He sighs. "I don't know how to use it. I don't know where to start. I suppose we could go and talk to everyone on the list... but we don't know who's truly important, and in what way. It would take too long, and it would be too expensive for us to accomplish. I mean these names... these people are all over the world. I wish he would have given us instructions."

Julie shakes her head and sips her coffee.

"Or a magic eight-ball. You know, the kind you shake and it gives you the answer to your questions? Like, where do we go next, what do we need to do, that kind of stuff?"

I frown. That suddenly gives me an idea. Having lived with Tom all that time, I know there's a lot more of the stuff I read in comic books as a kid that's actually possible than one would be inclined to believe.

"Is there someone on that list that can predict the future? Maybe they'd know what we need to do."

They both stare at me, and for a while, I can't tell if they think the idea is genius or stupid. I think it's pretty cool, myself. Julie turns to Dow. He blinks, and has a small smile. Good. Looks like my idea was a good one. He starts looking at his computer again.

"I'll find out. There's a database with power listings, so all I have to do is find someone that fits our criteria, and we're good to go."

Julie takes another gulp of her coffee, and puts it down, looking at me.

"Good. Now why don't you go wake up your friend Jimmy so I can send him shopping? I need fresh underwear, and as funny as your outfit is, you look like a douche bag."

I try to glare at her, but I find I don't have it in me. I'm just too tired. I put down my coffee with the cup still half full, and look at the stairs. I think about just getting up and climbing them, but of course I know better than to try it. For some reason, I feel embarrassed as hell that she thinks I look like a douche bag, which pisses me off, but I'm just too worn out to bite her head off. I pick up my cell phone and call Jimmy. I suppose it's just as well that I can't get up and go and wake him up personally. Who knows what they're up to, up there?

I look at the suit Jimmy bought me, and I suppose it could be worse. It's not like I can go out and get a nice tailored one right now, and I know how bad his taste is when it comes to clothing, so I'm glad for the two gray vests and pants he got me. The shirts are white, and plain, and he didn't get me any ties, but at least everything matches and nothing stands out too much. Dow is still wearing what he had on last night, but he made Jimmy get him some clothes too, a couple t-shirts and some jeans, though I suppose he should have been more specific, because he ended up with *Angry Birds* shirts. Julie's the one who's the least satisfied, but I guess that was to be expected, what with her being a girl and everything.

"These are granny panties!"

"Look, it's bad enough you make me buy girl's underwear, I wasn't going to get the frilly lacey stuff!"

"I'm not saying I wanted a matching Victoria's Secret set, but if you were gonna pick up a Wal-Mart six-pack, at least you could have picked the bikini cut!"

84

"Well is it my fucking fault that women's underwear is so fucking complicated? I mean, when I pick underwear, all I gotta wonder is, boxers or briefs, and that's done. You guys have like twenty different kinds! You should be more specific, if there's something you want!"

She rolls her eyes and throws her hands up in the air, and I refrain from telling her how much worse it could have been. I can't imagine the stuff she would have ended up with if she had asked him to pick up a dress or some girly clothes. There's a small advantage to her lack of taste, I suppose. I look at Dow, who seems completely oblivious to the whole exchange.

"Anything yet?"

He makes a face, which tells me that it's not good.

"Well, yes and no. I've only found one that has a good ability to read the future, and he's in Africa."

"We can go to Africa. What's the problem?"

"It doesn't say where in Africa."

"Oh."

I think about it. My last geography lesson's really far away, but as far as I remember, Africa is a really, really big place. Not the kind of place where you just drop off randomly and start asking 'hey, have you seen this guy?'

"So... it doesn't even say which country?"

85

He shakes his head. "No. If only there was at least that, it would be a lot better. I've been cross-referencing with every other document in here to see if there is another reference to this guy, but I can't find anything."

He runs a hand through his hair, sighing loudly, puffing his cheeks. I have to admit that this is discouraging. I guess Future Tom overestimated our capacity for planning.

"So... what now?" I say.

"I don't know. I've tried using every database I have access to as a prosecutor to locate this guy, but he doesn't seem to have any sort of paper trail. I'm stumped."

"Maybe we're going at it the wrong way."

I turn to see Julie, who seems to finally want to join the conversation, holding up a pair of white cotton panties, looking discouraged. She tosses them on the coffee table before going on.

"This is about people with superpowers. Alex was right to suggest someone who can see the future. What about someone who can find people? Does that sort of power exist?"

Dow blinks at her, and shrugs, hoisting up his laptop on his lap again.

"I guess we'll see. Give me a second."

We both stare at him while he types and clicks on his computer. He looks up at us a couple times, clearly uncomfortable with our staring, but doesn't say anything. It's not that I want to put pressure on the guy, of course, but it's not like there's anything else to do at this point. After a couple minutes, he raises his eyebrows, and I know we've done it just by the relieved expression on his face.

"Yeah. There's a guy in Italy. He can find anybody in the world."

"Does it say where exactly?"

He nods.

"I don't have an address, but I do have a name and a city."

I lean back on the couch, relieved.

"Finally! Looks like we're getting somewhere. So, we're headed to Italy!"

"Let me make sure I locate him first, but yeah, we're headed to Rome."

"Good. Hey, Jimmy, does Eric have a credit card?"

He raises his eyebrow at me, twisting his mouth. "How the hell should I know?"

"Well, then, do you?"

"No. What the hell do I need a credit card for?"

I sigh. Of course he doesn't. He often boasts at how proud he is to be completely off the grid, having had no paper trail to his name since his birth certificate. Even his driver's license is fake. It has its good and bad sides, but when you kill as many people as Jimmy has, it's certainly a plus to be virtually untraceable. Julie frowns at me.

"What's all this about credit cards? Don't you have a credit card?"

"Well, yeah, but if we're being watched, we're probably being monitored, so we can't use our cards."

"Oh. Right. But why need one?"

"We'll need plane tickets. I guess maybe I can send Jimmy directly to the airport with some cash."

"Hey, don't talk about me like I'm not there, man."

"Sorry. Will you go?"

"I guess. Won't you guys need like, passports and stuff?"

"I've got one in the emergency bag I keep in a locker at the airport."

I look at Julie, and she shrugs.

"All I have to do is teleport directly onto the plane. No customs. I don't like being felt up by guards, anyway. They usually have body odor."

"I guess that just leaves Dow and Tom. Jimmy, would you go pick up my bag and use it to get us a couple tickets? Get a flight that leaves soon, but give me at least 24 hours to work out something for passports."

He nods, and stands.

"I got a nice forger who works miracles pretty quick. Want me to give him a call?"

I should have expected that. He's a lot more resourceful than I ever was. I wonder what makes him want to keep me as his boss. He's better at this than I am.

"Yeah, do that. And let me know."

MAY 20ᵀᴴ, 1:37 PM

I take another look at my cell phone. Lupino insisted on driving us to the airport, and he's usually on time, but he's a couple of minutes late, now. Jimmy's sitting next to me, on the porch, smoking, my bag at his feet. Everyone else is still inside, getting ready. We had to leave most of our possessions behind, and buy the clothes we need, so all of us have pretty small bags. We have no idea how long we'll be gone, or when we'll be back, but everyone's agreed we'll probably be a lot safer overseas than anywhere here.

A limo pulls up in the driveway, and I'm reminded of just how much money Lupino has. I look around at the state of Erik's house and its landscaping, and I'm ashamed that he has to see where I'm hiding out. Jimmy helps me stand, discreetly, and I say nothing because no matter how much I hate needing someone's help, I'm sure as hell not going to show Lupino how battered and hurt I still am. Once I'm on my feet, I grab the crutches, and I make my way to the limo on my own while Jimmy carries my bag. The driver steps out and walks to open the door of the limo, and Mister Lupino stands up, smiling at me.

While Jimmy hands the driver my bag, Lupino claps me on the upper arms, and I lean down so he can hug me. He's the only person I allow to do that, the only one since Lori that doesn't make me feel awkward or self-conscious when they touch me.

"Alex, my boy! You are looking a lot better. How do you feel?"

"I'm good, Mister Lupino. Really."

"Good! Good. You will see, Italy is a wonderful country. I cannot wait for you to eat some real food!"

Jimmy walks back to the house to get the others. As usual, he and Lupino ignore each other. It's what they could agree on that would be polite and tolerable for both of them.

"I thought Rosanna's food was pretty decent," I say.

"Oh, it is, of course. But you have not tasted real food until you have tasted home-made pesto made from fresh herbs grown under the Tuscan sun."

I smile. He looks happy, which makes him look young, and healthy. Losing his son all over again three years ago was a tough blow, and it made him look a lot older, but what surprised me was how it affected him when I gave up my own son. I guess he'd come to care for him like family. This is the happiest I've seen him since then.

"I'll try and find a place that has that, then."

"No need! I will show you."

My jaw drops. Did I hear him right?

"Did you say you will show me?"

"Yes. I have packed my bags. I will be coming with you."

"Mister Lupino..."

I don't know what to say. He can't be coming. Doesn't he know how much danger we're in? How do I tell him without sounding offensive or condescending?

"Mister Lupino... as much as I would love to visit Italy with you, we're not going there to visit. This is going to be dangerous. I don't think..."

He raises his eyebrows, as if daring me to go on, and I have to stop.

"Alex, my boy, you are not suggesting I stay here because it is too dangerous, are you?"

I think I'm sweating. Why can I never get my way with him?

"Well..."

He waves a hand dismissively at me. "I will not hear of it. There is no danger in this world that will let me miss an opportunity to go to my home country with you. Besides, I have already made arrangements for our stay there."

I refrain from sighing. If he's that decided, there's usually no talking him out of it. He chuckles when he sees my face, and claps me on the upper arm again.

"I'm glad to see the prospect of my company pleases you so."

"No! No, it's not like that at all! It's just..."

He smiles kindly, and rubs my arm as Julie, Tom, Dow and Jimmy come out of the house, walking towards us.

"I know. You do not need to worry."

Julie whistles when she sees the limo.

"Wow! We're going off in style! I've never ridden in one of these. Does it have a mini bar?"

She just gets in without waiting for an answer, leaving her bag on the ground. Tom picks it up, and gives it to the driver with his own, before getting in the car without a word. Dow nods at us, eyebrows raised.

"Well, whoever said that crime doesn't pay clearly has not spent time with you."

I give him a look, but he just laughs and hands his bag over before getting in the car. Lupino looks at Jimmy, and then pats my forearm one last time.

"I will wait for you in the car."

As he gets in, I turn to Jimmy, who's lighting a cigarette.

"So, that's it, then? You're off?"

I nod. "Lupino too, apparently. You'll be all right?"

He just looks at the limo, and back at me.

"Of course I'll be all right. What, you saying I can't take care of myself?"

For a second I think he's really offended, but then he cracks a smile and gives me a playful nod with his chin. Then, his face goes back to being serious.

"You be careful, though. I won't be around over there, and I don't like this superhero battle shit. It might look good and end well in the movies, but really, it's just messy in real life."

He doesn't say it, but I know he's worried, probably 'cause I still look like crap from the beating I took, so I try to act cool.

"I've had worse. You don't need to worry about me."

He rolls his eyes. I think he's embarrassed, like he didn't want to be caught caring.

"Will you just get out of here already?"

I grin, and nod, and lean my armpit on my crutch to punch him in the arm.

"Yeah, yeah. I'll have my cell phone. If I change numbers, I'll call you. Keep me informed if something goes on."

He nods, and since we've said all there really is to be said, I get in the limo. The driver comes to help with my crutches, and then we're off to Italy.

MAY 21ST, 10:17 AM

The hotel mister Lupino booked is the fanciest place I've ever been in. Everything is gilded, and looks ancient. He booked us all luxury suites, with the largest single beds I've ever slept in. Everything seems golden, the curtains, the floors, everything; it's almost too much to look at. There are plenty of couches, with almost too many pillows on them to allow for a person to sit. I haven't been to that many hotels in my life, granted, but I know enough to know that this must have cost him a fortune. I'm awake now, and I don't know if it's the jet lag or the fact that I'm probably lying on the most comfortable mattress I've ever slept on, but I just can't get up.

I squint, and I see that mister Lupino's bed is empty, next to mine; that wakes me up all the way. I sit up, pushing the fluffy duvet comforter aside with some difficulty, and I see him, sitting on the huge couch, reading a newspaper. I relax, and I hesitate as to whether or not I can go back to sleep, when he folds his paper to put it on the coffee table, turning towards me with a smile.

"You are awake. How do you feel this morning?"

I stifle a yawn and carefully swing my feet off the bed. The pain in my thigh isn't so bad, it just burns and pulls whenever I move it. My ribs hurt most of all, but I think I can manage to both move and breathe at the same time, so I must be doing better.

"I'm better. I guess the air here really is good for you, huh?"

That makes him smile, like I knew it would.

"I am glad to hear it. Are you hungry? I would like to have breakfast."

"Oh, yeah, I mean, yes, I'm starving."

"Would you like for me to order it in, or do you feel good enough to go to the restaurant downstairs? They have a very nice terrace."

He must want to go, if he's mentioning it. I'm pretty sure I can make it.

"The restaurant sounds good."

He nods, looking happy. "Good! Do you need help?"

I shake my head, but I still let him bring me my crutches, though I make every effort not to show how much it hurts to stand up. After a few steps toward the door of the room, I realize that my ribs hurt much more than my leg, and I try taking off the crutches, leaving them against the wall. It makes it more bearable.

"Are you sure you should be walking? Your injury is fairly recent."

"Oh, yes, I feel much better."

I smile at him, and I must be real reassuring, because he nods, and he doesn't seem worried at all. We make our way, slowly, to the elevator, and then to the restaurant downstairs, which is every bit as fancy as the room is, with white silk tablecloths and fresh roses in the middle of the tables. We sit down, and when the waiter comes, Mister Lupino orders our breakfast in Italian, which seems to be much the same kind that I eat at his house regularly, with brioches and croissants and jams, and cappuccinos. When the waiter nods and walks away, he turns to me, smiling.

"And what are your plans for today?"

I shrug. We haven't really talked it over, me and the others.

"Well, we gotta contact our man, but we don't exactly know where he is, so the first thing is to find him, then we'll see."

The waiter comes back with baskets of fresh-smelling baked goods, and a small tray with five different kinds of jam. Mister Lupino helps himself to a bun, breaking it open before smearing a sweet-looking red jam on it. I take a look at what else there is on the tray. There's more choice than there usually is at his house, but there's nothing salty. Most of these things I would eat as dessert at home. There's even a couple different kinds of cookies.

I pick one up and start chewing on it. It's pretty good, and sweeter than I expect for breakfast. I look at Mister Lupino to try and see if I've made some kind of faux-pas, but he's just smiling at me like everything is normal, so I grab another one.

"I trust you will let your friends do the walking and the fetching today?"

I blink at him, unsure what to answer. What is he getting at?

"Uh... why?"

He raises his eyebrows like I've said something stupid, and then looks down at my leg.

"Oh. Right. Well, if there's a lot of walking involved, they'll do it. But I'm good at the talking part, so I will want to do that with them."

"I am sure a prosecutor is more than capable of convincing someone of the validity of your cause."

"We'll see."

He nods, like he agrees to leave it at that. We eat in silence for a little while longer, and he watches the street through the window. It's made of cobblestones, but they look like they're well-maintained and surprisingly even. When he's done eating his first brioche, he picks up another one, and looks at me.

"There is something I wished to speak with you about, actually."

"What is it?"

"As you recall, some time ago, I spoke to you of retiring."

I nod. That was about two years ago, before all that business with GenEx started.

"I have begun to take steps to make this happen in the following months."

I stare at him, and catch myself, grabbing another cookie and stuffing it in my mouth to give myself time to think. He's gonna ask me if I made a decision about continuing in the business or not. With everything that happened, with Lori and Nicolas, I didn't really give it much thought, and now that I have to make a decision, I have no idea what I really want, no matter what I told Jimmy.

"But as I am doing that, I have come to realize that it can get very lonely for an old man to have no one around when he begins to spend his days being idle."

I frown at him. This isn't what I expected. Is he going to ask me to move in with him again?

"I would not wish to lose this relationship I have with you. I have come to cherish it."

I listen, chewing my cookie slowly. He hasn't looked up at me for a while, not since he started on this train of thought.

"In fact, as you may know, I have begun to think of you as my own son over the past few years."

I have to swallow, because the cookie is mush in my mouth, but I grab another one to eat right away. This is usually the part where I say something really, really dumb, and this feels real important, so I don't want that to happen this time.

"And so, I was wondering if... you felt the same way about... our relationship."

What the hell is he saying? We don't talk about feelings. At least, I don't talk about feelings. Not with Jimmy, not even Luke, and certainly not Mister Lupino. Does he want to discuss how we feel about each other? I don't know if I'm comfortable doing that, and if I was, I wouldn't want to do it in public. He glances up at me, sees I have my mouth full and probably a very confused expression on my face, and he has a small smile that barely touches his eyes.

"In short, I was wondering if you would consider changing your last name."

I frown. Is he saying what I think he's saying? I have to be mistaken.

"Changing my last name?"

He nods. "Yes. To Lupino. I would like for you to become my son. Officially."

I swallow, and manage not to stare at him with my mouth hanging open like I usually do. Become his son? Be able to call him father? Did I pass out again? Am I going to wake up at the hospital? I knew I should have been more doubtful of this cookies-for-breakfast business. He looks up at me again, and seems to think my face is funny, because his eyes twinkle and he can barely repress a chuckle. I finally say the only thing I can think of that won't make me sound like a complete idiot.

"Really?"

His eyes are still happy, and soft, but there's just a hint of sadness in them.

"I am old, Alex. I will not be here very much longer. The time I have left... I would like to spend it like I wish. Exactly like I wish. And when I am gone, well..."

He looks down, and takes a sip of his coffee. I don't know what to answer, so I let him go on.

"I do not want my name to die with me."

I just stare at him, while he puts another bit of brioche in his mouth, chewing it. He looks up, sees me staring, and smiles. The silence stretches out until I have to say something. I really should have earlier, but what is there to say? How can I express what I'm feeling? I don't deserve this, and yet, there are very few things in the world I want as much as this, right now. To wear his name, call him father... there is no other man I would ever call that name, and I have no attachment whatsoever to the name of the man my mother made me with.

"I... I don't know what to say, Mister Lupino."

He chuckles a bit. "Well, it would be a good start to let me know whether or not you accept."

"Of course I do! Just... are you sure? I mean... me?"

His eyes soften again, and I see that look of pride he gives me sometimes when I do something that makes him particularly happy.

"I am very certain, Alex. I would choose no other man to wear my name."

I have to clear my throat, because I'm getting stupid emotional again.

"I'm so... thank you, Mister Lupino."

"Please, call me 'papa'. And the pleasure is mine. How about we celebrate, tonight? I will take you and your friends out to a nice restaurant. Nicer than this. What do you say?"

I open my mouth to say he doesn't have to, that it's all too much, but I know how he feels when he gives me something and I protest, so I just nod.

"It would be great. I'm looking forward to it."

103

"Hey, handsome. You're a tough guy to find, for someone who has restricted mobility."

I look up to see Julie plop down into the chair next to mine. I'm sitting on the terrace of the restaurant, smoking. Lupino has gone to walk around town and find us a place to have dinner, and he insisted I stay here so I wouldn't get hurt, so I just stayed exactly where I was, since I could both smoke and order refills of coffee.

I think it's a little embarrassing to have her sit next to me in such a fancy place looking like she does, though, with her baggy Iron Maiden t-shirt, her jeans with a hole at the right knee, and her trench coat, but when she actually leans her chair back to prop her feet in their unlaced army boots on the fancy table, I want to crawl somewhere and hide. She notices the look on my face, and smirks.

"What? At the price your boss is probably paying for this crap, we should be allowed to do what we want."

I give her a level look. "That's not how this works."

She raises her eyebrows at me, smiling insolently. "Oh? How's it work?"

"There are other people here, who have also paid an obscene amount of money to be here. They want to enjoy their stay. If you disrupt it, it doesn't matter how much you're paying the hotel, they're not going to lose other customers to accommodate an undesirable."

She grabs a toothpick from the dispenser on the table, and starts chewing on it, still grinning at me.

"Undesirable, huh?"

I feel my face get warm. Am I blushing? Why the hell should I be blushing? It defies any logic. She should be embarrassed, not me!

"That's... not what I meant. I just meant..."

"That you don't desire me."

She has that wry grin again, her eyebrows raised. She's baiting me, of course. Why am I responding to it?

"Whatever."

She shrugs. "I have to admit I'm certainly not at my sexiest right now, but that's no reason to call me undesirable."

I get annoyed, and sigh. "Was there something you wanted?"

"Well, I was coming here to let you know that Dow has located the guy, and him and Tom are on their way to see him."

"What? Why didn't you come get me?"

"Well, we couldn't find you. Plus, I ran into your boss, and he said to leave you alone."

I sigh, and light another cigarette. "Fine. Are they at least supposed to call when they get there or something?"

She shrugs again, like she doesn't care. "Maybe. Who knows? All I know is, in the meantime, we got time to kill. So whaddya say we get back to my room? I got a bath the size of a pool table."

I stare at her. Is she suggesting what I think she is? My cock reacts immediately, ten times faster than my brain, bringing up all the images of her sleeping in her underwear at Erik's place that I didn't think I remembered so clearly.

She lets her feet down, and leans with her elbows on the table to get closer to me. I can smell her shampoo again, and I notice how shiny her hair is. Damn. And I almost had my brain working again, too.

"Not so undesirable after all, am I?"

I realize that my mouth is open, and I close it, and I lean slightly away from her. It's easier to think without smelling her hair.

"Uh... No thanks."

She looks slightly disappointed. "Why not?"

I try to think of something to say, without having to explain.

"I don't... do that sort of stuff."

"Oh. You're gay?"

"What? No! Why would you think that?"

She raises an eyebrow. "Well, you just said..."

"That's not what I mean. I'm not gay. I'm just... not interested in a relationship, right now."

She stares at me, a huge smile forming on her face, and then she just cracks up and starts laughing. I feel my face heat again, and as embarrassed as I am, I'm pissed as hell, too.

"What?"

"I'm not asking you to get married, I'm asking if you wanna get naked in a hot tub with me. Geez, lighten up, kid!"

That's it. I don't care how much it hurts, I stand up and storm away. Well. I limp away. But I do it with an attitude.

MAY 21ST, 3:44 PM

There's another knock at the door and I sigh. I ignored the first two, because I don't really want to see Julie, and Mister Lupino wouldn't need to knock to come into his own room, but then I hear Tom's voice on the other side.

"Alex? I know you're in there, I can hear you think. Can we come in?"

I guess there's not much I can say to that. "Yeah, sure."

I stay exactly where I am, sitting on the couch. The door's not locked. I twist to see over my shoulder, but then that hurts my ribs like hell, so I just turn back around and watch the TV like that's what I intended to do all along. That way they can't see me make a face. Tom comes to sit next to me, looking at the TV.

"What are you watching?"

I shrug. "No idea. Some soap opera, I think. That's what it looks like, anyway. I've seen more dramatic gestures in ten minutes than in one entire episode of *Passions.*"

108

Dow doesn't sit, just stands next to the couch, frowning at the TV.

"I found a couple English channels, this morning. My room has the BBC. Doesn't your room have any?"

I shrug again.

"Maybe. It doesn't really make a difference."

"Well, maybe if you didn't have it on mute, you'd understand better."

I grab the remote and turn off the TV; I don't really feel like discussing this with someone one I just met.

"So, I hear you went after the guy. Did you talk to him?"

Dow finally sits down in one of the comfy chairs next to the couch.

"We found out all we could about him. His name is Marcello and he lives at the other end of the city, but we couldn't speak to him. We went to his house, but according to his wife, he's gone to Naples to visit family. He should be back tomorrow or the day after."

"Do we know where in Naples?"

"No. And honestly, it was nearly a miracle we figured out where he was at all."

"What do you mean?"

"Well, I don't speak Italian. Thank goodness Tom was there, because I wouldn't have managed it with the phrase book."

I raise an eyebrow at Tom. "You speak Italian?"

"Not really. But thoughts aren't just words, so it makes it easier to understand what someone is saying."

I look from one to the other. "So... what do we do now?"

Dow shrugs, glancing at the TV.

"I guess we wait for him to come back. I gave the woman the name of our hotel, and the room number."

"All right."

We stay quiet for a little while, and then Tom nudges me with his elbow.

"Come on. Aren't you going to invite us?"

I frown at him, and then I remember the dinner. Dow leans forward, his elbows on his knees.

"Invite us where?"

"To dinner. My boss... I mean... Mister Lupino wanted me to invite... my friends, to dinner."

"Dinner? Where?"

"I'm not sure, exactly. He wanted to pick a really nice restaurant."

"Just for fun, or are we celebrating something?"

I look at Dow. Was he always this perceptive? Why do people always seem to know what's going on in my life? I decide I want to keep a little mystery. I look at Tom. Well. Keep it a mystery from Dow, anyway.

"Kind of. It's... a little private."

Dow chuckles, shaking his head.

"Fine. I suppose we'll find out tonight at the restaurant." He gets up. "Did you need anything, while I'm here?"

I blink at him, wondering what he means, and then I realize it's because of my leg.

"No, thanks. I'm good."

"Well, I'll be going. I'll see you then. Tom?"

Tom looks at Dow, and then me, and stands up.

"See you tonight, Alex."

MAY 21ST, 6:17 PM

I walk out of the elevator carefully. I'm trying not to limp, so I take my time, but my leg hurts like hell. I managed to not use the crutches all day, so there's no way I'm going back.

I find Lupino sitting at the bar with Dow, and I head over there. They're both having some kind of dark red cocktail in a small glass, chatting. When I reach them, Lupino nods at me. He looks truly happy, his eyes kind of shining, happier, I think, than I've ever seen him before. Dow raises his glass towards me, smiling.

"Hey! Congratulations!"

I reach the bar and sit down on a stool. "For what?"

"Your boss... sorry, I should say your father, Mister Lupino, has told me the good news."

"Oh."

I smile awkwardly. I still feel like I don't deserve it, and it's hard to think about. I hope I get used to it soon, because it really does make me happy.

"Thanks."

"Of course! It's always a happy time when you expand your family, no matter what the occasion."

He looks at something behind me, his eyebrows raised. "And speaking of occasion..."

I turn around, and I'm just awestruck. I don't recognize her at first, or rather, my mind can't wrap itself around the fact that it's her, but it really is Julie, coming towards us, in a little black dress, matching heels and gloves, pearls around her neck and a black shawl wrapped around her shoulders, her hair done up in a French twist. She's all made up, too. She joins us at the bar, sitting on the stool next to me, smiling. Her lips are red, and fuller than I remember.

"Hello, boys."

She sees me staring, and puts her elbow on the bar, leaning on it. I don't know if it's done on purpose or what, but her shoulder strap slides off, drawing my attention to the perfect curve of her collarbone. She grins.

"Still think I'm undesirable?"

I glare at her. I don't really have the patience for her stupid banter tonight. She laughs at me, of all things, and looks at Lupino and Dow.

"What's that you're drinking?"

Dow lifts his glass.

"It's called a *negroni*. Mister Lupino says it's the only way to start a good meal. Want to try one?"

Mister Lupino nods in approval, and Julie shrugs.

"Sure, if you're buying."

Dow waves the barman over. "What about you, Alex?"

"Huh? Oh, no. Just a Coke. I don't drink."

Julie rolls her eyes at me. "Boy, you're just all sorts of boring, aren't you?"

I sigh, audibly. What is her problem, anyway? Mister Lupino comes to my defense.

"Alex is a perfectly pleasant young man. He has his reasons not to drink."

She shakes her head, smiling. Dow orders our drinks, and then turns an appreciative smile on her.

"So, all dressed up for the restaurant?"

She smiles again, ruefully. "Actually, I have a date, later on."

I feel anger build up in the pit of my stomach, and I breathe through my nose to keep calm. I wonder what's pissing me off so much. I don't have the leisure of exploring it, though. Not if I don't want to set anything on fire.

Dow lifts an eyebrow. "A date? Who with?"

She lifts her eyes to the ceiling, as if remembering wistfully.

"Some guy named Arturo. Or Antonio. Something like that. He speaks some English. He's got upper arms the size of my thighs."

I concentrate my sight on a napkin dispenser on the bar. Keep calm. Don't think about this Arturo guy, or how much you could kick his ass. Why is this pissing me off so much? She can do whatever she damn wants.

One of the napkins starts darkening, and smoking.

"He's taking me to the opera."

Her drink comes, and she takes a sip from it. The barman puts an empty glass and a can of Coca Cola in front of me, but I don't pay attention. I'm trying to not let the napkins catch fire. Dow keeps his end of the conversation going.

"You like the opera?"

"I guess we'll find out. I do like Arturo's arms."

"Or Antonio."

"Whatever."

"Everything all right?"

There is silence for a little bit, and I realize that Dow's last comment was directed at me.

"Huh?"

"I asked if everything was all right. You seem to be trying to burn those napkins."

I look up, and everyone's staring at me. The napkins are a bit blackened, but not on fire.

"Uh. No. It's nothing."

I stand up, too quick, and my leg hurts. I guess my face shows a bit of the pain, because Dow frowns.

"Where are your crutches? Should you be walking on that leg?"

"I'm fine. Where's Tom?"

"Over there. He's found an old-fashioned pinball machine, and he's figuring out how to play it."

"Fine. I'll go help him. Get me when you're ready."

I walk away as quickly as I can with my injured leg and without looking like I need help. I leave stunned silence behind me, but I don't care. I don't want to see her leave with stupid-named big arms opera-going Italian guy. In fact, I don't want to see her at all, right now.

MAY 21ST, 7:44 PM

The ride in the limo could have been more pleasant, but at least I sat next to Lupino before Julie could take the seat next to me. I guess that let me cool off a little bit, even if I did have to watch her flirt with Dow the whole way there. The restaurant really is nice, and the chicken I ordered is good and juicy. Dow and Lupino seem to be getting along really well. Turns out Dow is a chess player, and they start talking about that, kind of shutting out the rest of us, so I'm left with Tom, and Julie. Tom is still behaving a little awkward, and Julie sees I'm still mad at her, so she leans towards him, an eyebrow raised in that flirtatious expression she has way too often.

"So, Tom, turns out, you're gonna be pretty bad ass when you grow up."

He stares at her like she just called him a no-dick son of a bitch, and then shakes his head.

"You know, Julie, I know what you think, and there is absolutely no call to be that offensive."

She shrugs, taking a sip from her wine. "I could say the same to you. There was no need to be offended."

"You think I don't know you only say that to get a rise out of me? I'm sixteen; I've done most of the growing up I'm going to do, and you're sorely mistaken if you think I actually want to become that guy."

She rolls her eyes. "Fine, fine. Forgive me for wanting to find out if you actually had some feeling under all that weirdness." She looks at Lupino and Dow, still wrapped up in their discussion, and then looks at me. "So. New dad, huh?"

I nod, looking at her suspiciously, wondering where she's going with this.

"What happened to your old dad?"

I shrug. This is something I never talk about. With anyone.

"He's dead. I think."

"You think? You don't know?"

I shrug. "He was in critical condition when I left home. With any luck, he didn't make it."

"With any luck?"

I give her a level stare. "That's all I got to say about this."

She shrugs. "Fair enough. How'd you meet Lupino, then?"

118

I look at him. He's listening to Dow talk about his mother. He sees me looking, and smiles at me, his eyes twinkling with a certain complicity. I return the smile before turning back to Julie.

"It was a few years ago. I had just taken over the operations of the Borodinski group, in Newport."

"The what?"

"The Russian mob."

She lifts her eyebrow incredulously. "A few years ago? No offense, really, but how old were you?"

"Fourteen."

"And you took over a whole mob? By yourself?"

"Well, no. I had Jimmy with me."

"Just the two of you?"

I have a satisfied smile, and I remember what Jimmy said, what seems like ages ago. Just a kid and a crazy guy.

"Yeah, just the two of us. Essentially."

"How'd you do that?"

"Well, it all started when I freed some kids from a brothel that the Russians owned. It was kind of a self-defense thing. They tried to take me, too." They succeeded, but I leave that part out, of course. There's really no need

119

to talk about it. "So I killed everyone in charge, and since the kids all had nowhere to go, and I didn't either, I decided to stay there. Of course, the place made a lot of money for the mob, so they kept sending people after us. I needed Jimmy's help, and for a while, we were able to fend them off."

"Does Jimmy have some kind of superpower?"

I shrug. "I guess you could say that. He's got a taste for blood."

She frowns, and I can tell that she's wondering tons of things, but I don't talk about Jimmy's private business. He's one of the people that got fucked over the most by the Russians, and I respect his privacy as much as mine.

"Anyway, after a while, he helped me take down the head of the gang, and take it over from there. He'd been working for them as a contract killer, so he was kind of an insider."

Julie shakes her head, and takes another sip of her wine. I can tell she's impressed.

"Where does Lupino come in? It wasn't his gang you took over, was it?"

"No, but we drew attention. Also, when you try to take over a syndicate, you have to deal with a lot of guys you don't know very well yet, and betrayal and assassination is something you're gonna have to contend with. The Chinese and the Irish respectively tried to muscle in on my territory, and I was able to keep them out for a while, but eventually the Lupino family got involved. They came to me with a deal, and at first, I turned them down, because I never intended to do this for a living."

"And then?"

"Then, one of my own guys, a guy I trusted with my life, tried to kill me. And I realized I needed more help than just Jimmy could provide. But I wasn't gonna deal with a middle man, so I broke into Lupino's house."

Julie chuckles. "You broke into his house?"

"Well, his yard, really."

"And now he loves you like a son?"

"Hey, I can be charming."

She shakes her head again, still laughing. "I know that. So what happened?"

"He was having breakfast. He wasn't even scared to see me come. Might have been because I was bleeding from my gut, but he just invited me to join him. And then, instead of talking about money, or power, he started talking about the kids. My kids. About how I could protect them."

I look at Lupino. Even the first time he ever saw me, he got me, he knew who I was, and why I was doing the things I was. Of course, it's because he had my permanent record. After mentioning the kids, he explained why he understood what I wanted. How he knew about the abuse.

The broken bones. The injuries that no one else ever seemed to notice or care about. He did. And he promised me that if I worked for him, my life would be better. I had no idea how much.

"So how come he made you his son?"

"Because we get each other. And we both have no one else. That should be enough."

She looks at me, and then at him, and shrugs. "I guess I can get that."

She glances at her watch, and puts her glass down, standing.

"Oops. I'm late. Well, I'll catch up with you later. Congratulations, I guess."

She stands, slinging her purse over her shoulder, and waves at everyone, walking away. I watch her go, and the warm feeling of quiet joy I had been having by remembering how I met the most important person in my life just vanishes. Why do I let her affect me so much?

MAY 22ND, 1:36 AM

Julie is standing in the doorway, wearing that pink and black bra, this time with matching panties. She has her arms crossed, leaning on one leg, her other foot behind her, against the doorframe.

"Hey, handsome."

I sit on my bed, and then she's standing over me, putting her hands on my shoulders.

"Julie? I don't..."

"Shh."

She pushes me down and kneels on the bed, straddling me. The phone rings.

"Julie..."

She covers my mouth with hers, pressing me down against the mattress with her body, and the phone rings again. I open my eyes. It's dark, I'm lying on my stomach on the bed, and my dick is so hard it hurts. I hear Mister Lupino stirring in his sleep, so I make my hand wake up and reach for the phone, promising myself to bite the head off whoever it is that's calling me at such a crappy moment. I look at the caller ID to prepare myself.

It's Julie.

I answer, mumbling something as I sit up. I'm too sleepy to remember to take it slow. I have to bite my tongue to keep from screaming as I just throw my legs over the side of the bed and stand up, way too fast. Julie's saying something on the other end of the line. I take shallow breaths to try and calm down.

"What? I didn't hear you. What do you want, Julie?"

"Come get me."

Did I hear that right? I turn to look at Mister Lupino, and he's stirring again. I push through the pain, and manage to walk all the way to the bathroom, going in and closing the door not to disturb him with the sound of my conversation.

"Come get you? How come? What's going on? Where are you?"

Her voice sounds funny, all slurred and muffled.

"... that's too many questions at once. Pick one."

"What's going on?"

I hear her sigh. She almost sounds like she's drunk. "This guy... he wasn't a nice guy. I'm stuck in a closet. Come and get me."

"What do you mean, stuck in a closet? Where are you?"

"I dunno. I'm in this... building. I guess it's a nightclub."

"And you're in a closet?"

"Yeah... next to the kitchen."

"What happened?"

"It's a long story. Come and get me?"

I'm really pissed off at her right now, but that last request sounded so pathetic I can't really say no. "All right. What's the name of the nightclub?"

"It's *Bella Notte*. It's right next to the opera house."

"How do I find you? Which closet are you in?"

"I dunno... some kind of back room. Janitor's closet type thing."

"Can you teleport and meet me outside the nightclub?"

"Dumbass. If I could teleport, don't you think I would have? Seriously, you can be so dense."

125

"You know, it's usually good policy not to insult the people you're asking for help."

"Whatever. Are you coming?"

"Yeah, I'm coming. I'll be there in twenty minutes."

"Good. Hurry up, ok? I feel like... like I'm... I don't feel good."

"Fine."

I hang up on her, and limp back into the room as quietly as I can, dressing as quickly as my ribs will permit. Then I go downstairs, and get a cab to take me to the opera house, glad as all hell that Mister Lupino made me learn Italian.

MAY 22ND, 2:03 AM

The *Bella Notte* night club is vaguely reminiscent of *Fellini's*, back home, and I get a bad feeling about it when I walk inside. It seems to be some kind of Goth club. Everyone inside is wearing dark clothes, and looks at me weird when I pass them with my limp and my regular-person suit. I make it all the way to the back, near the bathrooms, when I get out my phone and call Julie.

She doesn't answer, and I don't like it. I keep calling, once, twice, and I realize I need an alternative solution. I want to slip in the back, but the only way I see is behind the bar, and I guess I must be real conspicuous. Everyone is watching me with weird expressions, like they think I'm funny-looking and they're waiting for me to make a wrong move.

I head down the hall that leads to the bathroom, like all I'm doing is going to take a piss. There's a couple guys standing there who stop their conversation when they see me, like they were talking about something secret. I walk past them, and I spot some plastic doors at the end of the hall that look very well like they could lead to a storage area. Right next to it is an emergency exit, so I make like I'm heading for that, taking my cigarette case out of my pocket. The guys see me, and I guess they assume I'm gonna go smoke, 'cause they turn around and resume their conversation in a low voice. I stop by the exit, make sure they're not looking, and then I discreetly slip through the storage room doors.

It's dark on the other side. I can't really make out anything, but I don't want to make any light 'cause the guys outside might spot me. I don't know who they are, but I can smell trouble a mile away, and they're definitely trouble.

There's a lot of shelves with all sorts of things, like big pots of olives, kegs of beer, and crates of bottles on them, and I think I can make out a couple of doors at the back. I head for there, calling out softly, even though I'm sure she won't answer me.

"Julie? Julie, can you hear me?"

I pick up my phone and try calling her again. She's still not picking up, but I think I can hear her ringtone from the other side of the middle door, so I head for there.

The knob turns, and the door even moves a little bit, so I can tell that it's not locked; she must have jammed something on the other side to prevent it from opening. I try calling her name again.

"Julie? You in there? It's me, Alex. You called me, remember?"

There isn't a single sound. Full of doubt, I call her cell phone again, and the ring is definitely on the other side of that door, so I look for something to break it down. I find a crowbar and use it as a lever to force the door open. It takes some jiggling, which is mostly due to how much this is making my ribs hurt, but I get it at last, and with minimal noise. When it's open, I have to squint a second, and then I see her, lying in a heap on the floor, in a position that can't be comfortable, obviously unconscious, her cell phone on the floor next to her hand.

I put my phone in my pocket, and use the door handle to help lower myself down to her level, as quick as I can, despite the pain. I start by checking her vitals, and see that she's breathing and that though her pulse is a little fast, her heart is still beating strong. I pick her up and slap her gently with the back of my hand on the cheek, to wake her up.

"Julie? Can you hear me?"

She moans a little, but doesn't wake up. I give her a shake, not too hard, because her head is rolling on her shoulders in a way I don't like, but she's still not waking up. I pick up her phone and purse, and try bringing her up as I stand, but my leg is nowhere near ready for that kind of an effort, so I stand, lean on the doorframe, and drag her up by the arm awkwardly until I can wrap her arm around my shoulders and start walking, dragging her.

The pain in my ribs is just unbelievable, but it's nothing compared to having to lean both her weight and mine on the injured leg, no matter how small the steps I take. I look for an exit. I'm already starting to sweat, and I'm in no shape to fight off whatever it is that put her in that state on top of having to drag her around. There isn't a door, at least none that I can see, which means I'll have to make my way to the hallway I was just in. Damn. I hope those guys aren't still hanging around there.

By the time I reach the plastic doors that lead to the hallway, I'm sweating like a pig, and completely out of breath, which makes my ribs hurt even more. I look out into the hallway. Looks like I'm out of luck; the two guys are still standing there. I rub the wound on my thigh, 'cause it's getting itchy on top of being painful, and my leg feels wet. When I look at my hand, I can see it's covered in blood. Great. Awesome place to pop a stitch and bleed, trying to get out of a night club while carrying an unconscious girl.

I look back up and there's suddenly three of them. They're still talking, but they're getting more into it. Why can't they just leave? Who goes to a night club to hang out in the hallway that leads to the bathroom?

Julie's head rolls on my shoulder, and her hair tickles my face. It smells really good. Is she wearing perfume? I've never seen her look as good as she did tonight. Why hasn't she ever wanted to dress up like that for me? Why that stupid big-arms Italian dude? I get pissed off again, and the fire gives me an idea.

There are sprinklers in the hallway. I concentrate on a piece of decorative tapestry, and start heating it. I don't want to burn it, really; just get it to singe enough to produce a good smoke. I keep it up, maintaining the heat at exactly the right temperature, until the smoke is thick enough to attract the attention of the men at the same time as the sprinklers go off. I take advantage of their distraction to slip out of the back room, and limp to the exit door halfway down the hall. As I reach it, I hear one of them calling out, and I don't wait to see if it s me he noticed before heading out, going faster.

I just limp as fast as I can, not caring about the pain in my leg or my ribs. There is no way I'm getting in trouble in a foreign country, especially since I still have no idea what happened to Julie. I've pushed through pain before, and now I'm protecting someone, which makes it easier. The door leads to an alley, so I half-run, dragging Julie against me, making for the street.

By the time I reach it, there's guys coming out the door, but even if they're faster than me, it doesn't matter; there's two cabs here, the drivers leaning on the first one and having a cigarette. I make for the door of the car and get inside, while the drivers start berating me in Italian. I say nothing, and I'm too exhausted to try and understand, so I just dig into my pocket and take out a hundred-dollar bill, and throw it in the driver's seat. They look at each other and the driver finally gets in the car, too slow for my taste. I look towards the alley, but the guys haven't reached us yet, or have abandoned pursuit. I finally let myself breathe when the car drives away. I've made it. She's safe, and with me.

MAY 22ND, 3:17 AM

The ride cost me 200 bucks, because I gave the driver another bill to apologize for bleeding all over his back seat. It's pretty hard just to walk back into the hotel, first of all because I have to avoid all the bellboys that look at me weird or try to help me, and second, because I'm starting to have a real hard time walking on my own. By some miracle, I do manage to get up to her room, and I have to rummage through her purse to find her keycard. I stumble in, and make it all the way to the huge, king-sized bed to drop her off on it. She's still not awake, and it worries me, but her pulse seems even better than it was earlier, and she's breathing strong and deep, so I figure she's gonna be all right. Probably better than me, actually. I sit on the bed and look at the trail of blood I've left behind, probably in the hall too. I feel dizzy, but I've felt worse, so I know I'm not bleeding to death. Not yet, anyway. I light a cigarette so I can finally relax and think.

I take off my pants, and let them fall in a heap on the floor. I'm gonna need to call room service to pick them up and clean them, because blood is hell to get out of clothing once it's dry. I sit back down on the bed, looking at

132

her, and think about how awkward it would be if she woke up now, what with me having no pants on and her passed out next to me. I'm pretty sure she'd understand. I limp over to the bathroom and grab a hand towel, and then get to the closet, where I get a clean sheet before making it back to the bed. I sit on it, and make myself a makeshift bandage, with the towel to absorb the bleeding. I don't want to try and find a doctor in Italy, and besides, it's not that bad, so I'm sure it'll be all good by the time I wake up tomorrow morning.

As I tighten the sheet over the towel around my thigh, I steal a look at Julie. She's lying down awkwardly, but she's started to snore, so that's a good sign. She's probably not passed out anymore, but just sleeping, which feels considerably less dangerous. Her left leg is hanging off the side of the bed, which pulls her tight dress high, revealing almost all of her thighs and a little bit of her underwear. She must have gone shopping for a while today, because she's not wearing the white cotton granny panties that Jimmy got her, but black lace, which covers considerably less. I lean back on the bed, watching her. She looks so peaceful, you wouldn't think anything bad happened to her tonight. My eyes travel back down to her thighs, and I have to resist the urge to touch her.

I shift on the bed, which sends pain all the way down my leg, but that's preferable in every way to the ache that's forming in my balls. She grunts in her sleep and tries to roll over to her side, but she obviously hasn't got enough strength for it. That's what finally convinces me. If she wakes up while I'm lying next to her with no pants and a hard-on, she'll flip. Or jump me. Either way, I don't really want that to happen. Add that to the fact that I'll

133

never be able to sleep if I sleep in the bed, and the choice is simple; I pull a blanket over her, limp over to the couch, lie down there, and sleep. Or try to, anyway. I don't think that she's breathing any louder than usual, but every time she exhales, it feels like she sighs, and it makes me think about what the texture of her skin would be like, so it's a really long time before I can get any sort of sleep.

MAY 22ND, 7:19 AM

I try to dispel the fog from my mind as I reach for the phone on my nightstand. Except there is no nightstand. The phone is ringing from farther away, and I'm lying on a couch. Why am I lying on a couch? I hear Julie's voice groaning from the other end of the room, and I remember. Julie. Her legs. The bar. Right.

I sit up, and remember my ribs are broken, but all that disappears when I swing my legs onto the ground and I'm hit by a ridiculous pain in my right thigh, so much I have to bite my hand not to scream. I take a look at the makeshift bandage I made last night, and see that in addition to the blood, there is a yellow-green pus-like substance seeping through the cloth. I try to stand to go get the phone, but it's too painful, and I sit back down on the couch with a moan. I've missed the call anyway; I can hear my voicemail alert.

"What the hell are you making all that noise for?"

I turn around and see Julie, sitting up in bed, her hair frizzing out of its French twist, her make-up smeared, and

135

the blanket covering her legs. Her eyes are puffy, bloodshot, and have bags under them. She looks around herself, slightly confused, and then at me.

"What are you doing here?"

"You called me so I could come and get you last night. Remember?"

She seems to think about it for a second, and then just scratches her head.

"Yeah... a bit. What happened?"

"Actually, I was going to ask you."

She seems to think about it, real hard, and then her face contorts in anger.

"Right. That prick."

I wait for her to go on, but she doesn't. "What did he do?"

"Put something in my drink."

She stands and paces a bit, as if looking for something. She finds her purse on the floor and looks through it, sitting back down on the bed. After a few seconds, she tosses it on the floor, sighing, but looking satisfied that whatever it was she was looking for is still there. She sees me looking, and raises an eyebrow.

"What?"

"Well, not to be indiscreet or anything, but how did you end up in a closet, calling me?"

She shrugs. "I was feeling myself slip, and I knew I couldn't make it all the way back to the hotel, so I decided to teleport to somewhere I could hide until someone could get me."

"And you called me."

She shrugs, but doesn't look at me. I get the feeling she's not too proud of what happened. And of the fact that it was me she called. Why didn't she call Dow, then? It would have been less trouble for him to get her, what with being able to be invisible, and not having a gunshot wound to the leg.

She stretches, stands, and reaches behind her back to unzip her dress. She lets it fall to the floor, wiggling her hips to help it on its way as she removes the pins holding up her hair with both hands. She has a matching black lace bra and panties, and I stare at her perfect, taut belly as she shakes her hair loose. She catches me looking and grins, running a finger along her collarbone all the way to her shoulder, lowering her bra strap.

"I'm gonna take a shower, but if you want, you can come along... you earned it."

I was starting to feel uncomfortable, but that last sentence sounded so much like Lori, it's not even a little hard to turn away anymore.

"No thanks. Can you just toss me my phone?"

137

She shrugs and leans down to pick up my pants. She makes a face at the blood.

"What the hell?"

"Long story."

"Are you ok?"

She walks to me, still in her underwear, holding the pants away from her, between her thumb and index finger. I shrug.

"Probably. It's not anything new, it's just my thigh again. I had to do some running yesterday. While carrying you."

She drops the pants on the couch, and leans over it to inspect my leg. She screws up her face.

"Eew! I don't think it's supposed to be this color. Is it?"

"I'm fine."

She raises her eyebrows at me incredulously, and bends further so she can poke it. For a second, I can smell a bit of her perfume, but underneath it, is the soft, earthy smell of her skin, and I close my eyes to cool down. Then, my leg hurts like hell as she pokes right into the wound.

"Ow! What the hell did you do that for?"

She gives me a level look, raising an eyebrow. "Fine, huh? I think you gotta get that checked out."

I roll my eyes, retrieving my phone from my pockets.

"Whatever. Weren't you going to take a shower?"

"Yeah. And the offer is retracted. I don't want you oozing all over me."

She turns and walks to the bathroom, while I check my phone for who called. It's Mister Lupino. I don't even bother checking the voice mail, I know what he wants. He woke up and I wasn't there; I owe him an explanation. I hit the callback button, and he picks up on the first ring.

"Alex. Where are you?"

"I'm in Julie's room. Don't worry, I'm fine."

"I was worried about you. Did something happen?"

I sigh, quietly. How do I even begin to explain it? "She needed help in the middle of the night, so I went. It was just easier to stay there."

"Oh. It was, was it?"

I open my mouth to explain that I'm really ok, that nothing bad happened, when I realize that his tone is amused, not worried. I almost groan when I think of how what I said sounded.

"Oh. Uh, it's not like that. It..."

"Oh, you do not have any explaining to do. Please, forgive me for bothering you. I will go have breakfast downstairs. Join me if you like, but take all the time you need."

"Mister Lupino..."

"Good-bye!"

I sigh heavily as I hang up. I shouldn't have told him I was with Julie. Now, who knows what he's imagining? I hear her turn on the shower, and I slide to the edge of the couch, carefully, trying my leg again. I almost scream with the pain as I try to lift myself off the couch, and I resist the urge to throw my phone against the wall to shatter it. This won't do. I can't even stand up anymore. I'm gonna need at least my crutches. What should I do?

I try calling Lupino again, but he doesn't pick up. I don't have Dow's number, and Tom doesn't have a cell phone. I try to think. Maybe Tom's still in his room. Didn't he say he already knew what Dow was thinking because we lived next to him? It's worth a try. I close my eyes, and concentrate on him.

Tom.

It takes a few seconds of concentration, and then I hear his voice in my head, sounding annoyed.

What do you want? I'm sleeping.

I try to tell him that my leg hurts, that I need my crutches, that Mister Lupino isn't answering his phone, and at the same time I think of Julie and what happened last night, and before I have time to sort it all out, I hear him in my mind again.

Wow, wow, ok, I got it. Just stop thinking and relax, I'll get you your damn crutches, all right?

I grab the remote and turn on the TV, muting the volume, to try and clear my mind. I concentrate on the image for a little while. It's an old black and white movie, and some guy is doing all sorts of weird tricks to please a girl in a white dress who doesn't want anything to do with him. The girl is short, and dainty, and has curly black hair and 1930s make-up, but I can't help imagining Julie, even though she's tall, strong, blonde and a total tomboy. I wonder what the guy is trying to tell her. I wonder what he sees in her too; she seems so uninteresting, with her vaguely flirtatious yet prudish manner. She seems really dumb, too. I'm relaxed enough that I've almost forgotten Julie's naked in the shower just a couple yards from where I'm sitting, when someone knocks on the door.

"Come in!"

The door opens, and it's Dow that walks in first, holding my crutches. Tom is trailing not too far behind him, hands in his pockets, looking in a better mood than I've seen him in for days. I raise an eyebrow at them.

"Hey, Dow. You turn yourself into Tom's mule?"

Dow lifts an eyebrow and looks at Tom, who just smirks and shrugs. I guess he hadn't noticed, or didn't care until someone else had. They look at each other for a couple seconds, after which Dow just shrugs and hands me my crutches. In doing so, notices my leg.

"Has it been looking like that for a while?"

I shake my head.

"I had to walk on it last night, fast; I guess I popped a stitch. It's fine."

He wrinkles his nose in disgust. "I don't know about that. It looks infected. Maybe you should see a doctor."

"It's probably just the strain."

"Strain, huh? What have you been doing to occasion such a... strain?"

He has a slight mocking smile, and I roll my eyes. Why does everyone assume I had sex with Julie, just because I'm in the same room as her in the morning? Can't they see I'm on the couch?

"It's not like that. I just... helped her out, last night. Nothing happened. Besides, I feel fine. I don't want to see a doctor."

He looks at Tom, as if seeking confirmation of what I'm saying. Tom nods, and Dow shrugs.

"I suppose it's your decision. But if you start getting a fever, I think you ought to see a doctor."

"Fine, whatever."

I prop the crutches on the floor, and hoist myself up onto them. The pain is excruciating, but I do manage to stand. When I've finished catching my breath, I look down and notice the flaw in my plan.

"Huh. I guess I should have asked you for pants."

Tom laughs and shakes his head. "Well, Lupino's gone now, so you'll have to give us your key."

I start looking through the pockets of my pants and fish out the key card. I hear the shower being turned off, and I suddenly remember that Julie is naked in the bathroom.

"Uh. Maybe you could help me get back to my own room?"

Tom shrugs. "Well, I don't know. I think it would be more useful to talk to the both of you, and besides, you probably shouldn't walk too much on that leg."

I look up at him to protest, but I see he's got a playful grin on his face, and I realize he's having me on. I give him a look that says 'don't fuck with me,' and I know he knows it because he can read my mind, but he just looks up innocently at the ceiling like he has no idea what's going on. The door to the bathroom opens and Julie steps through, holding a towel against the front of her body. Her hair is wet and tangled, and the water drips from it down her bare back, her legs, the curve of her ass... She stops dead in her tracks and looks at us, raising an eyebrow. She lets go of one side of her towel, revealing even more of her body, and puts a hand on her hip.

143

Her eyes are no longer puffy and bloodshot; she looks fully awake.

"What's this? I think you could tell a girl you're planning to throw a party, especially if it's going to be when I come out of the shower naked."

Dow turns to lift an eyebrow at me, an appreciative smile on his face, and I look down, my face flaming, but not before I take a look at Tom and realize that he's as hot and bothered as I am.

She turns her back to us, and completely drops the towel to start dressing right then and there. I stare at her butt while she's slipping underwear up her perfect legs, but when I notice that Tom and Dow are doing the same thing, I grab one of my crutches and whack them both with it. They start, and have the decency to look a little embarrassed. Dow clears his throat, and turns to the TV.

"What is it with you and watching TV on mute?"

I shrug, not caring too much about privacy for the moment, glad for the distraction from Julie and her body.

"It's how I always watched it. When we were kids, my sister and me, we used to get up early so we could watch it before the man my mother made me with got up. We had to watch it on mute, or else it'd wake him and he'd get pissed off."

Tom sits down next to me, and Dow just frowns at me, like I said something really weird.

"The man your mother made you with? You mean, your father?"

I glare at the TV. This is why I don't talk about things. It gets way too personal.

"That man was never a father to anyone. Lupino's my father, now."

I see him open his mouth to ask another stupid question, but I'm quicker than he is.

"I'm not going to be talking about it, so you better forget it."

He shuts his mouth, and I'm satisfied. I don't talk about that stuff, and I'm certainly not about to start with an obviously privileged guy who had such a happy childhood that he still eats dinner with his mother three times a week.

Julie walks over to us, wearing her stupid jeans with the hole in the knee, and a baggy AC/DC t-shirt.

"Way to sour the mood, kid."

I roll my eyes, but I don't respond to the bait. I gesture at Tom with my chin.

"Why don't you hand me the room service menu? I'll order us some breakfast."

145

Dow looks at his watch. "Well, actually, I wanted to take advantage of the spa. Did you know there is a full-service spa and massage parlor in this hotel?"

Julie grins. "Ooh! Fancy hotel breakfast, hot tub, sauna, massages? That sounds like my kind of day. You in, Alex?"

The hot water stings my leg as I slip into it. It's full of chlorine though, so I guess it must be good for healing wounds, right? Tom slips in the hot tub right after me, sitting in a spot and spreading his arms on either side of him on the edge of the tub. Dow looks at him and nods, grinning like an idiot. Julie is already settled, her head leaning back on the edge, eyes closed. Dow smiles at me.

"So? Feeling good? Glad I convinced you to go?"

I have to admit it's really relaxing, and it's even making my ribs feel better, so I nod, closing my eyes and leaning my head back just like Julie. We stay quiet for a little while, and then I feel something brushing against my uninjured thigh and I look down. It's Julie's foot, and she's grinning at me with her eyes half-closed. Dow also has his eyes closed, but Tom is frowning at her, so I twitch my leg away from her touch, clicking my tongue. She rolls her eyes, but she's still smiling, like she thinks it's funny.

Tom sighs. "You know, it's really, really annoying."

She lifts her head, looking at him. "What is?"

"You. Thinking about sex. *All* the time."

She shrugs, smirking. "What? It should be pleasant."

"Oh yeah? How would you like to watch porn all day? And I mean, all day? Without interruption?"

She shrugs. "I guess it would get old, but it's not like I can control everything I think about."

"Well, you should try, at least, because it's really irritating. And don't tell me you are, because I've been doing this long enough to tell the difference between conscious and unconscious thoughts, and yours are *way* conscious."

She rolls her eyes, shrugging again. "Whatever. You should learn to relax."

"That's it. I'm leaving. Antoine, I'll be getting a massage."

Dow opens his eyes, like he didn't notice the argument going on until now, and shrugs. "Fine. I'll come with you. At my age, you get wrinkly really fast, anyway."

They both step out of the tub, water dripping from them. I'm thinking 'don't leave me,' but I don't dare say it in front of Julie, and I'm not gonna get out of a place that's finally making me feel good after all this time, so I just shut up and look at her. She watches them go and leans forward, half-walking, half-swimming until she's

148

practically sitting on my lap. She wraps one arm around my neck, grinning at me. I frown at her.

"What are you doing?"

She shrugs, looking innocent again. "Weeell... we're alone in a private hot tub. We should be taking advantage of that time."

"I told you, I don't do that."

I think about pushing her off, but I'd be touching too much skin, so I just move away from her instead. She rolls her eyes, and sighs loudly.

"Look, I don't care that you're a virgin, I'm not gonna judge you on your performance."

"I'm not a virgin."

I want to glare at her, but I'm just so tired right now; I wouldn't even have the energy to get up out of the tub and walk away, so I stay, and I discuss my fucking personal life with someone who has no filter, no sense of decency, and no shame.

She raises her eyebrows at me, smiling derisively, like she doesn't believe me.

"Oh, really? That's hard to believe."

I'm starting to get mad. What is wrong with her, anyway?

"Why? You're always after me. Is it so hard to believe that someone else would be, too?"

She shrugs, still mocking me with her smile.

"I've never seen you with a girl before, and you say you're not gay. What, do you have some kind of secret girlfriend somewhere, that nobody knows about?"

For some reason, I keep picturing Lori, holding our baby. I'm starting to feel sick.

"No. I don't have a girlfriend."

"Have you ever had one?"

"Yeah, I have, and it's complicated, and I don't wanna talk about it. Ok?"

She purses her lips, like she's considering something, then shrugs, and stands to walk out of the tub.

"Fine. I'm gonna go get a massage too. Have fun playing with yourself."

She grabs her towel and wraps it around herself before walking away, leaving me alone. I'm a little pissed off and flattered at her persistence, disappointed that I wound up alone in so short a time, and relieved that she's gone. I thought after living with Lori for over six months I'd finally come to a place in my life where I understood women, but I guess I just never will.

150

MAY 22ᴺᴰ, 12: 36 PM

Mister Lupino waves at me when he sees me walk into the restaurant. It's not like I wouldn't have found him anyway; I mean, the place is small enough, but I humor him by nodding at him and heading over to his table. I sit down with some difficulty, and the pain in my leg makes me cringe, but I don't think he notices.

"Good afternoon, Alex. I see you are back with the crutches."

I look at them as he mentions it, and shrug like it's no big deal.

"Yeah... I woke up this morning and my leg hurt."

The corners of his lips twitch up in a barely concealed smile, half way between amused and collusive.

"Well... perhaps there are certain things you should not be doing right now, with your injury."

151

I frown, wondering how he knows what I was doing last night, and then it hits me, that he doesn't, and he thinks I spent the night in bed with Julie. I feel my face heat, no matter how hard I try to stop it.

"Oh! No, it's really, really not what you think."

"Is it not?"

"No, really, I meant what I said this morning, she got in trouble with her date, she needed help, and she called me."

He frowns at me, like he's about to reprimand me.

"You did not get into trouble with the man she was with, did you? Get into a fight?"

"No! No, of course not. He just... well, he slipped something into her drink, and she found a place to hide until I could pick her up."

He smiles, eyebrows raised, looking halfway between impressed and happy.

"So. When she was in trouble, and she needed someone to trust, she called you."

I frown. I know he's trying to tell me something, and I'm not sure I see what it is. So what if she called me?

"Uh... yeah. Why?"

"It would seem that she trusts you."

He chuckles when I look blank. We've fought together on more than one occasion. We're comrades-in-arms. It only makes sense that she trusts me.

"Well... yeah."

He's still smiling, like I'm doing something funny. And endearing. It's annoying.

"Women find it very important that a man be someone they trust, Alex."

I stare at my plate, not answering. So that's what he was going on about. He thinks she likes me. I guess I should probably set him straight.

"Is something the matter, son?"

I look up, and I find myself smiling. I know now that when he calls me son, it's not some vaguely patronizing term of endearment, but really what the word means; his son.

"It's nothing. Just... She's not interested in me that way."

He raises an eyebrow, looking amused. "Oh? Is that so?"

"Yeah."

"She seems interested, to my eyes. Very. But maybe I am just old. Maybe things have changed."

"Well, I mean, she's interested in..."

153

I feel my face heat again. Damn, why am I such a wimp lately? And in front of Lupino, too. But I don't see myself mentioning it to him; he's right, he is older, and I never talked about sex with him. Yet he still has that amused face.

"In...?"

Great. He's gonna make me say it. Guess I don't have a choice. "She just wants to sleep with me. It's not anything serious."

"Ah. And what makes you think it is not serious?"

I shrug. "She behaves that way with most of the other guys she met. I mean, even with Tom. And he's barely sixteen."

"So, why is it that she did not call Tom to her aid, last night? Why you?"

I frown. I suppose he's got a point. Tom is as trustworthy as I am, possibly more, because he's smarter, and powerful. But I guess he couldn't get into a night club. He's way too young, and it shows; I may be only eighteen, but I know I look older.

"Many reasons, I guess."

"I think you might misjudge her. You young people, these days... you let physical things sometimes get in the way of what the heart wants. The body has needs, of course, but it can prevent you from talking about what matters."

154

"What do you mean?"

"She is a bit like you. Strong. But strength does not have to mean hardness. And because you are both strong, it is possible that she does not wish to show you the weakness of her heart."

I try not to sigh, and think about what he's saying. He's awesome, and smart, but I don't get why being that way makes people have to talk like Yoda. Why can't he just say what he means?

"I'm not sure what you mean."

He chuckles. Again. "I mean, correct me if I am wrong, but you are not one to get emotional. About anything."

I shrug dismissively, but don't answer. It's true I don't like to get mushy. So what?

"I have known you for a very long time, and have seen you go through intensely emotional ordeals, and you have never shown emotion. Not once."

"So?"

I can't help myself. I get defensive when I detect someone has found a kink in my armor, even if it is Lupino. That makes him smile, like I'm validating his point.

"So, is it possible that you associate emotion with weakness?"

I shrug. The man my mother made me with always told me that crying was for wusses, and wimps, and that real men are strong. Maybe I did let it affect me, but then, having done the things I needed to do, I couldn't really sit down and talk about my feelings, could I? Not with people like Jimmy.

"...maybe."

"Well, everyone needs to talk about their emotions. Not all the time, of course, but there are moments when it is necessary, especially when love is involved."

I pick up a piece of bread from the basket in the middle of the table, and put it in my mouth, chewing on it so I have a little time to think. It's true that Lori always wanted to talk about how she felt. But I was never good at that. I always thought she was indestructible, because of the things she had gone through and laughed away. If I had made time to talk to her about stuff, I might have known she was dying inside, and I might have been able to help her. Save her.

But what about Julie? She doesn't seem to feel what normal people feel. She just has fun with everything. She likes to hit stuff, and have sex, and that's all I know about her.

"I don't know about that."

"Oh, she is a strong one, like I said. After all, as I gather, you do like them that way. But everyone has feelings, and everyone needs to discuss them... if only with the person they trust the most."

There is that trust thing again. I feel like he's trying to make a point, and I can't see what it is. "What are you saying, exactly?"

"I am saying, that maybe she would like to discuss certain feelings with you. But that she does not feel like they would be received very well."

"Why not? I've been nothing but nice to her."

Haven't I?

"I am sure you have. But being nice is not always enough. Sometimes, with someone you like, you need to do something that you, in particular, are not especially fond of doing, even though I suspect you sorely need to."

"What is it?"

"Open up."

I frown at him. I really don't see how it would help for me to go and spill all my secrets. "Why? I mean, why is it important?"

"Because to really connect with someone, you have to discuss what is really important to you. And all those things you keep locked inside your mind... that is what is important to you."

"No, it's not."

I glare at a spot on the tablecloth. With the price we're paying for this food, you'd think we'd at least get a clean tablecloth. Why is he telling me all this stuff?

"Is it not? Think about it. Why are we close, you and I?"

I try to think about it. It's true that he knows all my secrets. And we've discussed them, at least sort of. And I've been able to talk with him about some things that hurt. And he didn't make me feel like less of a man because of it.

"I guess... because I trust you."

"And you trust me because...?"

"Because... it's hard to put in words. I guess you know things about me, and... you still think I'm good enough."

He smiles, kindly, with a touch of condescendence. Well. It's not really condescending, I guess... maybe it's just the kind of look fathers give to sons they love. I wouldn't know.

"Yes. I know a lot of things about you, and I do still care about you. You also have not seen me at my best, and I do believe that you care about me, as well."

I smile at him, and nod a bit. It's true that I've seen him during some difficult times in his life. But why would that change anything?

Oh.

158

Is that what he was trying to make me see? He nods, as if he's reading my mind. I guess my face is a lot like an open book.

"So you see... love is about being able to trust someone enough to let yourself be vulnerable to them."

I stare at him. I hope I'm half as wise as he is when I get to be his age. I have to try to work out what that means for Julie, though.

"Thanks, Mister Lupino."

"I have told you before, please, call me papa."

"Thanks... papa."

I hear the knock again, and wake up completely. I look around, disoriented for a little while, before I remember that I'm in the hotel in Italy. The knock comes again.

"Alex? Tom told me you were in here."

"Yeah, yeah, come in."

I rub my face. I guess I must have passed out while watching TV, because it's still on, and it's day outside. Did I sleep the whole day and night away, or did I just doze off for a few minutes? Dow comes in and joins me in the living room, sitting on the comfy chair. He eyes me weirdly, and I notice he's staring at the bunny I'm still holding in my hand. I drop it on the couch, and look at him like I'm daring him to say something. I guess having seen me with a bunny really trumps my intimidation skills, because he does.

"So... is that your special friend, or something?"

"No. Was there something you needed?"

160

He nods. "Mister De Luca's wife called. He's back from Naples. He said it was ok if we went to see him."

"Who?"

"Marcello De Luca. The man we're here to see."

"Oh. Ok. Is that all?"

He raises an eyebrow. "You know, I get that you're trying to look tough and all that, but seriously, you could be less abrasive. I'm sure it wouldn't hurt."

I glower at him. "Where do you get off telling me how to act?"

He shrugs, but he's not getting up. I guess he's decided he was talking with me for a while.

"I'm not. I'm just telling you how I'd like to be treated. I realize I might not have had a choice to team up with you guys, but I think you could try being friendly once in a while."

"I'm perfectly friendly."

"Yeah, right. There's not a single time I tried to start a conversation with you that you haven't ended up telling me off in some way."

I open my mouth, but realize I'm about to tell him off, so I shut up and just sigh. He's right, I guess. I've been caught up in my own shit, and I haven't had time to think about anything else.

"It's not personal. Well, it's not about you, anyway. I just don't like it when people ask me personal questions."

"Yeah, I'm getting that. Tom says you've got a lot on your plate. That's not good, for someone your age. How old are you, twenty, twenty-five?"

That makes me smile. It doesn't happen very often that someone overestimates my age. Well, I mean, I'm sure it does happen pretty often, but mostly, I notice the times when someone calls me 'kid' a lot more.

"I'm eighteen."

He looks genuinely surprised, which only makes me feel better. His eyes go to Nicolas' bunny again, and I realize he really does think it's mine, and that I have some kind of childhood issue. I mean, I do, of course, but not that way.

"You had to grow up really fast, huh?"

"That's not... mine. It belonged to..."

I pick up the bunny, and look at it. I don't really know what to say. I don't want to bring up Nicolas, because in the realm of personal subjects, it's kind of at the top of the do-not-discuss list. Dow frowns at it, and he seems to catch on.

"Tom said you had a lot to deal with... I only imagined... someone as young as you... that it would mostly be from your family. Tom said they weren't very nice to you."

I put the bunny down. Compared to Nicolas, the people who made and raised me seem almost like an easy topic, and I'm glad not to have to talk about my son. Let him think I have childhood issues. At this point, I'd rather that than have to admit to a stranger that I was as incompetent a parent as they were.

"Well, not everybody's fit to have kids, you know. They weren't. That's pretty much all there was to it, and it's nothing to make a big deal about."

"Where are they now?"

I shake my head. It's odd; I haven't really talked about them in a really long time. Now, compared to everything else, it's not that painful anymore. Maybe it is true, what they say; time really does heal everything.

"I have no idea. I haven't seen or heard of them in what, four, five years?"

"That long? What happened?"

I open my mouth to speak, and he sighs, reading something in my expression, I guess.

"Let me guess. You don't talk about that."

I blink at him. Maybe I am that predictable. I frown, trying to think of some way of not saying that, but I guess there really is only one way. I shrug.

163

"They weren't nice, like you said. I left. I had to. I never looked back. We were all better off without each other."

"Ah. I'm sorry to hear that."

I think of what to say to that. Everyone's always pried, wanted to know all the sordid details, like they got off on it, or knowing exactly what my birth parents did to me would help them quantify my pain, put some kind of value on it. Well. Everyone but Mister Lupino.

I'm really surprised that Dow's not even putting theories out there, but what is most surprising to me is I don't feel anything at all. I haven't tried talking about my own childhood, and everything that happened, since Mister Lupino brought it up. I was younger then. It's only a few years, but they feel like decades.

Have I finally made peace with it?

"Uh. That's fine."

He smiles, kindly, and I don't even detect a bit of pity in his expression. Sympathy, maybe.

"I can't imagine what that's like. My mother... she means the world to me. So did my father. I admired him a great deal. He died when I was a young man. I had my problems with him then, as I suppose most young men do with their own fathers. When he was alive, all I ever wanted to do was to be free, rebel, do everything my own way. When he died, all I wanted was to be like him."

164

I frown. I've never had anyone just start telling me their whole life story, just like that. Well, maybe Lupino, once or twice. But not someone I barely know. Then again, I don't think I ever knew anyone whose biggest problems simply revolved around rebelling against authority.

"So... I guess your dad was a nice guy?"

"Yes. He was. He sometimes had very firm ideas, but he was a righteous man. He always did what was right. I admired him a lot. That's what inspired me to study law. I wanted to perpetuate his legacy."

I think about that. The man my mother made me with had nothing anyone would ever call a legacy. Well. Unless you can count an unimaginable amount of empty beer bottles. So I don't really understand what he means by that. I think of Lupino, and the main reason I've continued in the work I do, way past the time when it was an absolute necessity. Maybe I do understand.

"So... I guess he was a lawyer?"

"A prosecutor, just like I am now. One of the best."

"Well, that must be nice. Having something in common with someone like that."

"I'm sure you know what that feels like."

"How'd you mean?"

"Well... Domenic and you, you are in the same line of work, right?"

I raise an eyebrow at him. I get that we're doing the bonding thing and everything, and I don't want him to feel excluded, but even if the subject didn't make me feel crappy because I don't know what I'm gonna do with my work, he has to realize I can't talk about that with him. Plus, since when are mister Lupino and him on a first-name basis? He looks puzzled.

"What?"

"Look, dude, even if I was inclined to talk about my work, which I'm not, with anyone, unless it really needs to be done, I definitely wouldn't talk about it with someone who makes a living getting people like me convicted, you know what I mean? Nothing personal."

I expect him to act all offended and hurt again, but he just shrugs, and smiles, then takes a look around at the fancy hotel room, like he's never seen it before.

"Hey, you can't blame me for being curious. After all, now that I see how the other half lives... I just wanted to know how it feels to make that kind of living. You know. The choices you guys make."

"Well, I'll tell you one thing. It's never easy."

He nods, and takes another look at the bunny. I can see that he's burning to ask me about it again, but he doesn't. Instead, he looks at his watch, and stands.

"We should go. I don't want to interrupt his dinner. Do you want to join us, or would you rather give your leg a rest and stay here?"

"No way. I'm bored out of my mind. I'm coming. Besides, I speak better Italian than any of you, so I might as well."

I start to struggle with my crutches, and then notice he's holding out his hand to help me. He doesn't do it in a patronizing, or 'I'm-better-than-you' way, so I take it, and let him help me up.

MAY 22ND, 3:42 PM

The taxi stops on a street so narrow it's almost an alley. The houses are all pretty tall, and so close together that a lot of them have strung clotheslines over the street. It should be dark, because of how small it is, but since the buildings are all varying shades of orange and yellow, it seems bright.

The house we're headed to is a dark cream color, and as I pay the taxi and manage to pull myself out of it after the others, Dow and Tom reach the door, while Julie waits for me. She says nothing when I join her, just moves at my rhythm, and by the time we're at the door, Dow is already knocking. It opens almost immediately, and a sour-faced man in his sixties stands there, arms crossed. He frowns at us like he's surprised to see us, but still looks extremely put out. He begins speaking in Italian, mumbling a bit.

"You're not the same people that came the first two times. Still, I will say it again, I want nothing to do with you or your organization. Go away!"

He makes a shooing gesture with his right hand; Dow looks puzzled and on the edge of panic. He searches through his phrase book, but the man is already closing the door. I step in, finding myself being grateful to Mister Lupino, again, for making me learn Italian. Who knew I'd need it for something other than impressing him someday?

"Sir, we are not from any organization. We are here to speak to you because we need your help. We know nothing of the men who came here before us."

I look at Julie, discreetly, and I'm suddenly hoping my accent has gotten good enough to impress her. Dow looks at me, his eyebrows raised in surprise, and Julie is just grinning at me like I took my shirt off. I turn back to the man, who is pursing his lips repeatedly, like he's chewing on something with his front teeth.

"You're not with them, then?"

I shake my head. My leg is starting to seriously hurt, and I decide to use it to my advantage.

"Like I said, we have no knowledge of anyone coming to see you. There are not more of us, and we are only here to ask your help. If you don't mind, could we perhaps continue this conversation inside, or at least somewhere where we could sit down?"

He looks at my crutches, examines my friends cautiously, and gives me a curt nod, leading the way inside. Julie elbows me softly in the side, still grinning.

"You're pretty sexy when you speak Italian."

169

I ignore her and hurry up to walk in after him, not waiting to see if the others are following, just hobbling up the small stairs with my crutches. The pain in my leg is still there, but it's a bit duller now, so it's not so bad. I stumble as I limp over the threshold and Julie catches me, releasing me as soon as I get myself upright again so it doesn't get embarrassing.

The house is pretty, if a bit gaudy, and not as small as the claustrophobic alley made it out to be. The kitchen is at the back, and is a lot bigger and nicer than any kitchen I've ever been in. It's even bigger than the one at Lupino's house. Of course, he has a dining room, so I guess he doesn't need that much space; the table here is in the same room. There is a gray-haired woman sitting at the table, and she springs up and hurries to an elaborate coffee machine when she sees us walk in, like she didn't expect us and now she has to make us something. The man sits at the table, making as small and quick a gesture as possible to tell us to sit at the other chairs, and folds his arms, watching us with a guarded, even suspicious, expression.

I sit down and take a short moment to introduce all of us, just naming the others while they sit. It's a large enough table, and there is space for us to all sit around it.

I look at the others. I know I have to be the one doing the talking because, well, I'm the only one who can, but I should probably have discussed what we were gonna say with them. I don't really have a clue how to be subtle about this. I'm used to intimidating people into doing what I ask them, not being nice. The guy, who has to be Marcello De Luca, beats me to it, wiping the corners of his mouth with his thumb and index finger.

"What do you want with me?"

"We... need to locate someone."

That should at least get his attention, and maybe even give him a hint at what we know about him. He raises an eyebrow, and looks at me and my friends again. I can understand why he'd be suspicious of us. We look like a weird and unlikely bunch. Tom looks even younger than he is, and is wearing a t-shirt with the Coliseum on it, which he bought at a tourist store, and cargo shorts. Julie is wearing her usual, unappealing Black Sabbath baggy shirt, torn jeans, and unlaced army boots, though she at least left the trench coat at the hotel. Dow is the only one who looks like he could be in a group with me, because we're both wearing suits, though he's at least twenty years older than I am. I scratch my head, and look back at Marcello, who seems to finally be inclined to say something.

"Who are you looking for?"

I look at Dow for him to give me the file, but of course, he doesn't speak Italian, and he has no idea what I want, so he just looks at me with a confused face.

"Can you hand me the file?"

He nods, taking it out of his briefcase, and passing it to me over the table.

"Can he help us?"

171

"I'm finding out."

I open the file and look for the picture of the African guy who can see the future. I unclip it from the paper, and slide it over to Marcello, watching for his reaction.

He picks up the picture, frowns at it, and then at me, putting it back down, leaning back in his chair and folding his arms with a closed-off this-discussion-is-over expression.

"I do not know this man."

I don't pick up the picture, still staring at him. "I didn't think you would."

I notice that his wife is looking at us too, a bit nervously, while still getting busy making the coffee. He raises an eyebrow, unimpressed.

"Then why ask me about him?"

"Let's just say... I have heard you have a knack for finding people."

He looks at his wife, and in the exchange of glances they have, I think I can see how afraid they both are, so I lean forward.

"Sir... I don't want to make you uncomfortable. But we really do need the information. There are... circumstances."

He shakes his head. It looks like he's getting angry again. He taps his index finger on the table. "I do not know you, and you presume to come into my home and ask me things like this?"

I blink. I didn't think this would be offensive. "We just..."

"You just thought you could come here and pretend like you have nothing to do with your partners, and you just happened to hear about me, and make me admit what I can do, is that it?"

I look at my companions, but remember from their neutral expressions that they have no clue what's going on. Dow seems worried, and is looking through his phrase book, but when he sees he's got my attention, he frowns at me.

"What is he saying?"

I almost answer, but I can see Marcello glaring at me. I get the impression that if I start consulting my friends in a language he doesn't understand, it's not going to help his mood. I see Tom rolling his eyes, and sighing, and then abstract images of my memories of how GenEx first contacted me flood my mind. I'm pretty sure it wasn't just me remembering, so understanding, I turn to Marcello.

"These men... who are they? Did they leave any information about themselves?"

He looks at Dow suspiciously, like he thinks we just shared some kind of secret instead of just his confusion, and then stands. He walks to a hand-painted letter holder and leafs through it for half a second, before retrieving a

173

small business card from it and walking back to the table. He purses his lips again, considering me, but I already know what the card is going to say before he hands it over.

It's all in German, I think, with a European phone number on it, but one word is definitely recognizable. GenEx. I see Julie is looking at me expectantly. From Tom's grim expression, he's already figured out what was going on, so I slide the card over to her. She looks shocked when she sees it. Marcello watches us carefully.

"You know of these people?"

I nod, refraining from sighing. This is turning out to be a lot more complicated than I thought it would be. At the same time... the enemy of my enemy is my friend, right? Maybe I can use that to my advantage.

"We have all had dealings with them in the past. They're out to harm people like you. Like us. We are trying to prevent them from doing something that could seriously hurt not only all of us, but the world, as well."

He seems to consider it. At least, I think he does. I've never seen anyone look more neutral and sour at the same time than this man, and that's saying something. His wife brings us each a little cup of espresso while we sit in awkward, heavy silence. Finally, he reaches to take his own cup, takes a sip, and puts it back down.

"What do you want from me?"

"We need you to find this man we are looking for. We came all the way from America for no other reason. We know about what you can do. We're trying to prevent a catastrophe from happening. Only this man can help us."

He looks at the picture again and gives me a look that nearly scares even me.

"What do you know about me? And how?"

I hesitate, but then slide the file of all the information we printed from what Future Tom gave us. He glances at me, and picks it up, looking at it. He frowns, as if increasingly concerned by what he's seeing. I have no idea what he understands from it, since it's all in English, but I wait.

"What is this?"

"We got all this information from an... ally of ours." I glance at Tom, remembering how he looked in the future, but he's careful to avoid my eyes. "He told us that a war is about to erupt between different groups of... extraordinary people." I have no idea how to say superpowers in Italian, so I hope this carries my meaning. It seems to, because he purses his lips.

"Extraordinary?"

I nod. "Yes. People with... extraordinary abilities. As I said, we are like you."

He doesn't say anything. He seems to wait, his arms still folded on his chest, so I extend a hand, concentrating, making a small flame in my palm. His wife drops

175

something on the floor, behind me, and gasps. He just frowns further, and then turns to Dow, Tom and Julie as if really seeing them for the first time. Dow looks at him, then me. I nod and he seems to take my cue, because he concentrates for half a second and becomes invisible. Julie shrugs and disappears from her chair, appearing next to Marcello's wife. She ignores her strangled shout of surprise, bending down to help her pick up shards of porcelain. I don't know what Tom is doing, but it has Marcello suddenly look at him, eyes wide.

Dow reappears and stares at me with an air of trying to communicate by thought, and I realize I should probably say something again, so I look back at Marcello.

"Abilities like these, for instance. The men we're fighting against... the ones who came to see you... they would harm all of us."

"And you heard about me from..."

"From our ally, who asked us to stop this catastrophe. He has a list of all the people who will be involved in this, forcibly or not."

"Which includes me."

"It does."

I keep looking at him. I don't want to give him too many details, because I don't know how it could affect what's about to happen. Now that I've got him believing me, I also don't want to come off as a lunatic. He looks into my eyes and sighs, picking up the picture. Then he seems to realize something.

"This man, your ally, who knows all these things... why could he not tell you where the man you are looking for is?"

I scratch my head. How do I explain that?

"His way of communicating with us is... limited. We just know we have to find this guy, and we know you are the only one that can do it. Will you help us?"

There you go. That's direct, a yes or no kind of deal. He's gotta answer me now. He looks at the picture and sighs again.

"Is it possible to narrow down my search, or am I finding him anywhere in the world?"

"We only know he is somewhere in Africa."

He nods, and calls for his wife to bring him his atlas, then picks up the picture. He stares at it, concentrating for a few moments, then closes his eyes.

Nothing happens for a little while, then his wife comes back into the kitchen and drops an atlas on the table. Dow looks at Tom and Julie, then leans over the table to whisper to me.

"What's going on?"

I take a look at the guy, who seems to still be concentrating really hard. I don't want to disturb him, so I lean over the table to whisper back to Dow as quietly as I can.

"I think he's doing his thing."

It lasts a long, uncomfortable time, during which even I'm not sure of what he's doing, and then, finally, he opens his eyes, puts the picture down, and picks up the atlas, starting to look through it. He still seems focused, and I don't know if I'm going to throw off his concentration if I say anything, so I wait quietly. It's not something I'm good at, and I'm dying for a cigarette, but I sure as hell am not about to light up in here when we're right about to have our answer.

Finally, he seems to stop leafing through the atlas and settles on a page. He stares at it for a little while, and then flips it over to show it to me, pointing at a particular space by tapping his finger on it.

"He is here. You will find him here. In a village near this town."

I pick up the atlas. It's some part of Africa, called Kenya. He's pointing at the western part of the country. I squint at what's written. I have no idea if I'm even pronouncing this right.

"...Kaka... mega?"

He nods with an air of satisfaction. "That is what I saw. I am sure of it."

I sigh in relief. It's not as exact as I imagined it would be, but at least, it's not looking for one man with just one name in all of Africa. I smile at him, and take another look at the atlas. Dow drums his fingers on the table, then just spreads his hands in an expectant and impatient expression.

"So?"

"Our guy is in some place called Kaka..." I have to take another look at the atlas page to read it. "...Kakamega. So all that remains to be done is to go there and look for him, I guess."

Julie shrugs. "Until he tells us what to do to save the world, and all that. That should be considerably more complicated."

I frown. Finding that guy had such a finality to it that I had almost forgotten why we were looking for him. There is a knock at the door, and Marcello's wife goes to answer it. Dow looks at Marcello, and smiles in the awkward fashion of someone who really can't communicate but still wants to look friendly.

"Ask him if he wants some compensation for his work."

I raise an eyebrow at Dow, but I suppose he's got a point, so I turn to Marcello.

"Is there something we can do in return for you granting us this favor? It really was helpful to us."

He shakes his head, waving a hand dismissively. His wife comes back in the kitchen, a puzzled look on her face.

"Marcello, the men are back. Should I tell them you are busy?"

He looks at us, and then frowns at her. "The men who left the card? Did you tell them I was here?"

I look at the others, and Tom seems pale and nervous. He's straining his neck to see the door, but of course, he can't, the angle is much too awkward. Julie leans back, balancing her chair on its two back legs, taking a look at the door too.

"What's up? Why is everyone looking like they've lost their puppy?"

I look at her, and try to make my voice as low as possible. "It's GenEx. They're here."

Marcello doesn't answer his wife, just looks between me and Julie, and I realize he's expecting us to do something. I stand up, leaning on the table, trying to do it without my crutches. It's painful as hell, but I push through because I know that looking like a handicapped guy is not going to help me intimidate these freaks away. Tom stands too, obviously knowing what I have in mind, and so does Julie. Dow looks at us all, confused.

"What's happening?"

"You wanted to know what we could do in return for him? Well, this is it. We need to get GenEx off his doorstep."

Dow frowns, standing. I start walking to the door. My leg is killing me, so I take it slow, and I hope the limp doesn't show too much. There are two guys here, and they seem confused and alarmed as they see us walking toward them. They're wearing matching, cheap suits, like some kind of a uniform; even their hair is the same, all slicked back with too much gel. One of them taps the other one on the upper arm, and they share a meaningful look. I stand in the doorway and hope they'll speak English; I don't know if I can do this on my own. I try my luck.

"You guys with GenEx?"

They look at each other, hesitating, and then the shorter one looks at me with an air of defiance. He does speak English, but his accent is thick, and definitely not Italian.

"This does not concern you. We have come to see Marcello De Luca. You are not Marcello De Luca."

I raise my eyebrows in a mock-impressed expression. "Wow! Smart, and a snappy dresser."

They seem taken aback, for sure, but I know their tactics. It's gonna take a lot more than intimidating these two guys to deter them from coming after Marcello. Even if I do send them on their way, they'll be back in no time. I need to do something more impressive, to have them away for a while, so that Marcello has time to get to somewhere safe.

The short one, who seems to be the leader, clears his throat and turns back to me.

"We are not looking to have a conflict with anyone at this time. All we want is to speak to Marcello."

"Well, you're not going to."

I fold my arms and lock my knees, trying to look as impressive as I can, which is pretty hard with how much my leg hurts. Maybe it'll be as simple as that. The taller one raises an eyebrow and folds his arms too, imitating my posture, and I can see this is going to turn into some kind of pissing contest. The smaller one takes a step forward, a smug grin on his face.

"We are here to speak to Marcello, not you. And our discussion is now over."

He flicks his fingers at me, and suddenly, an invisible wall pushes me to the side. It makes me lose my balance, and I fall to the ground and halfway down the four steps to the street; in trying to remain upright, I strain my leg, and the pain rips through me like the gunshot all over again.

I'm caught by the same wall before I fall all the way, and it's the weirdest thing I've ever seen; I can feel that it's there, it's hard as rock, but I can't see anything, not even the sort of nothing you see when you look through glass.

I can see that Dow, Tom, and Julie are also pushed aside by the same invisible force, and the small guy just starts walking into the space he's cleared, looking smug as hell. Julie glares at him and teleports out of the space she's in, appearing directly in his face. He has time to look shocked before she hits him square on the nose with a punch as hard-looking as any I've seen Jimmy throw.

The guy takes a step back, holding his nose, and I guess his concentration is shot because suddenly there's nothing to keep me from tumbling down the rest of the way, which I do. I see from the corner of my eye that Marcello is behind us, and retreating towards the back of his house. Just as I think 'someone should help him,' I see Tom nod at me and head after him.

Julie is advancing on the small guy, still wailing on him, but then the bigger guy teleports behind her and grabs her by the back of her shirt, yanking her away. She grabs him, and they disappear. I look around me and I can't see Dow anywhere, so I guess he made himself invisible to keep out of the way, which leaves me to take care of force-field dude. I try to stand, fail, and use the rage that pain brings to fuel my fire, throwing a blast at the guy.

He screams and throws up one of his shield things, I guess, because I can see my fire deflected right in front of him. The front of his suit is singed, so I guess I did take him by surprise. When I'm done, he looks at me, wide-eyed, then notices my predicament. He runs inside, well aware that I won't be able to follow him. I curse and scream with the pain, but I make it to my feet and manage to limp at a not-so-leisurely pace after him, not caring about who sees me in pain anymore.

I find him in the small living room, looking around like a man who's forgotten something. Tom is there, with Marcello and his wife. They're all standing in a corner, not moving, and Tom has an air of concentration on him. Force-field guy doesn't seem to see them at all, though, and he looks all around himself scratching his head like he doesn't know what to do. I don't know what Tom is doing, but I decide to use it to my advantage. Before I get to, though, Julie teleports right next to him, grabbing him by the arm. She looks up at me, grinning, but then her eyes widen.

"Look out, behind you!"

I turn around real quick and I see the other dude, the big one, standing about five feet behind me. He walks up to me, holding a large stick that I have no idea where he got. My instincts act even before I know what I'm doing, and I hold up my hands, summoning all the fire I've got through the sudden fear. He screams and takes a step back, and I think I got him good, even though something blocked my way. Probably more invisible walls from the shield guy.

There is a little confusion, though, because I think I heard him disappear, like Julie does, except I can clearly see his body fall down to the ground. I immediately turn my attention to where Julie was with shield guy, except she's no longer there, and Tom, Marcello and his wife are all staring at me with wide-eyed horror. I look around, but I don't see anything on fire; I did manage to be pretty careful. Then Tom just runs past me and kneels next to the fallen guy on the floor, and I finally realize what's wrong.

This isn't the guy. He's much smaller, for one. And he's got his hair in a ponytail... and the remains of a suit that was much nicer than the ones the GenEx guys had on.

This is Dow.

I gasp, and hurry over to him to check on him. He's lying face down, though Tom is turning him over when I get there. Half his suit is burnt off, some of it right into his skin. His skin... most of it is crispy. Blackened. Or red, blistery, and oozing. It smells horrible, like burnt meat. I haven't seen anything like it in a long, long time. Not since I burned the man my mother made me with.

I suddenly feel sick, and I turn away from him, standing, heading outside, never mind the pain in my leg, just trying to get some fresh air. When I finally reach the door, I lean over the threshold to throw up on the stone steps.

Dow. How could I not have seen him? Of course. He was invisible. I've never fought while having someone on my team that I just couldn't see. I should have thought about it. Why didn't I think about it? Those burns... he'll never recover.

I lean on the doorframe and realize that I'm sitting, though I don't know how or when I did. My head is spinning. I feel so dizzy... I look down at my feet. I realize I have puke on my shoes, but I don't care. I lean my head on the doorframe, and close my eyes. I don't want to think. Mercifully, my head doesn't seem up to it, either.

I don't know how long I'm there before someone touches my shoulder. It could be seconds, but it feels more like hours. I can't really tell.

I look up and see Tom. I hate the expression on his face; it's so full of pity, it's almost condescending. He's holding my crutches, and sits down next to me instead of handing them over.

"You ok?"

"Fuck me. How's Dow?"

He shrugs. "I don't know. Julie took him to the hospital as soon as she got back."

"Oh."

I hate myself instantly. It wasn't her job to do that; it should have been me. I sigh and rub my face with my hands. I want to ask if he's gonna be ok, but of course, he's not. Tom shrugs.

"You don't know that. They might be able to do something. We'll have to see."

I look at him, remembering that he can read my thoughts, and I sigh. I feel so heavy, and exhausted... he stands and hands me my crutches.

"Want to go to the hospital and see?"

I sigh. I don't really want to, but I could never forgive myself if I didn't. I pull myself up, using the doorframe, and take my crutches. My leg is covered in blood, again, but whatever. I've had worse. Dow has a lot worse. Tom nods.

"I called a taxi. I took care of Marcello and his wife, too. Told them they should find somewhere to hide, somewhere that can't be linked to them. Marcello said he knows where to go."

I nod, absently. I hadn't even thought of that. I guess I really don't know how to deal with stuff like this.

"Good, good."

Tom gives me a sad little smile as the taxi pulls up, but he knows better than to say a stupid platitude.

MAY 22ᴺᴰ, 5:39 PM

I guess hospitals always look the same, no matter where you go. It feels like they all have these stupid little blue plastic chairs that are supposed to mold everyone's butt, no matter your shape or size. I jiggle my good leg absently, staring ahead. Dow's still in ICU, and they won't let us see him because they're still working on him. Tom's gone off to who knows where, and I still haven't found Julie, so I wait in the waiting room that's meant for people who really care about the people that are being operated on. Not the people who hurt them. But where else am I gonna go?

I check my phone again. It feels like it's been so long already... when I see the time, I realize it's only been minutes.

I close my eyes and lean my head back against the wall. I try to clear my head, but all I can see is Dow's body falling, burnt, by my fire, hitting the ground with that horrifying sound, and the smell... I can't stop smelling the smell. I think it's on my clothes.

I feel someone staring at me, and open my eyes. Julie's standing not three inches in front of me, looking down at me, her hands in the pockets of her jeans.

"Hey there. You ok?"

"Why does everyone keep asking me that? I'm fine, I'm unhurt. He's the one that's not ok."

She makes a face, and sits down next to me. "He might be. Eventually. The doctors say we won't be able to see him for a while, and he won't be conscious for at least a few days... so I think we should go back to the hotel."

"What? You want to go to the spa, or something? Get a massage? I'm not going anywhere while he's not ok."

She shrugs. "You're gonna get kicked out if you stay here too long. Visiting hours are over, and we're not really supposed to be here anymore."

"I don't care!"

She rolls her eyes. "Look. We are absolutely not useful here. But at the hotel, we've got his laptop and documents, and we can look for a way to help him. They're going to keep him sedated, so there's no purpose in us staying here. He won't even know the difference. Besides, if you want to feel sorry for yourself, you can do that as well over there as you can here. So what do you say? Come with me."

She puts her hand on my wrist and gives it a light squeeze. I close my eyes, and the contact feels really, really good for a little while, then I remember I have no right to be feeling any sort of good at all, so I shake her off and stand. I mean for it to be dramatic, but it probably takes me a full two minutes to clamber back up to my crutches; my leg feels like lead. She doesn't say anything, doesn't even smile in that mildly mocking way that she has, and I find myself being grateful for it, though I'd never tell her that.

She waits until I'm on my feet, then she stands, stretching, like she had meant to wait all along. She walks at my rhythm, and looks down at my leg as we walk out of the hospital. I can tell she's dying to comment, but I'm glad she doesn't.

MAY 22ND, 6:07 PM

When we get to the hotel, she waits for me to catch up to her in the lobby, watching me. I can't exactly explain why, but I get the uncomfortable feeling that she's evaluating the way that I'm walking. I reach her, and she purses her lips as if considering something.

"You feeling ok?"

I know I shouldn't, but I get frustrated at her question. "Of course. I'm not burnt to a crisp, am I?"

She shrugs, as if she expected the outburst. "Wanna go get some dinner?"

I think about it. I don't really want to go face Mister Lupino just yet, because he'll know something is wrong, and then he'll make me talk about it. I can't lie to him, and even if I did, he always knows when I do. I don't really want to stick around with Julie, because she knows what happened and I have to look her in the eye, but I get a feeling she likes her privacy as much as I do, so she probably wouldn't pry. Besides, I am hungry.

"All right. Dinner sounds good."

She nods and takes me to the restaurant, walking slow so I can follow her without hurting myself too much. We don't look really good, and I realize that we probably shouldn't be sitting in a five-star restaurant looking like we do, so I stop before we get there. She stops too, and raises an eyebrow at me.

"What's up?"

"We look like crap, and the place is full. We should go somewhere else."

She shrugs. "Fine. Wanna go up to my room and get some room service?"

I don't know what my face looks like, but she looks at it and starts laughing, before holding up her hands.

"No funny business or hidden intentions, I swear."

"Fine."

She leads the way, calling the elevator while I catch up to her. We stay quiet as the elevator goes up, and all the way to her room. I sit down on the couch heavily while she picks up the menu and the phone, and orders us dinner. I don't really listen. I'm hungry, but I'm also nauseous and I feel like my stomach is caught in a steel clamp, so I might devour whatever it is she ordered, or I might not be able to swallow a single bite. I stay on the couch while she gets up and goes to change her shirt to an AC/DC tank top, and after a few moments, a hotel employee comes in

192

pushing a cart that has a couple of steaks, bottles of wine, and two glasses on it. I don't say anything, but after she's tipped the bellboy and he's gone, I look at her.

"I told you, I don't drink."

She rolls her eyes. "Oh. Yeah. Right. You hate fun. I forgot."

"I don't hate fun."

"Then why don't you drink? Or have sex?"

I stare at her. I feel like I'm boiling inside, and I literally have to say nothing and concentrate not to burn something. She sighs a bit, probably noticing how angry she just made me, and shakes her head.

"I just thought it would do you some good, after the day we've had."

"Alcohol has never done anyone any good."

She smiles at that, raising an eyebrow. "Oh? It does me plenty of good, on a regular basis."

"So you think."

"So I know. It helps me forget my troubles for a little while, and then I feel better for a while. Where's the harm?"

"It probably makes you act in ways you regret. Maybe you don't even realize it."

193

She shakes her head. "Nah, I'm not a horny drunk. I'm a talky drunk."

I frown at her. "What do you mean?"

"The kind of drunk I am. People are all sorts of different kinds of drunk, but they generally always act the same kind of way, depending on their personality. There's mean drunk, weepy drunk, talky drunk, clingy drunk... well, you know what I mean."

I don't look at her. She pours us each a glass, and takes one, though she doesn't offer me the second.

"You don't know what I mean, then? You must not have been around drunk people a lot, in your life. What makes you such a tight-ass about it, then?"

"I've been around enough drunks to know that it's something I don't want to be."

In truth, my parents were the only drunks I was ever around. They were both mean, in different ways. But I've seen Lori drunk quite a few times, and she wasn't at all like them. Maybe there is something to what Julie is saying.

"How often have you been drunk in your life?" I shrug, and her smile widens. "You never have, have you?"

"So what? It's not something that I want to try. Is that so bad?"

She picks up the second glass and offers it to me. "Try it. After a day like this, it helps you relax. You need it, trust me."

I think of the time I almost hit Lori. I wasn't drunk then. Is that the only thing that stopped me? "I'm sure you wouldn't like me when I'm drunk."

"I'm not telling you you should be drunk. I'm telling you, have a drink. Start with one. See where it takes you."

I take the glass from her hand and look at it. I guess one drink won't be so bad. I had one drink, once. Granted, it was roofied, but I conceived Nicolas with that drink, and that was definitely a good thing. I take a sip. It tastes a bit bitter, but earthy, and fruity in a way that's not sweet at all. It's really not that bad. Julie watches me with fake wide eyes, and I snap at her.

"What?"

"Wow. You're not dead."

"Oh, shut up."

I take another sip, this one larger, almost a gulp, and put the glass down, picking up the plate, balancing it on my knees, and starting to eat. She smiles, and sips her wine, watching me. I take a bite and pick up my glass again. I like this stuff better than beer. All right, maybe I only had the one taste of that, but I didn't like it as much as this. She was right, I guess. It is taking the edge off a little bit. I don't feel so tense and crappy anymore.

She opens her mouth to speak, and I put the glass down, interrupting her.

"No, it wasn't so bad. All right? It's actually kind of good."

"So I'm gonna take a wild stab in the dark, and say... your parents screwed you up over that issue?"

I glare at her. Why does she always have to ruin everything? "I don't talk about them. Lupino's my father, now. That's all you need to know, as far as I'm concerned."

She rolls her eyes. "Of course. It's all a big secret. Like everything else in your life."

She pours some more wine in my glass, and I drink again.

"Do you talk about your past all the time?"

"Well, I'm not obsessed about keeping everyone from making a personal connection, at least."

"It's not like that."

I finish the glass, and it takes the edge away from my anger. I watch her, and she's not looking at me anymore. Her eyes are wandering the room, trying to find something interesting to focus on, I guess. I find myself remembering the discussion I had with Lupino, about discussing my private stuff with others, but it doesn't feel right. This part of me is past. Buried. It's gone. Why rehash it?

I sigh. "Look, Julie... I don't like talking about it. It's personal, and it's about me. Can't we just leave it at that?"

She looks back at me and smiles. She sees my glass is empty, again, so she reaches for the bottle and refills it. I think about stopping, but the glasses are pretty small, so I can't have had that much, right? I have another drink.

She smiles and shrugs. "It's all right. I didn't expect much, anyway. I guess that's as good as I'm ever gonna get. I shouldn't feel bad. You never really connected with anyone, right? I mean, apart from your Mister Lupino?"

I rub my face, finishing my glass. My cheeks feel hot, and as I lean over to put the glass down on the table, I feel oddly dizzy and unbalanced.

"That's not true. I have friends. Like Luke. And Jimmy."

She snorts a laugh and shakes her head. "Jimmy! Oh, yeah, you have a real deep connection with him, all right. You obviously can't even deal with the fact that he's gay!"

I glare at her, but it's hard to get really mad. The only thing I could say is that it's not that I have a problem, just that I didn't see it coming, but I guess it's all the same.

She continues chuckling and refills her own glass, and then mine. Is it the first time she does that? I'm starting to feel warm. And kind of comfortable. I guess I'm starting to get it, about relaxing. I stay quiet, so I think she might let it go, but she doesn't.

"So, that's what you call connecting, huh?"

I'm the one that rolls my eyes, this time around. "We understand each other. What do you call connecting?"

"You know, talking about the real stuff. The stuff that matters."

"I do that. It's not like I know anything private about you either, you know."

"All right. How's about that for a deal? You tell me something personal, and I'll tell you something personal. Sound good?"

I frown. I don't know where she's going with this, and I feel foggy, but the more I think about it, the more tired I feel. Not physically, though I do feel a bit sluggish, but mentally. I'm tired of arguing. And I'm so, so tired of being lonely.

So I agree.

"You first."

She laughs and refills my glass, yet again. She's opening the other bottle. Is that a lot? I don't remember drinking half a whole bottle. Well, it's not that much bigger than a bottle of beer, I guess, so it can't be that much. It takes a whole lot of beer to be drunk, from what I remember. Right?

She leans back, leaving her plate half-eaten, and sips her glass while she thinks. I lean over the table to put my glass down and pick up my plate. As I move, the room seems to tilt. I blink it away, shaking my head, and I take another bite of the steak. I was right, earlier. It's having trouble going down, so I put it away again before picking up my glass. At least that's easy to swallow.

She finally looks at me again as she reaches for the new bottle to refill her own glass.

"You remember when we first met?"

I frown. There's really two events that could qualify. When I was first taken by GenEx, I was put in a cell that had a communicating air vent with hers. We spoke through there for a long time, getting to know each other, but it was weeks before we actually stood face to face to one another.

"What, like, when we broke out, or when I first got there?"

"When you first got there. You remember, you asked me something, and I wouldn't tell you what it was?"

I don't answer right away because I don't want to seem like I wondered about that for nearly the past two years, which I have. I asked her quite a few times, when all we had to do was talk, but she wouldn't say. Since I don't like to talk about my own stuff, I didn't press the issue, nor did I ever bring it up again.

"Uh... you mean when I asked you why you ended up in the cell? Why you stopped doing what they wanted?"

She nods. She doesn't have her usual mocking air, so I can see this is pretty serious for her. She's not looking at me, either. Her eyes are distant, looking straight in front of her at nothing in particular.

"Yeah. I didn't want to tell you, because it's not something I'm really proud of."

I wait. I know first-hand how hard it is to discuss something you really don't want to talk about. It can take time not only to get it out, but to find the right words. She holds up her glass to the light, looking into it.

"I was an assassin. For GenEx."

I lift my eyebrows. I expected many things, but certainly not that. She stays quiet, and I try to think about it. Sure, the ability to teleport is useful, but... an assassin?

"Why? I don't mean... I guess you probably didn't choose, but... why did they choose a teleporter?"

She gives me a small half-smile that doesn't touch her eyes, then looks away again.

"Teleporting isn't the only thing I can do. There's something else. Something I don't bring up really often. I'm a null. I can take away people's abilities by touching them."

I stare at her. Suddenly, some of the things I saw at GenEx, and even here, start to make a lot more sense.

I think about all of it for a long time, fitting all the pieces together, until I remember there was a second part to my question.

"You said you didn't want to do it anymore. Did something happen?"

She nods. "I was sent after people with powers. Dangerous people, mostly, that couldn't be controlled. I have no doubt they'd eventually have sent me against you, if we hadn't taken out the whole operation when we escaped. The tactic was simple; I'd teleport in, take away their ability, drop a grenade, and teleport out. Quick. Efficient. And then one time, it was different. And I couldn't do it."

I want to ask what was so different about it, but I take another drink from the wine instead, finishing the glass. It's weird, my face feels kind of numb. She goes on without needing to be prompted.

"It was a man in particular. As usual, I teleported at the time and place where they said he'd be most vulnerable. Unfortunately, or maybe fortunately, for me, that turned out to be when he was looking after his two little girls."

She looks at me like she's trying to justify herself, and I get the impression she's said those very words a couple of times before.

"They wouldn't have stood a chance. It's not their fault that their dad was superpowered, or out of control, or whatever made GenEx decide he had to be eliminated.

201

I couldn't do it. And it made me think about all the others. What if they had families, too? Who did they leave behind that would mourn them? I went back, and said I was done. That's why they put me in that cell. They thought they could make me change my mind. They were wrong."

We stay in silence for a long time. I never imagined something like that, any of it. But curiously, it makes me realize I have more in common with this girl than I thought I did. More than I thought possible to ever have with anyone, really. I've done reprehensible things for the sake of work I didn't really think I had a choice but to do, either, and I've regretted them... and I also have drawn the line at harming children, in any way.

I take the last sip from my glass and she looks at me before refilling both our glasses, emptying the bottle. She smiles at me, but it's the ghost of her usual expression. She lifts her foot and pushes me playfully with her toes.

"Come on, your turn. We had an agreement."

I shake my head a bit, and wonder what I'm about to say. What I wouldn't mind talking about. There are so many things I keep to myself... but it's obvious, of course. There is one thing that's always on my mind.

I put my glass down on the table and reach into my pocket to dig out my wallet. I open the back pocket and take out the picture. It's gotten soft and thin from being in there, and from me taking it out and looking at it all the time, but it still looks sharp. Nicolas is looking at the camera, smiling his wide, open-mouth, toothless smile, and

Lori has her face against his, also smiling. He looked so much like her. I wonder if he still does.

I look at it for a while, probably too long, and then I pass the picture over to her. She takes it, and frowns at it like she doesn't understand, before looking up at me with a puzzled expression. She doesn't say anything. Like I did, she waits for me to find the right words.

"I have a son. His name is Nicolas."

Her eyes open a bit wider. Even after the picture, she didn't come to that conclusion, probably because she still doesn't believe me when I say I'm not as inexperienced as she thinks I am with relationships. She looks at the picture again then hands it back to me.

"He looks like you."

"Thanks."

"So... how old is he now?"

"He turned two a couple weeks ago."

"I'm guessing he lives with his mother?"

I frown and pick up my glass again, taking a drink from it. This part is going to be the hardest. I haven't even said her name since it happened.

"No. I had to give him up for adoption. She... died."

She's still looking shocked, except even more so. "Oh. Wow. I'm sorry. What happened?"

I shrug, trying to be dismissive about it because if I allow myself to be emotional I'm gonna cry, and I can't let myself do that in front of her.

"She was a junkie. She relapsed while I was in GenEx. She was... it had happened by the time I came back."

There is a long, drawn-out, awkward silence between us. I don't dare look at her, because I couldn't stand to see pity in her eyes. Eventually, I feel a hand on my shoulder, and I look at it, but I can't look at her.

"I'm so sorry, Alex. I had no idea. I wouldn't have... I'm sorry."

I still can't look at her. I don't want to see her eyes. If I do, I'll have to be mad at her for pitying me.

I feel the couch shifting under me and she's suddenly sitting next to me, wrapping her arms around me, and leaning her head on my shoulder. I don't know what to do. Part of me wants to take off her clothes, and part of me wants to curl up into a pathetic little ball and cry like a baby. Neither option seems like a good idea, but it's taking all I have to do nothing.

We stay like that for what seems like forever, until I feel her start to let go. Before she does, I reach up and catch her hand, holding it in place, and she stops her motion. Finally, I gather up the courage to look at her face. Her expression is serious, but there's no pity in there.

There's a little sadness, but most of it is something intense that I don't think I've ever really seen before.

She curls her fingers around mine, slowly, squeezing my hand ever so slightly. Her skin feels warm. She feels warm; it's like I can feel how warm her body is even though it's not really touching mine. I can smell her, too, really clear and distinct, like I've rarely been able to smell in my life. She smells like nice soap, and summer, and all the soft things I've ever held.

She gives a soft, almost hesitant tug on my hand, and I let myself fall closer to her, against her chest. I lift up my face to look her in the eyes, and just as I notice how green they are, she closes them, leaning down toward me with her mouth half-open, really slowly. I can feel her breath on my skin, and it makes my chest feel like it's burning, my stomach heave almost like I feel sick, but not quite, and most importantly, my balls so tight they might make my whole body explode. To hell with good or bad ideas; I can't remember wanting anything more badly than I want her right now.

I close the distance between our mouths, kissing her, grabbing her upper arms to pull her closer. I shift so I can be on my knees on the couch, pressing myself against her. My injured leg stings, almost pulling me out of the moment, but I can ignore it. She moves too, sliding down under me, wrapping her legs around my waist, pressing herself against me. One of her hands makes its way up to my ponytail, grabbing the elastic and pulling it off, making my hair wrap itself around us, while the other starts unbuttoning my shirt with a lot more agility than I think I'd be capable of right now. Fortunately for me, she's just wearing a tank top, and all I have to do is lower its strap, and the one from her bra underneath, and before I know it, her nipple is in my mouth, she's pulling down my pants, and the feeling of her skin is so overwhelming my leg doesn't even hurt anymore.

MAY 23ᴿᴰ, 9:17 AM

.

I feel something moving against me, and I blink my eyes open. As soon as I do, I regret it. The light seems to burn through them to the bottom of my skull and I moan, bringing my hand against them to shield them. Somehow, my left hand is stuck under something heavy, soft, and warm. For a moment I think it's Lori, but then I suddenly remember what happened last night. Burning light or not, I open my eyes to make sure I'm good and awake.

She's lying half on her side, half on her stomach over my left arm, her own hand on my chest, her fingers curled around a strand of my hair. The blankets only go up to the small of her back, and I can see her smooth, flawless skin, and the soft curve of her breast pressed against my chest. Her mouth is slightly open, and her warm breath on my shoulders is sending shivers down my spine. Or maybe it's just cold. Is it cold? I can feel every inch of her body against mine, so acutely it almost hurts, making me aware of just how naked I am right now. It does hurt, actually. Is this what a hangover feels like?

I rub my face again, and she groans and starts to stretch, lifting her arm away from me, letting go of my hair, arching her back. There's the line of a small fold that forms at her waist when she does that. That never happened on Lori; she was always too skinny. I'm fascinated by it for a moment, and then she smiles at me.

"Hey, handsome. Sleep well?"

I watch her as she sits up in bed, stretching again, yawning.

"Yeah. You?"

"Oh yeah. I always sleep well after exercising."

She grins and winks at me, then stands up and goes fishing for her clothes where they lie haphazardly around the sofa. She pulls on her tank top without putting on a bra, and her panties, and then comes to sit next to me on the bed. She leans back on her hands, grinning slyly.

"You wanna go down for some breakfast, or should we order in and see if we're better at this when we're not so drunk?"

I stare at her, feeling my face heat. It's funny, though. It's like it feels... hotter. Not like when I blush. Which, I suppose, is something to be grateful for.

She looks at me, and frowns, suddenly. "You feeling ok? You look weird."

I shrug. "I feel weird. I guess it must be how much I drank last night, right?"

She's still frowning. "I don't know. How do you feel? Nauseous?"

"A little. My head hurts. Mostly, I feel really, really hot. And my skin hurts."

She brings up her hand to lay it against my forehead, then shakes her head and clicks her tongue.

"You're burning up! You're sick! Ah, shit, that means I'm gonna be sick too. You better not have stomach flu."

I raise an eyebrow. "I feel fine. You sure it's not just a hangover?"

"Hangovers don't give you a fever."

I try to sit up and swing my legs over the edge of the bed, but I just fall back down, so floored by the pain in my leg I can barely breathe for a little while. She sees me do it, and frowns, lifting up the covers. I have the urge to pull them back over me, because I'm not wearing anything, but after everything we did last night, there hardly seems to be any point to it. She wrinkles her nose in disgust.

"Eww!"

I look down. My entire thigh is red and swollen. The bandages are stained with blood, and something yellow, even green in some parts, is seeping through at the middle. Worst of all, it kind of smells.

"Gross, dude! Your leg is totally infected! We gotta take you to a doctor."

She picks up the room phone and dials the service button.

"Who are you calling?" My teeth are starting to chatter, and it's hard to speak.

"I'm getting the hotel to get us a wheelchair and a taxi. I'm taking you to the hospital."

"What? No! What about our breakfast plans?"

"Oh, shut up! You're so infected you actually smell!! You can't seriously be telling me you feel fine!"

I sigh. She's probably right. I recognize what I'm feeling, now. It's definitely fever, and I really, really hurt. I don't want to stand up again, so I guess I have no choice but to see a doctor.

"Fine. You can take me to the hospital. But they're patching me up and we're leaving, is that clear?"

210

MAY 23RD, 12:42 PM

Of course, it's not that simple. After asking me a thousand questions about how I got a gunshot wound, the doctor finally believes it didn't happen in Italy, and that it's already been looked at by the police, since it's evident that another doctor took a look at it and attempted to fix it. After that, he spends half an hour berating me for not coming sooner, and telling me that an infection this severe is really, really bad, and that all sorts of evil stuff could have happened to me. Only then does he give me a bag of some intravenous antibiotics, and goes away to have a nurse clean it and change my bandages. Julie sits and swings her leg through most of the interrogation, but then she gets up and leaves, telling me she's gonna go check on Dow. Everyone else leaves before she comes back, and then, Mister Lupino comes in.

I feel my stomach tighten. He's probably pissed as hell; I didn't give him any news last night, and here I am, a day later, in the hospital with one of my friends in the burn unit. I should have checked in. Or even called. I knew alcohol made you do bad things.

He doesn't seem too pissed, though. He just pulls Julie's chair closer, and sits down next to me.

"Alex, my boy. How are you?"

"Err... I'm all right."

He looks at me seriously. "I told you yesterday that you should have someone look at that leg. Did I not?"

I sigh, and look down. He's an awesome guy, but he does love rubbing it in my face when I'm wrong.

"Yeah, you did. I'm sorry. I should have listened to you."

He nods, firmly. "Yes, you should have. The doctor told me you could have lost your leg."

I refrain from rolling my eyes, because I would never do that in front of him. The doctor told me that, too, but I think it's ridiculous. Lose a leg from an infection? It's gotta be an exaggeration, right?

"It won't happen again, Mister Lupino."

He shakes his head. "I told you, call me 'papa'."

"Right."

He doesn't get that it's hard for me to say; he doesn't understand that I really don't feel worthy of being his son.

"I also wish you would have called me. I did not like hearing it from your friend Julie."

212

I blink, puzzled. "She called you?"

"She did. I understand you two are getting closer, but I would have liked for you to check in with me last night. I also would have liked for you to at least tell me you intended to spend the night with her."

I stare at him. Did she tell him everything? How much does he know?

"I... we... it wasn't really my intention to..."

He suddenly breaks out laughing, and I know he's having me on. He pats my hand, chuckling.

"Do not worry about it, Alex. I understand that boys will be boys, and young men do what young men do. I am glad that you are finally letting another woman get close to your heart. It is good for you."

I nod, looking away. I hope I'm not blushing. It's hard to tell with the fever. Then again, maybe I could blame that.

"Did she... tell you about that?"

He shakes his head. "Our rooms are close together. It was not hard to tell."

I cover my face with my hands. I can't believe he heard us. If he did, then surely Tom...

I suddenly realize that I haven't seen Tom since we got to the hospital together yesterday.

213

"Have you seen Tom?"

Lupino raises his eyebrows, surprised at the change of subject.

"Yes. We came here together. When I came out of my room, he joined me in the hall, and simply followed me. I asked him if there was anything I could do for him. He said he was taking advantage of the fact that I was going to the hospital to ride with me. He is a... very surprising young man."

"Oh. So... he's not here?"

"No. As I understand it, your friend Antoine was injured yesterday, in a fight you had with that organization you are working to stop."

I scratch the back of my head. Here is the discussion I ran away and hid from in Julie's room. In Julie's bed. I think about the way she looked when she was straddling me. No. Focus. You're talking to Lupino.

"Um, yeah."

He says nothing, just looks at me like he's expecting me to say something.

"I was going to tell you about it, it's just... it wasn't important."

"Are you in further danger?"

"No. And it shouldn't affect you, either. We've got it all under control."

He raises an eyebrow. "This is what you call under control? Half of you are in hospital."

"Well, yeah, but I'm only here because my leg got infected, which it probably wouldn't have if I didn't... well, I'm just going to refrain from... strenuous physical activity, or... whatever."

"Perhaps. What about your friend Antoine?"

I open and close my mouth. This is it. I either have to let him think we got our asses kicked, or tell him the truth. I can't lie to him, of course. I sigh.

"Well... that's... my fault."

He purses his lips slightly, and sits back in his chair like he's about to listen to a story. I hold back another sigh.

"There was this guy. He could teleport."

He squints his eyes. "Teleport? That is when you disappear from one place and reappear in another?"

"Yeah. And he appeared right behind me, and I threw some fire at him. Only Dow was between me and him, but he was invisible, so I... burned him."

"Invisible?"

"Yeah. That's what he does. He becomes invisible."

215

"Hmm."

He taps his mouth with his index finger, considering. "And I presume you are feeling quite guilty about this, yes?"

I look at the blanket. I wish I could have just told the story and left it at that. Why does he make me talk about my feelings all the time?

"...yeah."

"You do know that you should not, yes?"

I frown. "I did this to him. He's suffering and it's my fire that burned him. How could this not be my fault?"

"Because you had no way of knowing he was there. Is that not true?"

I don't want to roll my eyes at him. Like that makes any difference at all.

"So what? It was still my fire."

He sighs and shakes his head. "Alex, you have to stop carrying the weight of the world on your shoulders. It was an unfortunate accident. But as I see it, what happened is as much his fault for being between a man who can summon fire at his fingertips and his target, as it was yours for making the fire. If you do not let things like this go, you will die before your time."

I click my tongue. I guess he's got a point. But someone I know might not survive because of something I did. How do you get over that?

I start thinking about the man my mother made me with. The first man I burned. I was defending my little sister, does that make it right?

"Alex?"

"Huh?"

"What is on your mind?"

I shrug. If there's something I don't want to discuss, it's what happened to that man. What I did to him. I didn't know what I was doing, and I had no idea I could make fire back then. I was just a kid. Everyone thinks I left home because of what he did to me, but the truth is it's because of what I did to him.

"...nothing. Just... I wish it didn't have to happen that way."

He nods, but he's watching me in a way that tells me he's not entirely convinced. He seems to think about it, wondering whether or not he's going to press the issue, and I put it out of my mind so that my face doesn't betray me. It seems to work; he lets it go.

"Of course, it is very unfortunate. But there is no use to dwell on the past, is there?"

"Oh, no, there really isn't."

He nods once, and stands. "I will go see whether your friends would like to see you now. You would like that, yes?"

MAY 23ᴿᴰ, 2:42 PM

The TV is real small, but at least there is one in the room. I'm watching some kind of game show, but since I prefer it on mute, I don't really know what's going on or what the stakes are. There seems to be a lot of guessing, and word-writing, and whatnot; it looks halfway between Jeopardy and Wheel of Fortune.

Tom walks in, followed by Julie. I look for some kind of sign of what happened last night on her face, but she just immediately looks at Tom. Is something going on? She hasn't been back here since she left this morning. Granted, I wasn't sure I was ready to start a relationship with anyone yet, but now that we have, what's up with her? Isn't that what she's been chasing me about?

Tom, who of course, can read my mind, waves at me to get my attention.

"Hey, Alex, focus. We're not here to talk about sex."

I glare at him and look away. "Fine. What are you here for?"

219

"We've done some research. In the files, about the people involved, with superpowers, around the world?"

"Uh... ok?"

"Well, there is a guy that we found. A healer. He's just a boy right now, living in France, but the file says he can heal anything."

I frown, and wait to see where he's going with this. What good is the guy, if he's that far away?

Tom rolls his eyes. "France isn't really that far from here. It's pretty easy to get there. Julie and I have booked a flight to make a round trip and see if we can get him to help you guys."

"You mean Dow."

"No, I mean you guys. You're in pretty bad shape too, and before you get your panties in a bunch, yes, you are, so stop thinking about contradicting me."

I frown at him, my mouth open. This is crazy. I wasn't even thinking that yet. Is he getting weirder with this thought-reading shit?

He sighs, and folds his arms. "Don't even get me started on that."

Julie throws up her hands. "Well, while this one-sided conversation is super informative for someone who can't read minds, we have a flight to catch. Coming, Tom?"

I look at her, and wonder again what's wrong with her. They're leaving right away? She could have at least given me a bit of a warning. Tom looks at her, then at me, and starts walking out.

"I'll be in the hall."

Julie watches him go then turns to me, folding her arms and tapping her hand on her elbow. Does she look nervous?

"So, uh, you gonna be ok by yourself? You want me to bring you something to read, or some crossword puzzles or something?"

I raise an eyebrow. Why is she so ill at ease with me all of a sudden? From my admittedly limited experience, I've found that once you've seen a person naked, especially in the context of sex, it gets more comfortable to deal with that person. Doesn't it?

"Uh, no, that's not my kind of stuff. Do you have my cigarettes, though?"

She smirks playfully, and I finally see the girl I know.

"Nah. Gave them to your boss-dad. I told him you have the habit of lighting up in the hospital, so he's managing them."

I stare at her with my mouth open. I knew she liked to tease, but she's never been a bitch.

"But... I never smoke when he's around!"

221

She chuckles. "Well then, I guess you'll have no choice but to count the seconds until we come back. On that note, toodles!"

She wriggles her fingers at me in the mockery of a wave, and hops out of the room.

MAY 24TH, 11:14 AM

I pick up my last bishop before I know what I'm doing, and move it to a spot that seems like a good idea. I have absolutely no concentration, and though he's been incredibly patient with me, I can tell Mister Lupino is annoyed. He looks at the board, frowning, like it actually takes conscious thought on his part to beat the crap out of me.

"So, have you taken advantage of your stay here to visit your friend downstairs?"

I frown and stare at the board, pretending to focus on the game. "Um... no. I'm not supposed to walk, so I haven't had the opportunity."

The truth is, I'm kind of happy to be in my predicament. It's the perfect excuse. I haven't seen Dow since the battle, and I really, really don't want to look at the damage, which is not only selfish but stupid, because I'm eventually going to have to.

Lupino nods, picks up his queen, and moves it across the board. "Well then, it is good I am here. Checkmate. I will go find a nurse and a wheelchair."

I sigh as he leaves the room. He's been really good at keeping me company. I'm usually not a great chess player, but since yesterday, I suck way more than usual. I look at the door until he comes back, which I know takes about ten minutes, but I find that time passes way, way too quickly. As the nurse helps me get in the wheelchair without having to move my leg too much, I wonder why Lupino's on such a mission to make me connect to other people. I mean, I'm connected to him. Really. Isn't that enough? Now that he wants to make me his son, why is he so eager to push me towards others?

The nurse leaves, and Lupino wheels me all the way to the burn unit. He stops at the doors. "Do you wish me to come in with you, or would you rather I let you do this on your own?"

I chew on the nail of my thumb. "Is he awake?"

I see him shake his head even though I'm not looking at him. "No, I do not believe he is."

"Then why are we here? I mean, he won't even know we were. What's the use?"

I don't dare say it out loud, but all I can think of is whether Lupino is punishing me for doing something he said wasn't my fault.

224

"Because this man is your friend. Friends worry about each other, they spend time with each other. Especially when the times are hard."

I bite the inside of my cheek. I really wish I could have a cigarette right now.

"Why is it suddenly so important to you that I make nice with everyone else? That I start getting... connected, and all that stuff?"

"It was always important to me to see you grow into the man I know you can be."

"Well, you never made a big deal about it before."

He smiles down at me. "You are my son, now. It is a father's duty to ensure that his son is happy, and becomes a good man. Besides, I do not like to think that you will be alone, when I am no longer here."

I frown at him. He's been talking like that a lot, lately, like he's not going to be here much longer. I mean, I know he's old, but don't people live to be like ninety-five and perfectly healthy?

I chew on my thumbnail again, and stare at the door. "What am I supposed to do?"

He smiles, and shrugs. "Whatever you wish. But it will become easier to see him when he is conscious if you have seen him before. Perhaps you may even want to talk to him."

I wipe my hands on my hospital gown. My palms are sweaty. I knew I didn't want to go see him, but I didn't think it would have made me this nervous. Whatever it is I'm gonna do in there, whatever my reaction, I don't think I want Lupino to see it.

"All right. I'm gonna go in by myself."

He smiles again, and nods. "I will be waiting for you out here."

He goes to the waiting area, sits down on a blue plastic chair, and picks up a newspaper. I take a deep breath, press the button to make the doors open, and wheel myself in.

I stop at the entrance to his room. It's dark inside, the curtains are drawn. I can see the shape of his feet, covered by a light green wool blanket. I slowly, slowly roll in.

He's lying on his side, on the bed. Most of his upper body, and his face, are covered in bandages. I remember from what I saw during the fight that a lot of his back got burned, and some of his side, too. I reach the side of his bed where he's facing. He's still unconscious, and I'm really grateful for that. He's hooked up to all sorts of IVs, and he's got a tube down his throat.

I sit there, and look at him. It's not as bad as I thought it would be. I mean, he's pretty bad, I can't imagine the scars that this is going to leave, but... for me, it's not that bad. Looking at him. My stomach feels like it's in a vice grip, but I can make myself look at him and mentally prepare for when he wakes up and I have to face him. I'm glad Mister Lupino made me do this. When Dow wakes up, the hardest thing I'll have to face will be the look in his eyes.

MAY 26TH, 6:52 PM

I take another slow, satisfying drag on the cigarette. I've had to cut back severely, these past few days, because Mister Lupino made it clear he wasn't going to buy me another pack. All I can do is hope that Julie makes it back here soon. She would get me some, right?

It's frustrating to think of her right now. She hasn't given me so much as a phone call or a text message since she's been gone. I don't know if she made it there, if they found the boy, if anything is going right or wrong, if they'll be back today, tomorrow, or in a week. It kills me not to know. All right, it would probably be a lot less bad if I didn't know I was running out of cigarettes, but still. I mean, her plane could have crashed, and I wouldn't even know!

"Hey there, handsome."

I turn around, half-convinced that I'm hallucinating, but it's really her. She's standing at the entrance of the balcony, leaning on the doorframe, wearing a Black Sabbath t-shirt and her stupid trench coat. She's smiling

228

in a mocking, cocksure way, and I just know everything went well.

"Julie! Hey!"

She grins and walks toward me. She grabs my cigarette, throws it over the railing of the balcony, and leans down to kiss my forehead. I'm so glad to see her I don't even care.

"How was everything? Did you find the kid?"

"We sure did. And we brought you back some magic healing potion."

She reaches into her coat pocket and pulls out a sixteen-ounce metal flask, handing it to me. I frown at it. "Magic potion?"

"Yeah. One little drink and you should be all better."

I raise an eyebrow and unscrew the cap, bringing it to my nose. The stench hits me right away, and I pull it away from my face.

"Are you fucking with me? This is piss!"

She laughs, slapping her thigh, as I screw the cap back on, feeling my face heat. Why the hell is she making fun of me? "Yeah, it's pee. It's also what's gonna make you feel better."

"This isn't funny."

229

"Actually, it really, really is. And it's not a joke, either, this is the real deal."

"You mean you seriously want me to drink piss?"

"Yeah, I really do."

She looks at my face and starts laughing again. I wait for her to calm down, doing nothing, trying to concentrate on keeping myself from becoming too furious. Eventually, she wipes a tear from her eye and stops laughing.

"All right. So we find this kid, right? And it turns out he really can heal, but it's not some kind of Jesus crap where he lays his hands on you and you feel all better. It's more like, his bodily fluids can heal you. All of them. Sweat, spit... anything. So we had him pee in a bottle and brought it back, figuring this was the best way to get enough for both of you."

I wrinkle my nose at the flask.

"I think I would have been better off with spit."

She laughs again. "Come on, one little sip and you'll be all better. It's not that bad, is it?"

"Yes, it is that bad!" Why won't she stop laughing? "What, you're telling me you would drink it?"

She shrugs, still chuckling. "I don't know. But I'm not the one who's hurt, am I?"

I glare at her. "Well, I'm not drinking it."

230

She rolls her eyes, but she's still grinning. She holds her hand out for me to put the flask back in it. "Fine! Suit yourself. Enjoy your slow healing process. Us, we're leaving for Africa tomorrow morning."

I frown, and look at the flask. It's true that, in my condition, I'm just not fit to go trekking through the jungle. But drinking piss?

I start unscrewing the cap. If I don't get better, the others will be going alone. And though I know Julie can take care of herself, I've got the most offensive power out of all of us. Dow is mostly defensive, and Tom, scary as he can be, doesn't have that much training or experience.

On the other hand, since Julie is a pretty good fighter, I won't hesitate to punch her if this is all an elaborate joke and it does nothing. Probably.

I squint my eyes shut and take a swig. It's every bit as vile as I thought it was going to be, though granted, that probably has a lot to do with the fact that I know what it is. I take as small a sip as I can swallow, then pull the bottle away from my face, gagging.

"Gah! That is so fucking gross!"

She's laughing at me again, bent over, holding her sides, and for a moment, I really think this is just a joke meant to humiliate me. Then it happens. The dull ache, the pain I've been feeling in my leg for the past week, is gone. I don't feel it at all. I lift the part of the hospital gown that covers my leg, and I take a look. There's not even a scar, not a dent, not a spot, nothing to say that I ever got shot there; it's as if it never happened. I stare at it until she calms down, and then she stands and wipes her eyes as she peeks at my thigh.

"Well! Looks like it does a pretty good job, doesn't it?"

I nod, put the cap back on the flask, and hand it to her again. "Yeah. I'm gonna go get my pants. You go get me something to drink."

She smirks, taking the flask and putting it back in her coat. "What do you want?"

"Anything. Anything that isn't piss, that is. Coke would be nice."

She nods and walks back in. I stand, and that's when I notice it, that sweet, sweet feeling I've only had a few times in my life before; the complete absence of pain. No headache, no pain from healing bones, even the old phantom pain in my arm from when the man my mother made me with broke it in two places and it never healed properly, even that's gone. I just stand there, enjoying it, eyes closed, and then I walk inside, leaving the wheelchair on the balcony. Halfway down the hall, I stop, facing the elevators, but looking down at the direction that'll take me to the burn unit. Julie raises an eyebrow.

"Curious?"

I frown at her. "Vending machines are that way."

She sighs, and rolls her eyes at me. "Well, in case you are, yes, we did give it to him. Tom is with him. I'm sure he's all better."

I don't look at her, but I can see her walk away from the corner of my eye. I look at the elevator button for the longest time, then finally gather up my courage and walk toward Dow's room. Right after I cross the plastic doors leading to the burn unit, I know something is happening, because there's a big commotion. Probably all the nurses of the entire floor are there, talking excitedly, staring into his room. Tom is standing in the hall, and from his expression, I can tell it worked, though I still have to see for myself. He turns towards me, smiles, and motions with his head for me to take a look in the room. I walk, standing as far as I can while still being able to take a peek.

I can see that a nurse is helping him sit, while another is removing his IV, and yet a third is unwrapping his bandages. They're all gasping and exclaiming, and I can understand why.

He doesn't have a single mark on his body. Not a rough spot, not even something that might look like a sunburn. The only thing that can prove what happened to him is the lack of hair on the side of his face that got burned.

As soon as I've seen, I take a few steps back, turn around, and walk away as fast as I can, not making eye contact with Tom. My legs feel weak, my throat feels tight, and just because he probably knows what I'm feeling right now doesn't mean I have to let him see me get all emotional.

I take advantage of the small cab to sit in front and not have to look Dow in the eye, or really talk to anyone. By the time we get to the hotel, they seem to have caught up to what's happened. Without needing to interact, I find out that the trip to France had no complications except having to deal with the worried and surprised parents of a twelve-year-old. Also, Dow has not only no pain, but no memory left of the whole business either, which should be a relief but somehow isn't.

Lupino is waiting for us in the lobby. He stands when we get there, so I figure either someone called him without my realizing it or he was just hanging out here and happened to see us come in. By the way he comes toward us, I can see it's definitely the former.

He looks me up and down, and nods approvingly at seeing me walk properly, then he goes over to Dow and claps him on the upper arms.

"I am glad to see you have made a full recovery."

Dow smiles and runs a hand through the place on his head where there used to be hair, a little self-consciously. "Yes, well, there were some changes..."

Mister Lupino inspects him critically. "Hmm, I think if you cut off the rest, it will be much better than the haircut you used to have. Much more suited for a grown man."

I frown, thinking about what he's saying. Dow had long hair. Not as long as mine, but still... "Hey! Are you saying you don't like my hair the way it is now?"

Lupino smiles indulgently at me. "Of course not. You are young, you can afford to be more rebellious."

I frown, thinking about it, wondering what that means, exactly, but he doesn't leave me the time to reply. "Come. We have more than one cause for celebration. I have made a reservation at the restaurant. Join me."

We have the nicest table, and at this hour, a lot of people are actually finishing their dinner. By the time we get our food, the place is half-empty. We look a little bit like hell, what with my stained pants and Dow's weird hair and Julie's general style, but no one seems to want to give us a hard time, so I relax after a while. Dow and Lupino seem to be getting into more conversation. I don't really pay attention, but it seems like they might be talking about Dow's mother. Tom seems more relaxed than I've seen him since this whole thing started, leaning his head in his hand and chewing on his straw, but he keeps looking at Julie and then at me.

Julie's been acting a little weird; she was avoiding looking at me since the beginning of the evening, but now that she's had a few drinks, she's all warmed up. She starts giving me these playful grins, raising and wiggling her eyebrows at me. As he opens another bottle of wine, Lupino raises his glass and attracts our attention.

"My friends, I know you are planning on leaving tomorrow morning. I will not be going with you. I am afraid Africa is a bit too exotic for these old bones. However, I wish you all good luck in your endeavors, and to tell you that I am awed by what all of you have been able to accomplish. I am amazed and humbled right now to see how both Alex and Antoine have recovered from such severe injuries, and I am certain that you will succeed. I am also glad that new friendships are forming between you. You are special, miraculous people, and it would be very sad indeed for you not to associate with one another."

He looks at me, and winks when he's done his last phrase, and I glance at Julie because that has to have been what he meant. She's looking at him, though, as if she didn't get the double entendre. We all drink, to celebrate the toast. I'm having wine, but only the one glass; I'm taking really small sips so that it doesn't get empty and no one refills it. I understand that it's not going to kill me, and I didn't want to make a fuss. Besides, it seemed to make Mister Lupino really happy that I'm drinking, for some reason.

I watch Julie, and she's back in her weird not-looking-at-me mood, so I slide in my chair to gently kick her in the shin under the table. She looks up at me, her eyes already glossing over with drink, though we're only halfway through our meal. She blinks, surprised, then thrusts her chin out at me in a questioning expression. I frown at her.

"You ok?"

She shrugs, her features relaxing. "Yeah, just tired. Maybe that jetlag thing is finally catching up to me. I think I'm gonna head to bed soon."

"Oh."

I take another bite of my penne, then look up at her again.

"You sure? 'Cause you've been acting kind of on and off since... well, you know."

She raises an eyebrow. Is she actually going to pretend she has no idea what I'm talking about? I just keep looking at her, because I know she knows perfectly well what I mean, but she just shakes her head, puts her glass down, and stands.

"Well, I'm sorry, everyone. I feel like crap. I'm going to go to bed. Have a nice night!"

She waves at everyone and starts walking away. I just stare after her, my mouth open, and after a little while Tom kicks me under the table. I frown at him, and he gestures with his head that I should follow her. I'm even more confused, but he nods, as if reassuring me that this is the right thing to do. I look at Mister Lupino, and he gives me an encouraging smile. Is everyone in this room more aware of what Julie wants than me? I stand up and walk after her.

I catch up to her in front of the elevator, and unpredictable as always, she just turns to me and smiles. "What is it? You want some sugar?"

I blink, but before I can even think of what I'm going to say, the elevator light turns on, there's a soft bell, and the doors open. She walks in, turning around to lean her elbows on the golden bar, and grins at me. I follow, hit the button for our floor, and as I'm turning around to look back at her, she's suddenly standing closer to me, grabbing me by the tie, pulling me closer and kissing me. I was going to talk to her, but I'm not really sure what I was gonna say, and anyway, this is way better. She pushes me against the door, pulling my shirt out of my pants, and she's actually starting to work on unzipping my fly by the time the doors open. It takes me completely by surprise and I almost fall flat on my back, managing to catch myself and her in a couple of quick steps. She laughs, leaning her forehead against my chest, and for some reason, I feel ridiculous.

"What's with you tonight?"

She just shakes her head and keeps laughing, grabbing my tie again to pull me towards her room. When we get there, she pulls the keycard out of the back pocket of her pants and starts fumbling with it, while I try to get my thoughts straight. My mind really wants to ask her what the hell is up with her, but my dick is telling me to shut the hell up and that my questions can wait until morning. For a moment, I wonder who's gonna win.

"What's up with you? You're so hot and cold lately."

Looks like there's hope for my brain after all. She manages to get the door open, and turns around, grinning coyly at me, backing up slowly into her room.

"I'm hot, right now. Don't wanna take advantage?"

My stupid mind is really unsatisfied; I can still hear it wanting more over the sound of my own voice in my head telling it to shut up. I follow her, loosening my tie. She walks in, dropping her trench coat to the floor in a gesture so smooth I barely see it, then takes off her shirt, holds it between her index and thumb, and lets it drop to the floor. She looks at me over her shoulder, unbuttoning her pants, and starting to slide them off really, really slow. I swallow, and my mind finally shuts up.

I unbutton my shirt, my hands moving so fast I actually have a hard time with half the buttons, and walk to grab her hips, then press my chest against her back. She sighs, leaning into me, letting her pants drop to her ankles. She raises a hand to caress the back of my neck, tilting her head so that I can kiss her. As I do, she pulls one of her feet free of her pants, and runs it up my calf in the same gesture, making me shiver.

I break the kiss, grabbing her shoulders and turning her around, before pushing her down on the bed. Her other foot is still caught in her pants, and she trips, falling half-seated, half lying on her back on the bed, propped up by an elbow. I don't give her time to get up, but I grab her thighs, pushing her back a bit so she's in a more comfortable position for both me and her on the

239

bed, kneeling between them. She grins, sighs, and she's about to say something, but I kiss her again.

MAY 27TH, 1:37 AM

Julie snorts again, softly, lying on her back in the tangled sheets, her right hand leaning on my side. I have my fingers wrapped loosely around it, watching her sleep. I don't know why, but I can't sleep right now. Must be all that lying around in bed I did in hospital that took the tired out of me.

It's not exactly that she looks peaceful when she sleeps, because she has a lot of dreams both good and bad, and she makes all sorts of expressions and little noises. When she's not dreaming, she snores softly, not all the time, but by short bursts here and there. And she shifts a lot. She's changed positions so many times already I thought for sure she was waking and was going to get up, but I was wrong.

But she's... uncomplicated, when she sleeps. She's just beautiful, with her hair loose and messy and her face relaxed, and I don't have to try to figure out what she's thinking. She snorts again, tosses her head from left to right, and blinks her eyes open. She seems a bit confused as to where she is, then sees me, looks even more confused,

241

and sits up, rubbing her face. I let go of her hand when she does that. I don't think she noticed I was holding it.

"You're still awake? What are you doing?"

"Watching you. I couldn't sleep."

"Oh."

She frowns and stands, grabbing her shirt off the floor and pulling it on over her naked body. It's too big, but it doesn't fall too far past her waist, so that when she walks, I can see the curve of her butt under it.

"Where are you going?"

"Bathroom."

I watch her as she walks to the small bathroom and gets in, leaving the light off and the door open. I can't see her anymore, but I can hear her sit down and start to pee. I feel oddly shy, like I'm the one who should be embarrassed at what's happening. Lori never peed in front of me. Which, after watching her give birth, you would have thought would be all right, but no. This is a very intimate moment, and I find it really weird to be sharing it with Julie at this point.

She flushes and walks back to bed, scratching her head and yawning. She slides in between the sheets, leaving her shirt on, and lies down, curling up with her back to me. I watch her for a little while, that stupid sense that something is wrong creeping up in my gut again.

"Julie?"

"Hmm?"

"Is everything all right?"

She sighs, and rolls on her back so she can look at me. "Why are you asking?"

I shrug. Why am I acting like such an idiot, reading into her gestures and overanalyzing? "Nothing, I guess... just... you seemed like... it's nothing. Good night."

She watches me settle back down on the bed. "You know that this is all there is, right?"

I frown at her. "What?"

"This. You and me. Sex. And good friends. You know that, right?"

"What do you mean?"

"I mean, I think you're hot, great in bed, and I like to have fun, but I don't believe in monogamy."

I frown. I have no idea what she's talking about. I mean, I've heard the word before, but I was never involved in the conversation, and I wasn't curious or concerned enough to find out.

"Uh... what does that mean?"

243

She sighs, patiently, like she's explaining something to an idiot. "It means, I'm not a relationship kind of girl."

I run my hand through my hair. She's saying she doesn't want to be my girlfriend. Right? I really want to ask, but I can't formulate the words; I'm too afraid it'll make me sound like a kid, or an idiot. I feel sick, like a sort of squeezing nausea that's starting in the pit of my stomach and traveling up to my throat. She's looking at me for a response, and I don't know how to give her one. I just shake my head, and get out of bed.

"Where are you going?"

I shrug, putting on some pants. "For a walk."

I grab the rest of my clothes from the floor. As I walk out, I can see her, from the corner of my eye, sigh and flop down on the bed, on her back. I walk out into the hall and to the bedroom I share with Mister Lupino, being careful not to make any noise. He's lying on his bed, snoring softly. I know there's no way I'm gonna be able to fall asleep anytime soon, so I just sit down on the couch, turning on the TV, and putting it on mute. I don't even see what's playing. All I can think about is her, and what I did wrong. I try to shake it off a few times, telling myself that it doesn't matter and that I should just forget about it, but I can't. Why is this messing with me so much?

MAY 27TH, 8:17 AM

A hand shakes me awake, gently. I start and blink, and for a second I'm wondering why I'm not in bed with Julie when I remember coming here and sitting on the couch last night. I must have passed out while I was watching TV. Mister Lupino is looking down at me.

"Ah! You are awake."

"Uh... yeah. I must have forgotten to go to bed."

I sit up, rubbing my face, and then I realize I'm not wearing my shirt and pull it on real quick. Lupino sits in the comfy chair, and I can see there's a tray with some coffee, cookies and pastries on the small table in front of us. I guess he must have had breakfast brought in. He reaches and grabs a bun, breaking it open, smiling at me.

"Your friend Antoine came to see if you were here. He says you have to leave in one hour to get to the airport in time. I have ordered us some breakfast."

"Thank you."

I don't really feel like eating, so I reach to grab a cup of coffee. I sit, sipping it, lost in thought for a little while. Mister Lupino is eating his bun. I didn't even notice him spreading jam on it. When he's chewed and swallowed his bite, he reaches for the knife again.

"I would have thought you would be with your young lady this morning. Is something wrong?"

I sigh, putting the cup down. I tuck my hair behind my ear, and think about it. I don't know how to talk to Julie about it, but Mister Lupino seems to know a lot about women. Among other things.

"I guess you could say that... She... she said she wasn't into... monogamy."

I check for his reaction, and see that I used the right word. He frowns, and seems to think about it for a while, then shakes his head. "Young women these days are not the way there were when I was a young man, I must admit."

I wait for more, but it doesn't seem to be coming. I clear my throat. "So... uh... what do you think I should do?"

He raises his eyebrows at me. "What would you like to do?"

I blink at him. What does he mean? He chews, and I guess he sees how confused I am, because he swallows his bite and goes on.

"I am assuming you wish to pursue a relationship with this young lady?"

"...yeah."

"Have you made that clear to her?"

"...not so much. I don't really know what to say. I mean, if she's telling me she doesn't want to have a relationship, that means she doesn't want to be with me, right?"

"Why do you want to be with her?"

I take a sip of coffee to refrain from sighing. I hate that I'm talking about this with Lupino. It's true that I don't really have anyone else to talk to about it, and it seems to make him happy, but it makes me feel sick. I put down my cup.

"Because... she's like me. We... well, we're just alike."

He smiles. "Yes, I can see how that is true. She is strong, just like you. And, of course, she is a very beautiful young woman."

I nod. I hadn't really thought about how strong she was, but now that he's pointing it out, it's just another thing that I like about her. I guess I have to address the real problem.

"What if she just... doesn't like me?"

247

He smiles. "I do not believe that is the case. But should it be, at least, you will be settled, will you not?"

It makes me smile as I pick up my coffee mug again. I wish he was coming with us. As a boss, he was absolutely the best, but as a father... I didn't think I could have a relationship like this with anyone.

"I guess. Thanks, Mister Lupino."

He raises his eyebrows at me and doesn't say anything, but I know what he wants.

"I mean... papa."

MAY 27ᵀᴴ, 11:54 PM

The van we hired to take us from Kisumu airport to Kakamega slows to a halt, giving us a final jolt. I stand, wiping my forehead, and hurry to be the first one out of the van. The heat is oppressive, even this late. I've actually taken off my tie, jacket, and waistcoat, and I've unbuttoned my collar and rolled up my sleeves. I light a cigarette as soon as I'm outside, and look with some measure of dread at The Golf Hotel. I had to book online, and I was afraid I'd be sleeping in a hut, so I'm relieved at what I see; it's small, but looks modern and clean. Tom follows right after me, then Dow, and finally, Julie.

She's been doing that since we left Italy; sitting as far from me as she can, avoiding my eyes. I mean, I know I've been avoiding Dow, but I don't think I'm as obvious, and at least, I have a good reason. At the layover in Nairobi, while Dow and Tom went off to explore, she even sat at the other end of the row of plastic chairs from me. I only booked two rooms, though, so I guess she's gonna have to get over herself; they didn't have anything left with two beds.

The lobby looks like any hotel, and there's a bar and a restaurant, so I'm feeling better and better about this. I was really expecting something a lot more... rugged. I finish my smoke outside, letting Dow fill in the reservations and get the keys. I watch them interact through the front door, and Tom comes up behind me. I hadn't even noticed he didn't go inside. I nod at him, and he grins.

"This is great, isn't it?"

I raise an eyebrow. He can be so spooky with his mind reading sometimes that I forget he's also just a sixteen-year-old kid who was locked up in a tiny room and sedated for five years of his life. I look around. The hotel is in a town that looks pretty normal to me.

"Yeah, it is great."

He takes a deep breath through his nose, and I watch him. He smiles at me again.

"Think we're gonna get to see some giraffes?"

It hits me then. We're in Africa. Out there, really close, are rhinos, lions, crocodiles and all other sorts of beasts. I was just in Italy, and I didn't even see anything, like that falling tower, or the Coliseum. Tom and Dow did; they even got a few souvenir t-shirts. Maybe they have something when they say I'm missing out on my life because I'm too caught up in my own shit.

He grins at me and nods. "Now you're getting it. You have to stop and enjoy the scenery, even if you are on a mission."

I chuckle, and shake my head, finishing my cigarette. "Look at you, giving me your wisdom."

He shrugs, still smiling. "You know, when you go around reading everyone's thoughts, you get insightful."

"Tell me about it! I'm the one that has to live with you!"

I'm actually feeling weirdly proud of him right now. I remember the guy he used to be when I met him, and I think he's come a long way from there. Especially living with a tight-ass like me. He chuckles, and elbows me in the side.

"You're not so bad. And I guess you've kind of come a long way, too. You used to be really uptight and no fun at all. You're better now."

"I guess we've kinda been good for each other. It's hard to take yourself too seriously when you've got someone who can tell what you're really thinking all the time."

He grins. "Yeah. Hey, since we're all in appreciating each other mode, I've got a gift for you."

I raise an eyebrow, waiting for him to go on. "Julie. Try harder."

He winks, and taps me on the shoulder blade before walking in and joining Dow. They walk out of the common area together. I see Julie left there, looking awkward, holding a room key. She takes a look through the glass door, sees me standing there looking at her, and she looks away. Thinking about what Tom just told me, I can't help but smile.

I toss the butt of my cigarette and walk inside. She watches me come, and looks in the direction where Dow and Tom went, apparently wondering if she can escape there before I reach her. But of course, she can't; she has my key, and she's not a total bitch. I reach her, and she hands me the key.

"So, uh, I guess we're sharing a room."

I nod. "You know where it is?"

"Yeah, it's right next to Dow's. Over there."

She points, but I just stand there, so she sighs and starts walking. I follow her, acting like I didn't notice her behavior, and she takes me up some stairs and into a hallway. She stops in front of the last one on the right and opens it, walking in before me so quickly I think she's gonna slam the door in my face for a second, but she doesn't.

The room's comfortable, and not too small. It's nothing I would call fancy, especially not after the five-star hotel we stayed at in Italy, but it's clean, and it's a lot better than some of the places I've lived in when I was a kid. There's a bed, and a couple of comfy chairs, and even a little balcony that looks out over the yard.

As she takes off her trench coat and sits on the bed to remove her boots, I step out onto the balcony. It's dark, but I can still see that there are a couple of tiny huts in the yard. I wonder what's in them.

I keep my eyes open for beasts, but I suppose they probably sleep at night. Do they come to the town, like raccoons do back home? Even if they did, in this darkness, I can't see anything. I light another cigarette, watching the view. After a short while of seeing nothing, I turn around and see that Julie was watching me, though she jumps like she got caught, and stands to take off her pants. She does it quick and efficient, like she's probably done a thousand times when she's at home, and then slides into bed. I toss my cigarette, crushing it with my foot, and walk back inside. She avoids looking at me again, just staring at the wall. I sit in the chair next to the door, and fold my arms.

"How long are you gonna keep this up?"

She blinks and frowns at me. "What are you talking about?"

I roll my eyes. She can't seriously think I'm that thick, can she? Maybe she just thinks she's been slick about it.

"Avoiding me."

She blushes a bit, and glares at the wall. "...I'm not avoiding you."

"Oh. Sure. That's why you sat way in the back in the shuttle, even though all the luggage was there and you barely had room to move your arms. You haven't even looked at me since the last time we had sex. So, what's up with you?"

She frowns, looking pissed off, and seems to be making up her mind for a long time. I give her time to think. I've said what I want to say; I'm not the one who's been acting like a kid here. Given our age difference and the fact that she always calls me kid, it makes me feel a little smug, and really helps with my patience. Finally, she snorts.

"I don't have a problem. I'm not the one who left 'cause my little feelings were hurt."

I raise my eyebrows. "So, what, you're mad at me for leaving that night?"

She glares at me, looking like she's about to hit me.

"Stop being all mature about it. You're the one who couldn't deal with it."

"Couldn't deal with what? The fact that you don't want to be with me?"

There. I said it, it's out there, and it wasn't even that difficult. Now that I have, though, it's a lot harder to keep calm, 'cause my chest feels tight, and my heart's beating fast, and I hate feeling this nervous just 'cause I'm talking about my stupid feelings.

She clicks her tongue and rolls her eyes. "I never said that."

"What'd you say, then?"

"I said I didn't like relationships."

I raise an eyebrow, recalling the time she made fun of me in the hot tub.

"Oh? You ever been in one?"

She snorts and turns around so she has her back to me. It's so immature I almost laugh, but I can hold back because I realize I've probably done a thing or two like that. After a while, I figure she's just not going to say anything, but as I'm about to give up, she sighs.

"Fine. No, I've never been in a relationship. Doesn't mean I want one."

"Well, how do you know how something is going to be without trying it first?"

"I just like to have fun, all right? I don't want to be tied down to anyone."

I look down at the ground, trying to think of how I'm going to put it. I don't like talking about my feelings, again, but for some reason this time seems worse than usual.

"Well... don't you have fun with me?"

She sits up, like she's too restless to lie down, and folds her arms over her chest.

"Of course I had fun with you. You've got great pacing, and stamina. Why d'you think I wanted to have some more?"

I feel my face heat, and I guess I can't help it. but at least I can keep my expression neutral and serious.

"Do you still want to?"

"Yeah!"

"So, what would be so bad about being in a relationship with me?"

She shakes her head like I'm just too stupid to understand.

"It's not that I don't still want to have fun with you. But what about other people?"

Her words sting, but I stay cool. This isn't the time to lose control.

"What about other people?"

She sighs, and rolls her eyes again. "Well, I won't be able to have fun with them, right?"

I take a deep breath. I'm almost ready to say 'to hell with her' right now. I stand up and walk to the balcony again, lighting a cigarette. I try to think about what I see in her, but it's really difficult to do over how pissed off I am at her right now. I hear her stand, and her footsteps on the balcony behind me. I don't turn around, and she sighs.

"See? It's making you feel all bad. It's better to avoid it altogether."

"Who do you want to sleep with?"

"What?"

"Who do you want to sleep with, right now, other than me?"

"That's not the point."

"Am I bad in bed?"

She snorts. "Don't be stupid."

"Well, I think I have a right to know. Am I so unsatisfying that you'd need to look somewhere else?"

I glance at her, and have the satisfaction to see her blush and look away. She's barefoot, and only wearing her Black Sabbath t-shirt and underwear. It takes her a little while to answer.

"...no."

"Well, then, what's the big fucking deal?"

She frowns at me. "Well... I just... I like to have options!"

"Well, how is it having options if you don't have the option to have a relationship?"

She blinks, then thinks about it, then screws up her face. "What? What the hell are you talking about?"

"Well, it's like saying: 'I'm not gonna have that steak, 'cause a better steak might come along later.' Why not just have the steak now and see?"

She folds her arms again, shifting her weight from one leg to the other. It makes her hips stand out, and the curve of her waist a lot sexier.

"So what are you saying?"

"I'm saying, you were all over me to have sex with you because I should loosen up and try it. So what's so bad about giving a relationship with me a try?"

She throws up her hands in the air, and sighs, then walks to lean on the railing of the balcony. She seems to think for the rest of the time that I smoke my cigarette, and when she sees me throw my butt to the ground, she smirks.

"Fine. I'll go out with you. On one condition."

"What?"

"Quit smoking."

I stare at her. "What?"

"Quit smoking!"

"What the hell for?"

"You stink! And you taste disgusting. So, quit smoking, and I'll go out with you."

I sigh, and walk back inside. She's fucking with me. She's gotta be. Isn't she?

She seems pretty happy with herself. She managed to put the ball back in my court. Well, fine. If she wants to play that game, I can play too. I take out the silver cigarette case Lori gave me, which I always keep in the pocket of my shirt, over my heart. I look at Julie. It's a matter of pride, at this point. She still has that smile on her face, but she looks less sure. Good.

I open the case as I walk to the small bathroom, leave the door open so she can see me, take the first cigarette out of it, and flush it down the toilet. She loses her smile, looking surprised. I grab the rest of the smokes, and think for a second. I'm in Africa. Am I going to be able to get more if I need them? She sees me hesitate, and the smile is growing back on her face. That's it. I lock her in the eye as I throw them all in the toilet, and her jaw drops as I flush them away. My stomach tightens, and I immediately find myself craving a cigarette, but I can do this. I'm going to have the last word, here.

I lie down on the bed, ignoring her. I close my eyes, trying to calm down, telling myself I don't need a cigarette. If it's already starting, this is going to be really hard. I hear her come in and close the door, and her footsteps get closer to the bed. When I open my eyes again, she's standing over me, a serious expression on her face. I frown at her.

"What?"

"You'd quit smoking?"

"Isn't that what you wanted?"

"Just to go out with me, though? You'd quit smoking?"

I prop myself up on my elbows, half-sitting. "Yeah. I think it's kind of stupid and unnecessary, but if it's what you want, then fine."

She sighs, and kicks at something imaginary at her feet. She does that for a while, and then looks back up at me with a half-smile.

"I guess... if you're willing to do that much... then I'm willing to give this a try."

I find myself smiling, which, judging by how much I need a cigarette and how pissed off I feel right now, is saying a lot.

"Yeah?"

"I have one more condition, though."

I roll my eyes and let myself fall back on the bed, discouraged. "Seriously?"

"Yeah. I want you to take me on a date."

I lift my head to look at her. She's smiling, almost shy.

"A date?"

"Yeah, a date! The closest I ever came to one was big-armed, date-raping Italian dude and the opera. And, by the way, I hate the opera. Don't take me to the opera."

I grin. Lori never really wanted to go out when she was pregnant, and there was no time for it after the baby came. We had talked about going, when things calmed down, when she got better. And then... the time never came.

"I wasn't planning on the opera. I'll find something cool, as soon as we're out of this mess."

She nods, and seems to hesitate for a moment, then just climbs on top of me, straddling me. I raise an eyebrow. "So... I guess you're done avoiding me?"

She leans down close to me, and I feel her breasts brush against my chest, through our shirts. She's not wearing a bra.

"As long as you promise not to walk out as soon as we're done."

I grin, grabbing her waist and pulling her closer. "Promise."

MAY 28ᵀᴴ, 10:16 AM

I'm alone in bed when I wake up, and I feel really weird, like I can't wake up all the way. I pull myself up anyway, and walk out of the bedroom. When I step into the hall, everything is a little too bright, and there are open boxes everywhere. This is weirdly familiar. I make my way to the living room, and I can see Lori's sitting on the floor, packing some baby toys in boxes. She's sniffling, and I realize that she's got huge, dark streaks all over her cheeks and chin where her mascara has been running. I frown, slowing down.

"Lori? What's going on?"

"You don't need this anymore."

"What? I'm keeping all this stuff."

"You don't need it. You've given up. You've forgotten us."

"What are you talking about? I haven't forgotten! I'll never forget!"

She shakes her head, and keeps putting the toys in the box. I go and grab her hand to stop her. "Lori, stop! We can talk about this!"

She looks at me, and her eyes are dead and full of tears.

"Would you have given up smoking for me?"

I sit up in bed, screaming, my heart feeling like it's gonna explode. Julie, next to me, starts awake too.

"Alex? You ok?"

I nod, and I feel my throat being squeezed, my eyes stinging. I think I might not be able to hold it in, and then I stand and pull on my pants and head out to the balcony for a smoke and a little privacy. Once I'm standing there, I remember that I threw all my smokes down the toilet, and groan, leaning my elbows on the railing and grabbing my head. Am I being a dick by going for Julie? It doesn't really feel like I could ever forget Lori, or Nicolas, but what if I am? I mean, dreams mean something, right?

I rub my face, thinking how bad I need a smoke right now. Would I have given it up for Lori? I was trying, wasn't I? I had even cut back a lot. Was it for her, or him?

I hear the strangest noise I've ever heard, over my head, getting louder. It sounds like cawing, or moaning, from a thousand voices, and when I look up, I see a flock of huge birds flying right over my head. They're black, and white, and yellow, and have funny hair on top of their heads. This might be just the distraction I need.

"Holy shit! Julie, come see!"

I hear her shuffle in the room, and then she jogs out onto the balcony, wearing her t-shirt and underwear. She looks around, and then notices the birds.

"Holy crap!"

"Yeah!"

We stand there, on the balcony, staring up at the flying birds. There's a lot of them, and it feels like they're flying for a long time. I feel like I'm becoming more and more aware of her presence next to me, and by the time the birds have flown over, she's what has my attention. I'm watching the way her shirt doesn't quite cover her whole butt, and the way it falls over her breasts. Her smile is radiant when she turns to me, and there's a twinkle in her eyes that I don't think I've ever seen before; there's nothing mocking or superior about her expression, just pure joy.

"That was the coolest thing ever! I didn't expect to see anything like that!"

I nod, feeling myself grin at her too. I have to admit, this has done a lot to improve my mood. She reaches to touch my forearm, then apparently changes her mind and motions towards the lodge with her head.

"Wanna go back in and see what kind of food this place has for breakfast?"

MAY 28TH, 12:02 PM

It turns out that breakfast is mostly fruit. Most of them I recognize, like bananas, papayas, and pineapples, but there are a few I've never seen before, like these small little red and green ones that are halfway between a to-mato and a grape. We took it to go because, while we were sleeping, Tom and Dow rented a car to go and see some big rock that's supposed to be famous, and Julie wanted to go too.

Julie leans her head on my shoulder halfway through the ride, and I stop moving, afraid that if we hit a bump or something she'll straighten up. My shoulder and neck get real stiff after a while, but it doesn't matter. Her hair smells nice, and her head is warm, and it's nice to have it there.

It is a big rock. A really big rock. On top of a hill. With a smaller rock on it. Dow has a pamphlet about it and everything. They call it the Crying Rock of Ilesi, be-cause there's water coming down it on one side. Not a lot of water. But still, I can see where it gets its name. It's nice and big and everything, but I have to work not to show how bored I am. I mean it's really, really big, but it's a rock.

After they've spent way too long going around it and touching it, Tom declares he wants to go see something else, and he wanders off with Dow. Julie waits for them to go before taking my hand and leading me down the hill too. I just follow her. It feels weird and nice at the same time. Her palm is sweaty because it's really hot out, but it feels good to be holding her, even if it's just the hand. I've slept with this girl. Who knew that holding hands could make me feel just as close? Lori never held my hand when we walked. Not that we walked that much.

We reach the bottom of the hill, and then she stops, lets go of my hand, and turns around, taking out her phone and smiling at me. She points to a spot a few feet away.

"Go stand there! I wanna take a picture."

I shrug, and I do as she says. I don't really know what to do. People never take my picture. I got a mug shot when I got arrested for vagrancy when I was a kid, the first time I ran away, but that's pretty much it. I just stand there, awkwardly, trying not to look like an idiot. She positions her phone, and chuckles.

"You look like you've got a stick up your ass. What's wrong?"

I shrug, folding my arms. "I don't know what to do!"

"Do something funny!"

267

I scratch my head. I have no idea what she means by that, and I don't really want to do anything that makes me look like a jackass, especially if she's going to be taking pictures. She shakes her head, laughing, and motions for me to come back towards her. I do.

"You're no fun! I'll show you how it's done."

She hands me the phone and steps right in front of me. She puts her hands up in front of her, palms facing up. "Do I look like I'm holding it up?"

I blink and hold up the phone, seeing how the picture's going to look.

"Raise your hands a little... yeah, that's perfect."

She makes a face like she's really straining, but completely exaggerated; her eyes bulge out, her lower jaw protrudes like it's deformed, and the tendons in her neck become so taut I think they're going to snap. I take the picture, and she hops back to me, grinning.

"Awesome! I never thought I'd be doing this again. This brings back a lot of memories."

"What does? Taking pictures of giant rocks in Africa?"

She laughs, and leans back, taking a picture of me with her phone.

"Kind of. It makes me think about when I was little. My mom used to take me to famous landmarks and we'd have a funniest picture contest."

I watch her as she speaks. I can't help but wonder for a moment how I got here, in this wonderful, exotic place, with this awesome, sexy, intelligent, badass girl. When I left the place I grew up in all these years ago, I thought I'd be pretty lucky if I managed just to survive. I never thought I would be having all these adventures, doing all this stuff. Meeting someone like her. I suddenly find myself really wanting to know more about her, just for the sake of hearing her talk like that, relaxed and happy, with no innuendos and no complications. I don't know anything about her parents, except that they died when she was about the age I was when I left home.

"Tell me about it."

She shrugs, still smiling, and takes another picture of me.

"We didn't have a lot of money or anything, but once in a while, my mom used to take me on a road trip to see weirdly constructed houses, or the Liberty Bell. or the biggest ball or yarn, stuff like that. I loved it. We had a lot of fun, my mom and me."

"What about your dad?"

Something passes over her face, and I regret mentioning him. She starts walking away from the rock. slowly, and I follow her.

"My dad didn't live with us then."

I frown. I don't want to spoil the mood. "I'm sorry."

She shrugs, and she looks happy again. "Ah, it's all right. I barely remember him. He left my mom for another woman when I was real young. He left her without anything. She was a hero, really, my mom. Always made sure I had everything I needed, everything I wanted, really. She was awesome. I miss her a lot."

She stares at the sky. There's so much of it; it's so blue, and bright. Around us are mostly plains, but with plants and bushes I've never seen before. Tom was right; it is great to be here, so far from home and looking at things I'll probably never see in person again, but the only thing I can look at is her. She smiles at me. Did Lori ever look this happy? I try to push the thought out of my mind. I want to be in this place, in this moment. I don't want to think about anything else.

She turns to me, reaching out to take my hand. "What about you? Do you miss your parents, sometimes?"

I shrug. There's something I really didn't want to be thinking about. So much has happened that the memories feel distant, like something dangerous you see from a comfortable space, safely behind tempered glass, and they can't hurt you. I find I don't really mind talking about it, to her, in this moment, in this place.

"Not really. I guess sometimes I think about my mother. She had good moments. I liked it when she cut my hair."

She lifts her head and looks pointedly at my ponytail.

270

"Is that why your hair is so long? Some sentimental reason?"

I frown at her. "Don't poke fun at me."

She touches my cheek, smiling, though there's nothing derisive about it.

"I'm sorry. I really didn't mean to. I thought it was some kind of cool factor you were going for. I love that it's actually because you miss your mom."

I blink. She really isn't making fun of me. I think, at least. She walks backwards, still holding my hand, taking us away from the road and the rock.

"Tell me more about her."

"She was nice, when she was sober. I think in her way, she really did love me sometimes."

She frowns, slightly. "And suddenly, it's a bit less nice. What did she do to you?"

"Nothing, really. She was just... not that nice when she was drunk."

"What happened to her?"

"I don't know. I haven't seen her since I was thirteen."

"Why not?"

"I left home."

"Oh. Right. You told me this. Sorry. I just thought... you might have looked them up."

"No need. They're really better off without me."

"Why would you say that?"

I shrug. "They didn't want kids. They had them. I think they hated the experience."

She stays quiet, for a little while. "I'm really sorry. I understand a bit, though. Was your dad a bastard, too?"

I close my eyes, trying not to lose my cool. I hate talking about the man my mother made me with. "I told you before. He might have made me, but he was never my father. The only thing he knew how to do was scream and drink and hit. Other than that he ignored us, which was pretty fine with us."

She frowns. "You keep saying... us. You have brothers and sisters?"

"Just a sister. She's younger than me by five years."

"And I guess you don't know what happened to her?"

I shake my head. "I can't go back there."

"What happened?"

I look at the bushes and the foreign wilderness, trying to seize the moment again.

"I got into a real bad fight with... the man my mother made me with. It wasn't... it didn't turn out good."

I look at her. I don't want to be rude, but I can't go on talking about this.

"Julie... I don't..."

She nods, smiling. "I know. I don't want you to ruin your mood, either. My dad was a bastard too. He's still alive, you know. I'm pretty sure, at least."

I frown at her. I'm relieved not to be talking about my own stuff anymore, and though I don't want to make her talk about her stuff, I don't want this moment to end. So I say nothing, and just go on watching her.

"When my mom died... I kept hoping that he would come for me. I mean, it was my mom he left, right? He must have still loved me. But he didn't. He never came. And then I was sent to GenEx."

I watch her as we walk in silence. I might have been through a lot of shit but I can't imagine what that was like, waiting for someone. Hoping. I've never relied on anybody but myself. When I'm in trouble, it's on me, and I don't wait for anyone to get me out of it. I might have trouble trusting, but it's only because I never really gave my trust for anyone to betray. I think I understand her more, now. Maybe I just need to convince her that she can trust me. She seems lost in thought for a few seconds, and then she smiles at me.

"Well! Didn't mean to go that far down memory lane. Kind of lost the whole lovers in an exotic place vibe there, didn't I?"

I look at her seriously. "You know you can count on me, right?"

She smiles, and pats my cheek. "I know you're a decent guy. You know what else I know?"

"What?"

She stops, and steps closer, wrapping her arms around my neck.

"I find that a steady diet of frequent and lengthy sex has really helped you relax and grow as a person."

I chuckle, but pull her towards me anyway, putting my arms around her waist. She leans down to kiss me and the magic is back, just like that. We make out for long enough to leave me breathless, and when I break the kiss I actually start looking around for somewhere where we can lie down. As I do, I spot something weird. She sighs in discouragement when she feels me stop responding to her touch, and follows my gaze.

There seems to be a gathering of sorts. Of monkeys. Small ones, and lots of them. Around the monkeys are three guys with cameras that look like they could be shooting a nature film, except for one detail.

Dow is standing with them. Among the monkeys, sitting there like he's talking to them, is Tom. I look at Julie to see what she thinks of this, and she just shrugs, so I walk closer. I'm still holding her hand, though.

Dow sees us coming and waves us over like we didn't already see it, looking frantic. I can see that the cameramen are speaking together in hushed tones, completely fascinated by what they're seeing, and I can't say I blame them. There are monkeys all over the place, in and out of trees, all converging towards Tom, most of them sitting, observing, but all of them fascinated. Tom is just sitting on the ground, looking at the monkeys. I have no idea exactly what is happening, and I'm no psychic, but you'd have to be pretty dumb not to figure out something really weird is going on here. We reach the camera men, who see us and make wild gestures for us to stay back and be quiet. When we stop outside the range of their cameras, they relax and go back to watching like we don't even exist. Julie and I stay quiet, observing the odd scene.

After a short while, Tom just stops looking at the monkeys, and turns to me. As soon as he does that, the monkeys scurry away. "Alex. Hi."

I nod at him, and the cameramen stop their machines. "Hey, Tom. What's all this?"

Dow shakes his head, and motions to the cameras.

"Tom found the monkeys, and he decided to talk to them, and then these guys showed up and started recording it. But they can't use it unless he agrees."

Dow looks at them meaningfully, like he's trying to be threatening, and I have to say, failing miserably. The one in charge, a skinny guy with a really big jaw and stringy, curly hair, comes towards us with his hand held out. He speaks with a thick British accent.

"Hi! I'm Reggie Davis. Your friend is extraordinary! The monkeys love him, you would swear he was talking to them somehow! We would love to include him in our documentary."

I look from them to Dow, and when our eyes meet, I quickly look away. We still haven't talked about what happened, and it's still awkward, but I guess I can't really avoid this discussion without looking like a fool.

"Uh, well, I guess we should ask Tom what he thinks, then."

Reggie seems to hesitate, and looks sideways at Dow. "Aren't you his legal guardian? He looks underage, and I think we need a parent's permission."

Dow seems relaxed at that. "No, I'm certainly not."

I look at the British guy, raising an eyebrow. That'll teach them to underestimate someone's age. "I am."

He scratches the back of his head, and sighs.

"Well then, I suppose you can give us permission."

Tom comes to stand beside me and I look at him, wondering if he wants to be in the documentary or no. He shrugs, and I turn to Reggie.

"Well, I guess he doesn't care."

Dow clicks his tongue irritably. "Are you out of your mind?"

I want to get in his face about questioning my judgment, but I still can't face him. I can't stand this stupid awkwardness.

I swallow my retort, and think of something more... patient. "Why? What's the big deal?"

He runs his hand over his head. The side of his scalp that was burned has started to grow a stubble back, and the fact that he's mostly shaved the rest off with a clipper has evened out his look a bit. I can't stand to look at it for long; I keep remembering how he looked, burnt to a crisp, on that floor. He gets closer to me, speaking in hushed tones, while Reggie watches with an eyebrow raised.

"Well, isn't alerting the public to what we can do precisely what we are trying to prevent?"

I think about it for a while. I glance at Julie to see what she thinks about all this, but I can see she's just looking at me as if I have all the answers.

"I thought it was more about control. Didn't the announcement that there're people like us originally come from some big, orchestrated catastrophe?"

He frowns at me. "Yes, that's right, but..."

"Well, what if the circumstances were different?"

"What do you mean?"

"Well, what if they already know? What if we warn them first?"

"What, others like us?"

"No. Everyone."

He frowns, deep in thought. Tom clears his throat. "Uh, guys?"

We both turn around, and see Reggie watching us with a puzzled expression. I fold my arms at him and give him that level look that I learned from Jimmy. It works, too; he's shifting his feet.

"So... have you made up your mind? Can we use the footage?"

"Mind giving us some space? We're discussing it."

He rubs the back of his neck, hesitating, but when he sees that I'm not about to budge on this, he sighs and goes to instruct his guys to pack up their gear. I turn back to the others to see Julie staring at me, her lips pursed and a thoughtful expression on her face. I glance over my shoulder to make sure the camera guys are far enough that they won't hear before I resume the conversation.

"What's on your mind?"

"What about that guy, that we came here to find? Future guy?"

"What about him?"

"Aren't we supposed to ask him about what we do?"

Tom shrugs. "I guess one doesn't exclude the other. We can always get those guys to film it, and wait to speak to that guy to see if it's a good idea to release it. What do you think?"

Julie seems to think about it. "All right, fair enough. But how are we supposed to go about making enough people see it? And believe it, too?"

"Well they're making a documentary, aren't they? Maybe we can persuade them to change their subject."

She seems to think about it. "Doesn't it take a real long time to release a movie? I mean, it'd probably not be on time. What about YouTube?"

I raise an eyebrow. I've heard about it, but I almost never go on computers. Lori used to spend her time on them, going on the Facebook and all that, and Tom is on there all day long, playing things like *Angry Birds* and showing me weird videos, but I don't really know how it works.

"Would that work?"

Dow makes a face; he seems really unconvinced.

"I don't know. YouTube is great for the appeal, and lots of people can go there, and it's all pretty instantaneous, but it's also unreliable, and there's lots of

279

bullshit on there, too. I think the way to go would be a press conference."

I scratch the side of my face. Now it's Julie that looks unconvinced.

"I don't know. A press conference is well and good, but how do we get journalists to come see us? I mean none of us are famous, and what we claim can really be construed as bullshit anyway."

Dow sighs. "Right."

Tom looks up. "Well, how about both?" They look at him, and wait for him to elaborate. "Well, we each post a video showing what we can do on YouTube and announce a time and place in the near future for a press conference, and that'll make people come to see whether or not it's true. We should have our journalists then. Besides, even if we release it on YouTube now, it would give us time to decide whether or not it's a good idea to have the press conference."

They both look as impressed as I feel. Even Dow seems convinced.

"I think this just might work. Good idea, Tom."

I turn back to the camera guys. They're taking their time, stalling, like they've got all their stuff ready and they just don't really know what to do with themselves. Reggie looks at Tom, and then me, visibly anxious. I try a friendly smile, and it's apparently not an expression I've mastered because he really doesn't look reassured by it.

"I think we may have something better for you. Better than just that footage. How would you feel about changing the subject of your documentary?"

Reggie scratches the back of his head again, and then looks back at his crew uncertainly.

"Well, we're sort of on a schedule, here..."

Tom raises an eyebrow and looks him in the eye, saying nothing. Reggie's face goes white, and his body becomes very still. He stares at Tom, and nods, before turning around and going to his crew. Tom walks toward us, hands in his pockets, smiling. I raise an eyebrow.

"Show-off."

He rolls his eyes, but I can tell he's amused. "Ah, shut up. It was useful."

Julie gives him her mocking grin, and now that it's turned on someone other than me, I can see why it's funny. "Oh yeah? The monkeys too? That was useful?"

"Well, ok, that was just for fun. But they were calling to me, I had to stop and talk to them."

She raises an eyebrow. "I was kind of joking. You can actually talk to monkeys?"

He shrugs. "In their heads. They're not really that different from us, you know. They can't speak words, but as far as thoughts are concerned, they're kind of really similar to ours."

Reggie jogs back to us, a dubious look on his face. "Hey! All right. I've talked to my crew, and we'd be interested in hearing you out. No promises, though. We still have to know what it's about. Most people think their life is fascinating, but they're usually wrong."

I give him a smirk. "We're not most people, as I'm convinced you've realized. I promise that what we have for you is earth-shattering. I'm sure we can come to an agreement. But not here, though. I don't know about you, but I'm cooking in this heat. We should get back to our hotel. Want to meet us there? We'll buy you lunch."

MAY 28ᵀᴴ, 4:47 PM

I pace next to the jeep while the guys are packing up their equipment. They just got done watching the footage they took of Dow again. I thought this would take half an hour; turns out, filming stuff right is a lot more complicated than just point and shoot. I watch them put away all their junk, and I have to breathe through my nose not to explode in their faces. I have to remind myself that it's pretty nice of them to drive us to where we need to be, even if they are getting to film all sorts of stuff. Why are they taking so much time? I wish I could smoke right now. Dow comes to lean on the jeep next to me, watching them pack their material.

"You all right?"

"Fine!"

I almost bite his head off, and then I meet his eyes. It's still awkward, and I feel sick to my stomach. I look down at my feet, shoving my hands in my pockets.

"I'm fine."

"I notice that you're not smoking."

I grind my teeth to prevent myself from blowing up. "I'm quitting."

He raises his eyebrows and shakes his head. "Hell of a time to do that. You're pretty brave."

I shrug, irritably. Why do we have to be talking about this right now? I pace faster, staring at my feet. He's the last person I want to be talking about this to, on top of it all. Probably because I feel too bad about what happened to get properly mad.

He watches me, then kicks at the grass. "Look... I've noticed how you've been acting around me."

I roll my eyes, and scowl at the grass he just kicked. This is all I needed. A good long talk about my stupid feelings. Again. He watches me, and sees I don't answer, so he sighs.

"Please stop beating yourself up. What happened wasn't your fault."

I stop pacing, and look up at him. He looks serious. He's not being falsely indulgent, at least I don't think. I look back down at my feet, but I'm calm enough to actually lean on the jeep next to him.

"I threw the fire. I didn't look. I never thought you would be there."

He shrugs. "Even if you had looked, what could you have done? I was invisible. You couldn't have seen me."

I sigh. I'm all good and ready to have an emotional conversation with the girl I like, or the man who's just become my father, but with some dude I hardly know, it's something entirely different.

"What if they hadn't found the... the pee guy? You would have been stuck like... like..."

He shrugs, again, like it's no matter. "There's really no use thinking about that. It didn't happen, so let's focus on what did. Look, we can agree that it's both our faults. Would that make you feel better?"

"Fine."

"Things are good and square between us. Is that clear?"

I can finally bring myself to look him in the eye. "Yeah. That works for me."

Reggie finally packs the rest of his stuff in the trunk and comes towards us. He's walking fast, and talking faster, all excited like a little kid, a twinkle in his eye. He's been like that ever since he started filming our YouTube videos. He didn't believe what we said, at first, or at least he was reserved about it. Now that he's seen, and he's got it on camera, he's unstoppable.

"You guys ready to go hear your futures?"

I look at Dow, and sigh. He has a point about picking a hell of a time to quit smoking. I'm never gonna make it.

"Yeah. Fine. Let's go."

MAY 28ᵀᴴ, 5:42 PM

The drive is long and painful. We're way too many to fit comfortably in this car, but since we don't really have a choice, we squeeze ourselves onto the back seats, and I'm pressed between Julie and Dow with Tom sitting on the floor. We would absolutely get a ticket back home for this, but here, the guys seem to shrug it off.

It takes about an hour for us to get to where Marcello pointed on the map; there's a town or village there, but I have no more idea than that, just a point on a map. An hour's a pretty long time when you're squeezed in the back of a jeep, but Tom seems to be having a good time, pointing at stuff and exclaiming. At least, the road is paved, and I can be grateful for that. I can rest my head on Julie's shoulder and close my eyes for a while.

The Jeep slows down, and I open my eyes. I look around, but it doesn't seem like we've quite made it into the village yet. Then I notice why we've slowed down. There's a guy on a donkey in the middle of the road, traveling in the same direction we're headed. We're close enough to the village that I can see the buildings right ahead, and people walking around in the street. The guy on the donkey twists in his seat to peer in the windows of the jeep curiously, and he turns a bright smile on us. He seems to be native, but it's weird, I expected brightly colored attire like you see on the Discovery Channel. This guy's just wearing a striped polo shirt, cargo shorts, and weird sandals that look like they were made from an old tire. Reggie goes around him, but slows the jeep down so that the guy can talk to us through the window. Reggie leans down from the driver's side, apparently anxious to be the leader here.

"Hello, mate! Do you speak English?"

The guy smiles widely, and nods. "I do. Can I help you?"

"Is this Nambacha?"

"Yes, it is! I live here. Can I help you find something? Are you visiting someone?"

Reggie turns to me and I take out the picture from my pocket, handing it over through the open window.

"We're looking for this man. His name is Wanjala."

The man raises his eyebrows at the picture in obvious recognition, and nods, looking at me curiously.

"The Rainmaker? I know who he is. I can take you to him."

I take the picture and put it back in my pocket.

"Sure. Thanks. Reggie, can you stop the car? I think I'll walk the rest of the way."

"Ok. Don't forget our agreement, though!"

I nod, and step out of the car when it comes to a stop. It feels wonderful when I finally get to stretch; I hadn't realized how cramped we were in the jeep. The man gets off his donkey, just pulling it along by the lead, and nods at me.

"I'm called Wakhanu."

"Alex."

I nod right back as I pat my pockets for my smokes, which, of course, I don't have. I spot Wakhanu nodding at someone over my shoulder, and see that Tom, Dow, and Julie have all decided to follow my lead.

We follow the guy into the village, and Reggie parks the car while we stand around. This would be the perfect, perfect place to have a smoke. Dammit, why did I have to quit? I try not to look at Julie so she doesn't misread my expression and make a big fuss about it. I don't think she'd be the type, but with girls, you never know.

The village is a weird sort of place. It has modern-looking houses, but it also has a couple of hut things that look like they're right out of the *National Geographic*. There are people going about their business, though more and more, they're stopping to peer at us curiously. Mostly they just smile and nod and walk on, though a group of kids seems to be growing in numbers and coming our way.

Reggie finally gets all his equipment out of the car and comes to stand next to us with his two other guys, looking ready to go. I turn to Wakhanu.

"All right, can you take us to where this guy lives?"

He nods, and leads us and his donkey through the village. A lot of people stop to look at us, some waving and nodding in a friendly fashion. The kids have started to follow us, talking excitedly among themselves in a language I don't understand. The guy stops to tie off his donkey on a post. While he's securing the lead of his donkey, the kids surround us, and they start touching us. Especially me, it seems. Especially my hair. They all seem to want to touch my hair. Well, Julie's hair too, to be fair, but I guess between all of us, I definitely have the longest hair, and they're all fascinated by it.

Wakhanu comes back from his donkey and starts admonishing the kids and slapping away their hands, which makes them laugh and scatter, though they don't seem to go very far. He gives them a look that's somewhat stern, though there seems to be a playful twinkle in his eye. He makes sure they're keeping their distance, and proceeds to lead us to a hut at the edge of the village.

There's a bald, toothless old man sitting outside the hut on a small bench, as if he was waiting for us, and I imagine that if he is the one we're looking for, he must have known we were coming. He nods at us and Wakhanu, and gestures for us to take a seat; he's got a bunch of

290

assorted, mismatched chairs lying about in a sort of circle, five of them. The camera crew takes discreet, out-of-the way positions, continuing to film. I hadn't even noticed they had started.

The old man sees us hesitate, and gestures again, saying something in that language that the kids were speaking. At least, I assume it's the same language; he speaks so low, and mumbles so much, I think he could have been speaking English and I wouldn't have known the difference. I sit, and the others do the same. Wakhanu says something to him and starts to go, but the old man stops him, saying something else. They start apparently debating, not really arguing but more like disagreeing and annoying each other, and finally Wakhanu sighs and shakes his head and takes the fifth seat.

I look at the others, and they're looking at me, as usual, so I turn to Wakhanu and the old man. The old man doesn't really seem to speak our language. Who am I supposed to address here? Translator, or speaker? I decide to address the old man.

"Hi. My name is Alex. We're here to ask for your help. We have a problem, and we need to know what to do about it."

Wakhanu translates. The old man listens, nodding his head while still looking at me, and mumbles something again. His voice is so soft, his toothless mumbling so rapid, that I wonder how even someone that speaks his language can understand him. I'm really glad we're dealing with a translator. Wakhanu listens with an air of uncomfortable patience, like a kid who's forced to do something he doesn't want to, and sighs before he translates.

"He says that you have already begun to take the right path. He says that by coming here, you have already done what needed to be done."

I frown. "So... basically... what, we just keep up what we're doing? Do we go through with the press conference? Will that prevent the war?"

He raises an eyebrow at me like I'm talking nonsense, and I suppose that in a way, I am. But he translates anyway, the old man nodding along to his words, and then mumbling his answer. It takes a while, and I have the leisure to observe my surroundings. It kind of hits me then that I'm actually sitting outside a hut, talking to a sort of African shaman, waiting for him to tell me the future, and whether or not the decisions I've been making are the right ones. This is just like one of those movies or comic books about heroes with swords and destinies and stuff. I feel like when I get out of here, I should go off and fight a dragon or something. Wakhanu turns back to me to translate.

"He says you have to be careful when you do this conference. You have to survive until then, and after then, or everything will be lost, and the bad event will happen."

I nod, trying to think about what to ask next. I guess GenEx is going to come after us, if the whole world knows about this. We've been in danger since the beginning, there should be nothing different now.

But if he's mentioning it, there's a chance we won't survive, I suppose. Maybe I should ask about that.

"What can we do to make sure we survive?"

Wakhanu translates, and then the old man points a gnarled finger at Tom before saying his relatively short answer. Wakhanu scratches his head and shrugs, as if in apology.

"He says he needs to keep... becoming. That he knows. That's all."

I take a look at Tom, but he's glaring at the ground. I didn't know Tom could read the future. But if he can read minds and this other guy can read the future, then I guess it's all the same. He looks at me as I think it and rolls his eyes in annoyance with me, so I stop thinking about it, and instead wonder if I've asked everything I needed to. I look at the others to see if they have something to add, but they all stay quiet. I glance at the translator before looking back at the old man.

"So, if we go through with this, and survive, there will be no catastrophe, no war? Everything will be all right?"

I wait for my words to make it to the old man, and then he nods, repeating something twice in his language. Wakhanu looks at me, a confused look on his face as he translates.

"He says, for now. He says it's a work in progress."

I sigh. Isn't it almost over? I want to finally be able to get back to my normal life. I think about Nicolas again. I guess there really isn't getting back to completely normal. Not for me, at least. I look at the others.

"Anything else you guys want to know?"

Tom keeps staring at his feet, but Julie and Dow look at each other, shrugging, then Julie turns to me. "I think you pretty much covered it."

I nod and turn back to the old man as I think of the best way to sound grateful and respectful, both of which we really are. Well I am, anyway.

"We don't have any more questions. Thanks for... well, for this."

He nods, and says something again. Wakhanu breathes a sigh of relief and stands up.

"He wishes you well, and he thanks you too. Come on, let me show you around."

MAY 28TH, 9:47 PM

The ride back is a lot quieter than the way there was. It's incredibly dark out there, so there's nothing to distract us from the monotony of the drive. Dow is asleep in his seat, his mouth hanging open, snoring softly. Tom is playing with my phone, checking every few minutes to see if we have reception yet, which of course, we don't, and using up the battery playing *Angry Birds*. Julie seems lost in thought, and I don't really dare disturb her. It's a little while before she sighs, and leans her head on my shoulder.

"What are you gonna do, after this?"

"What do you mean?"

"Well, you know, when it's all over."

I shrug, but gently, so her head doesn't get too disturbed. "I don't know. Go back home and pick up where I left off, I guess."

She lifts her head and frowns at me. "You don't think you're just gonna keep doing what you did, do you?"

"...well... don't you?"

She stares at me like I'm stupid for a while, and I look away, grateful that it's dark enough she can't see me blush.

"I guess I didn't think about it that much."

She shakes her head. "You realize what's going to happen to us after the press conference, don't you?"

I frown. The man only talked about surviving. What's she going on about? I feel like an idiot for asking.

"What?"

"Well, we're going to be the first people to prove that we have superpowers. On record. In a press conference. With videos on YouTube anyone in the world can watch."

Holy shit, she's right. How had I not even thought about this? Because I thought about it like I do everything else in my life, of course. Get the job done. To hell with the consequences. She sees my face change, and nods.

"That's right. We're going to be world-famous celebrities. People are going to recognize us in the streets. And that means there is absolutely no way that either of us can keep doing the job we used to do."

She's right. What the hell am I going to do? I know I'd been considering retiring from what I do, but I hadn't really made the choice yet. I was only toying with the idea. I have to call Luke and Jimmy before it all happens.

Shit. I have to call Mister Lupino. What am I going to do? I don't know anything else. I'm uneducated and I've never had another job in my life.

Julie puts a hand on my shoulder, squeezing it reassuringly.

"Hey! Don't panic. It's gonna be fine. We're doing the right thing."

I nod, trying to school my face into neutrality, and it must work at least a little because she seems satisfied that I'm doing better. Tom isn't fooled, of course, but he just glances at me before looking back at the phone.

"You should talk to Antoine."

I look at Dow, who's still sleeping, and then at Tom again. "What for?"

"He realizes what we're doing too, and he's also not sure how it's going to affect his work."

I frown at Tom. "You know, you're always manipulating us non-thought-readers into saying specific things at certain specific times. Are we all your butt puppets, or what?"

He blinks at me and laughs. "Seriously? No one's my butt puppet. First of all, eww. Second of all, well, I don't manipulate anyone. I just try to help out when I see that my friends are in trouble and could use a hand. I mean, I know what you're all thinking. I know it makes you uncomfortable, but I can't help it, it's just the way it is.

297

I'd be kind of an ass if I let you all muddle around in the dark when I have the answers, right?"

It's tempting to think that he has some grand master plan, and that he just nudges us in the direction he wants us to go in, because that's what it feels like. At the same time, I know him, and he's a good kid. He shakes his head, smiling.

"Yeah, you better remember that."

I frown at him. Is he looking a little depressed? Before I have time to elaborate on that thought, the jeep finally slows to a halt and I realize I can see the lodge at long last. The driver turns to us as Julie shakes Dow awake.

"Here's your stop." Reggie yawns and stretches. "I'll ring you guys in the morning. If I have it in me, I should upload your videos tonight. Thanks again for letting us shoot the rest of your story, by the way. This is going to make a much, much better documentary than the mating habits of Bonobo monkeys. It's going to be a hit."

I nod. A few hours ago, those very words would have made me shit my pants, but in light of what we're preparing to do at the press conference, this documentary is nothing. In fact, I'm glad that Reggie gets the exclusive on everything we do. I know he's mostly helping himself, but he's also helping us a lot.

"Sure. Let me know when they're all uploaded."

He yawns again, waving us out of the car. "I'll ring you, like I said. I have your mobile number."

I nod, and step out of the jeep. I can't blame him for wanting us gone, especially if he's planning on working when they get to where they're staying. It's been a pretty long day. I stretch as the others walk out, and we all wave at them as they go before going in.

I look at Dow as we walk to our rooms, but he's like the walking dead, half-awake, so I decide to hold off talking to him about our options until tomorrow morning. After all, we did what we came here to do, and the conference is not for a little while. All we have to do until then is lie low, which I can't imagine doing better anywhere else than here. For all intents and purposes, we're on vacation here for the next few days.

Julie walks into our room, leaving the door open for me, and then flops onto the bed. I'm as exhausted as she seems to be, but there's something I have to do before going to sleep.

I plug in my cell phone to make sure the battery doesn't completely drain while I'm talking, and call Mister Lupino.

There's quite a few rings, but I don't worry, because it's late. Just as I think the voice mail is going to pick it up, I hear his voice.

"Alex? Is something wrong?"

"No. Not yet. Hi."

"Hello. What is the matter?"

I sigh, and go out to the balcony so I can let Julie sleep. "I... have to tell you something. Something important. It's going to happen tonight, and I don't want you finding out from someone else."

"I am listening, my boy. Go on."

I sigh, and really wish I could light a cigarette right now. Shit, when is this craving thing going to stop?

"We had an idea today, about how to... take care of our particular problem. How to get the people that are after us off our back... and how to prevent them from doing something that's going to be really bad for everyone in the future."

There's silence. I imagine him looking at me, looking serious and intent, and I go on. I know he won't interrupt until I'm done; it's not his style.

"Well... we've decided to tell the whole world. About us. What we can do. How different we are."

"You have." It's not a question. Rather, he's repeating because he's so shocked.

"Yeah. So the way that we're doing it... you know what YouTube is?"

"I have heard of it. It is... on the internet, is that right?"

"Yeah. People can post their own videos. Well, we made some videos of what we can do, and they're going online tonight."

"I see."

"And on the videos... well, we each give a date, telling everyone, if they want more, if they want proof, that they should come meet us. We're going to have a press conference. In a few days. And we're going to show the whole world."

There is a long pause. I can almost see his serious expression, his analyzing stare.

"And you have thought this through carefully, yes?"

I find myself smiling despite how nervous I am. He does know me pretty well. He would have guessed right, too, if Julie hadn't made me realize what it meant. But he should also know I wouldn't be calling him if I didn't know what it implied.

"Yes. I have. I understand what it implies. That's why I'm calling you."

There's another silence, after which the tone he uses sounds slower and more careful. "So, you must have come to a decision about the business, then."

"Yeah. I have. You can imagine that it's going to make me... a pretty high-profile person. Probably for a very short time, but still, too much for me to keep doing that."

I say it, and I thought I was going to be nervous, or terrified, or devastated, but all I feel is relieved. I guess it really had been weighing on me for the past couple years.

"Very well."

I take a deep breath. If he had been anyone else, this conversation would have been radically different. This kind of job isn't something you just quit. I'm lucky he trusts me so much.

"So... we're ok, right?"

"Of course, Alex. We did have this discussion some time ago, if you remember."

"I do. Thank you."

There is another pause.

"Alex... the family lawyer is going to file the paperwork tomorrow."

I frown. Paperwork? What's he talking about? "Um... what paperwork?"

"For the adoption. Making you officially my son."

"Oh."

"In light of your life changes... I... would understand if you did not want to go through with it."

I look for something to sit down on, and since there isn't anything, just turn around to lean on the balcony railing.

"Of course! I mean... do you still want to go through with it?"

I hear him sigh on the other end, and I hope it's relief. "Of course I do, Alex. Nothing would please me more. I will have him file the paperwork tomorrow. You are being careful, yes?"

I'm the one that's relieved at that. "Yeah. I'm fine. And I'm careful. We've got everything under control."

I hear him chuckle. "I have heard that before. Well, remember I will be very annoyed if something terrible happens to you."

"I remember. You don't have to worry about me, Mister Lupino."

"Good, good. Well, call me again tomorrow. I worry about you when I go days without news. Now, though, I must return to sleep. I am not as young as you are."

I smile. "Sure, Mister... I mean... papa." The word still feels strange in my mouth. "Good night."

"To you as well."

I hang up, sighing, and look at the savanna in front of me. I can see nothing, of course. I turn back to the room, and see Julie is fast asleep on the bed. I still feel way too

303

wired to sleep, and I check the time on my phone. It's way too late to call someone else. Wait. I'm an idiot. It must be... I don't know, afternoon-ish. I look at my phone for a while, debating who to call. I owe Jimmy explanations, so I really should call him first. I sigh, and dial his number.

It rings a couple times, and then he picks up.

"Hey, man. So you ain't dead yet?"

"Not as far as I know, at least."

"Good stuff. What's up?"

"Well... I sorta have to talk to you about something important."

"Uh... ok, let me get somewhere alone."

I hear some shuffling, some muffled voices, then there's silence a while, and then he comes back to the phone.

"Ok. What is it? Did something happen?"

"Yeah... kind of."

"What?"

I think about where to start, and shake my head. He hates long stories. There's no way he'd sit through that one.

"Well, a hell of a lot of shit. You won't believe where I'm at right now."

"Aren't you in Italy?"

"I was. Now I'm in Kenya."

There's a pause. "What the hell is that? Is that even a place?"

"It's a country. It's in Africa."

"Uh... Africa? Isn't Africa a country?"

"No. It's a continent."

"Oh. Seen some lions?"

"No... some nice birds, though. And monkeys."

"Heh. Monkeys. So, uh, I'm guessing what you had to tell me doesn't involve monkeys?"

"Uh, yeah. Well. It's about the job."

There is a pause while I gather my thoughts, but he's quicker than me.

"You're not coming back."

"No, I am coming back. Just, when I do, I won't be able to go back to doing the kind of work we do."

"Why not?"

I explain about the videos, YouTube, the conference. Surprisingly, he doesn't interrupt me. He's either really pissed, or really confused. I hope it's the latter.

"This is fucking stupid, man. I can't believe you're doing this. You have to be so much more of a dumbass than I thought you were."

"I have to, Jimmy. You don't understand. It's about the fate of the world. It's pretty important."

"Fuck that. What makes you think a couple of videos will make a difference in the world?"

"Because, this guy who can see the future told me."

"Holy shit, do you hear yourself? Are you fucking high?"

I sigh. "Jimmy, look..."

"Don't you fucking 'Jimmy look' me. I think it's ridiculous, and stupid, and I'm hanging up. Call me when you've come to your fucking senses."

He just hangs up on me. I stare at the screen of my phone for a moment, fuming, tempted to just hit redial and scream at him. Who the hell does he think he is, talking to me like that? I reach into my pocket to get a cigarette, but remember I can't. Instead, I just kick one of the posts holding up the railing three times, as hard as I can, hurting my foot. It's not as satisfying, but it does make me feel a little better. The post smokes a little, and I notice I've singed it, so I take a deep breath, and try to calm down. I look at my phone again, and dial Luke's number. It only rings twice.

"Hello?"

"Hey, Luke."

"Alex! Hi! I haven't heard from you in forever! How are you? Is everything all right?"

"Yeah, sort of."

"So... yes, it's Alex. No, he's calling long distance, he doesn't have time."

I smile. He's so good with the kids. "Tell them I'm going to send pictures from my cell phone as soon as I can. I saw some monkeys."

"I'll tell them when I hang up. Girls, go wait outside! ... Because I'm on the phone and you're bothering me. Shoo!" I wait for a second. "Sorry, Alex. I'm on the phone in the kitchen. Are you still overseas?"

"Yeah. I'm in Africa, actually."

"Really? That's amazing. The girls will flip when I tell them."

"Yeah."

"So... you're not calling me from Africa to tell me about some pictures."

"No."

307

I take a deep breath. I'm starting to get tired of telling the story, so as quickly as I can, I tell him about the videos and the press conference. I say just what he strictly needs to know to understand the situation, mentioning that the film crew is shooting a whole documentary about us.

"...so we're probably gonna get a lot of media attention."

He stays quiet for a bit, but I know Luke enough to know that he's just taking it all in, digesting the information to formulate an opinion. "Wow. Huh. You're ok with this?"

That wasn't what I expected. "... I have to be. I don't really have much of a choice in the matter. It's the best solution."

"Yeah. Sure. So how is it going to affect... what you do?"

Luke never likes to talk about my work. I guess what I'm about to tell him is going to make him pretty happy. "I... I called Lupino earlier to tell him I quit."

"Just like that? And he let you?"

"Yeah."

"You're sure he's not going to send someone to kill you? Should I hide out with the kids for a while?"

"No. No, everything is fine. Better than fine. He... while we were in Italy, he asked me to become his son."

There is another silence. It's been a while since I talked to him; I guess I've been way too busy to keep anyone posted, about anything.

"Seriously?"

"Yeah."

"Huh. Well. Congratulations, I guess."

"Yeah."

"So... what did Jimmy have to say about that?"

I click my tongue. I'm still so annoyed at Jimmy. "He said it was stupid. That I was stupid. That I shouldn't do all that."

"Well, it is dangerous."

"I'm not an idiot. I know that. He has to know that I look out for people other than just myself."

"He knows that. He'll come around. You know he always gives you a hard time about everything. He just needs to think about it, that's all. He'll be glad to be in charge."

I sigh. "What if he's right, though?"

"About what?"

I called him mostly so I would feel better about fighting with Jimmy, but I realize as I say it that that's the real reason I'm talking to Luke right now. I need to ask this of someone who knows me outside of my work. Who knew me before I became what I am now.

"Well... I know it's what I have to do, and what makes sense, and everything, but... what am I going to do now?"

"What do you mean, what are you going to do?"

"I mean, I don't know how to do anything. Literally. I've only barely made it to sixth grade. You know that. What the hell am I going to do with my life, now?"

"You don't give yourself enough credit. You're starting something big. You can try doing what you do best."

"What I do best? Set things on fire?"

He laughs. I can almost see him shaking his head. I hardly thought about him, about anything else than what needed doing all the time I was gone, but being this far, not being able to see him... it makes me miss him so much. Hell, I even miss Jimmy.

"No, numbskull. Help people. The way you helped us, here."

"What? You want me to become some kind of social worker? I'm pretty sure you need a high school diploma at least."

He laughs again, and I'm so glad for his ability to see things clearly that I can't even get mad at him for making fun of me.

"No. But what you're doing... when it's all over, a lot of people should come forward, from all over the world, no?"

"I guess, so?"

"So, a lot of them won't know what to do. Some will have explosive gifts, like yours. Some will just need someone who's been where they are. I'm sure you can find a way to help them out."

I think about it. Tom did mention something about talking to Dow. Maybe he meant something like that? I'll have to bring it up with the others.

"Thanks, Luke. I knew you'd think of something."

"Ah, what would you do without me?"

He's being sarcastic. He always is, when it comes to things like this. He thinks he owes me everything, that I saved him and the kids. I guess I helped, and Jimmy helped us a lot, but if it hadn't been for Luke, over the years, I don't know where I'd be.

"I don't know, Luke."

I take another look inside the room, and see Julie stir in her sleep. The bed looks so tempting; now that my anger and anxiety are gone, the fatigue is hitting me like a wall, and I can't wait to lie down.

"Anyway, I gotta go. I have my phone, you know. You can call me whenever, if there's anything. Don't worry about the fees."

"All right. Hey, when are the videos going up on YouTube?"

"Tonight. Or tomorrow. Why?"

"Are you kidding? The girls would never forgive me if I knew you were going to become a celebrity and they didn't get to see it all begin. We'll be watching."

I sigh. Of course. I didn't even think about that.

"Ok. But, for the press conference, can you try to convince them not to come, at least? It'll probably be really dangerous."

"I'll do my best. They're old enough to give me a lot of trouble now, I'm sure you know."

I've never lounged around naked in a hotel room with a girl and room service before, but I can see why rich people do it all the time. I haven't felt this relaxed in, well, ever. And that's saying something, with what's going on right now, with the videos and everything. I've ignored six calls today already, and I'm not planning on answering any, either. Well, unless Mister Lupino calls. I've been trying to reach him all day.

It's kind of extraordinary, when you think about it. I've known this girl for over a year and we've worked together on several occasions, but for all her flirtations, I never thought it'd come to this. And now, I can't really think of what it would be like to live without her. It feels like I want her next to me all the time, and I'm already thinking about what we'll do together when we get back home. I'm not sure I ever thought this way about Lori. As much as being with Julie makes me happy, that thought weighs me down like I swallowed a brick.

I lie down, with my head on her stomach, tracing circles around her bellybutton. Her skin feels soft, and warm,

313

and it smells like her sweat and like the sex we just had. It's so powerful it makes me want to do it all over again, for the third time today, and there's no reason not to. I let my fingertips trail, softly and slowly, down her navel and into her pubic hair. She sighs contentedly and parts her legs for me, but I take my time, teasing her until I can nearly taste her frustration. I move slowly, removing my hand and shifting my body so I can lick her inner thigh, and then I hear my phone ring with Lupino's ring tone. I turn my head slightly towards the sound. I want to ignore it. I really don't want to spoil the mood, but at the same time, I've been trying to reach him all day, and I've been kind of wondering if something was wrong. Julie sighs deeply, the tension in her body visibly diminishing, and I expect her to be mad for my distraction. Instead, she just puts her hands beneath her head to prop it up, and smiles.

"It's your Lupino guy, isn't it?"

I nod, unsure. She shrugs, and pushes me playfully with her foot.

"Go ahead. Pick up. I'm not going anywhere."

"You sure?"

"Hurry up, you'll miss it."

I decide to go for it and reach for my phone, which I left on top of the dresser on my side of the bed.

"Hello?"

"Mister Winters?"

I frown, and take another look at the caller ID. This is definitely Lupino's phone, but I don't recognize the voice. My mouth's suddenly dry, and I get this sinking feeling in the pit of my stomach. Something's happened.

"Who is this? Where's Mister Lupino?"

"We have the old man. You have until June 1st to surrender to us. If you go to the gathering you have called for on the internet, we will kill him."

"What? Who the hell are you? What have you done with him? Hello?"

There's not another sound, and when I look at my phone, I can see that they've hung up on me. I curse, and get up suddenly, going to get my pants. Julie sits up on the bed, frowning.

"What's going on?"

"They've got Mister Lupino. They're holding him hostage and saying they'll kill him if we do the press conference."

She just stares at me as I get dressed. She looks shocked, but she's making no move to get out of bed. I start getting ready to argue. She's awesome, and sexy, and perfect, but she can go to hell if she thinks for one second I'm gonna put my fun above Lupino's safety. Turns out I don't have to even try to convince her, though. She finally shakes her head like she's having a hard time assimilating the information, and starts dressing even quicker than me, looking at me with a concerned face.

"What can I do?"

"Get Dow and Tom. I have to make a call."

She nods, pulls her shirt on and walks out while I start calling Luke to tell him to take the emergency money and take a road trip with the kids.

MAY 29™, 5:22 PM

I'm trying not to, but every time my mind wanders to anything besides stopping myself from doing it, I end up chewing what little I have left of my fingernails. I have to keep resisting the urge to go hunting for a pack of cigarettes. Since I don't even know where I could buy any in this country, I thought it would get easier. Now, I just regret the smokes I flushed down the toilet, and I would crawl my way through broken glass for a mile to smoke just one.

Tom and Dow are sure taking their sweet time getting back to the hotel. What the hell was the idea to go hiking in the forest, anyway? Julie watches me, saying nothing for a long time, but after a while she apparently can't resist.

"You really care about him."

I look at her, confused. "What?"

"Your boss. Your new dad. You really care about him."

"Well, yeah! Why'd you think I'm becoming his son?"

She shrugs. "To be honest, at first I thought it was about the money. I mean he seems loaded, and if he doesn't have any other family, it all goes to you, right?"

I feel my mouth hanging open, but I'm too pissed off to say anything. How could she think that? It hadn't even crossed my mind.

"I don't give a shit about his money."

She studies me, and then smiles. "You really don't, do you? Well, I have to say, you keep surprising and impressing me."

I snort. I can't believe she even thought that of me. Who cares about money? Money's just a tool to make other things possible; it doesn't mean anything by itself. I have tons of it, more than I need. I find myself biting the nail on my index finger again, too short, and I make it bleed. By the time we get back to the US, I'll have chewed all the way to the bone. She lays her hand on my knee.

"Look, I'm sure he's going to be fine. I mean, he's pretty tough for someone his age. I'm sure you have nothing to worry about."

I sigh. What if he's already dead? Wouldn't they be capable of something like that? How are they treating him? I know he's tough, but he's old, and he's been needing a lot more rest lately. He doesn't complain much, but I can see in the way he moves that he's got all these aches and pains that he doesn't talk about. And all that talk about not being there for much longer... what if he does die, and I never got to tell him what he means to me?

Finally, Dow and Tom burst into the restaurant where we're the only ones waiting. The film crew is with them; the cameraman, I think he's called Dave, is filming them. Tom is hanging back behind everyone, staying out of sight of the camera. Julie frowns at Dow as he reaches us.

"Everything ok, Antoine?"

"No, it's not! They called me! They have my mother!"

I jump to my feet, unable to stay seated any longer. "They have your mother?"

"Yes! We can't do the conference. We have to get back home so I can go get her!"

"They called me too. They have Lupino."

His eyes are full of panic. "What do we do? She's an old lady! She's not that healthy! We have to do something!"

It's weird, but it feels kind of good to see him panic. It helps me focus on what needs to be done rather than what might happen to Lupino. Makes me feel purposeful, like helping someone is easier than taking care of my own problem.

"Of course we'll do something. We're not going to let them get away with this. Let's think about this logically. Mister Lupino was still in Italy. Your mother was still in New Cambridge?"

He nods. He looks a bit calmer now that I seem to know what to do. I don't, of course, but if I keep thinking about it enough I'm bound to come up with something.

"Ok. So first we need to figure out where they put them, and if they're still near the place where they were first taken."

He nods, looking at me expectantly, like I'm going to have the answer. I try to think. Why only us? Why not Tom and Julie? Tom shrugs.

"Well, we don't have anyone. You guys are our 'some-one'. We don't have family, or parents."

Julie frowns, and he turns to her, answering whatever it is she's thinking.

"What I mean is, we don't have anyone that's present in our lives. My parents might be alive too, for all I know, but I've been with GenEx since I was two, so there's no way to know. The only people I really care about are right here."

I sigh, annoyed, and look at Tom. "Stop answering us before we talk. It's confusing!"

He shrugs, lifting his hands up as if to protest his innocence.

"Fine! I just thought it would go faster."

I sigh, and glance at the film crew. Reggie is holding up a microphone to capture everything we say, and Dave is still filming. I roll my eyes.

"Come on, guys, this is kinda private. Do you have to be filming this?"

Reggie nods enthusiastically. "Of course! It's part of the story! This is great film-making. I tell you, this documentary is going to make history! Go on!"

I clench my fists and grit my teeth. I have to control my anger because these guys really are helping, so it would probably not be a good idea to punch one of them, especially on film.

"You're going to put that in the film?"

Reggie nods. "Think about it, mate. We've got it right on tape, here, how you're the innocent ones being persecuted by big evil corporation goons. This is as perfect for you as it is for us."

I pinch the bridge of my nose between my thumb and index, trying to focus on the matter at hand. The first thing to do is to find out where they are. How are we going to do that? It hits me so hard I have to slap my forehead.

"Marcello! Of course!"

Dow frowns, and then his eyes light up in understanding.

"Yeah! He can help us!"

321

I look at Tom. "You said he was going somewhere safe. Did you happen to catch where that was?"

He shrugs. "More or less. He didn't tell me."

"But you read his mind."

"Hey, you know I can't help it. Don't make me sound like a bastard."

"Fine. We need to get back to Italy. Like now."

Reggie pulls his headphones to uncover one of his ears.

"We can arrange that. Guys, it's a wrap for now. I'm gonna need you to go pack up your stuff. We're leaving on the first flight out of here."

MAY 30TH, 9:54 AM

The flight was a lengthy, agonizing nightmare that could only be topped by the pain of having to sit in the waiting room at the layover airport being filmed by Dave and Reggie while they ask questions about how this all started. If that wasn't enough, they try to get us to tell our life stories. I draw the line at that and only say that I've been on my own for a while and in charge of my own business, which happens to be not anyone else's business.

They seem a little put out by my lack of communication, but seeing as I'm much more forthcoming on the matter of how GenEx kidnapped me last year, I had to escape, and they came after us again and almost killed us, they don't seem to care that much about my past. Especially when I explain how Tom came from the future to stop them. They spend the entire taxi drive from the airport all over Tom, trying to get him to talk about how it made him feel. When he finally gives in, the answer isn't what I thought it would be at all, and I finally understand the attitude he's had about it since it happened.

"How do I feel about it? How am I supposed to feel? I've seen the person I could be if all my friends had died and I was left to fight a losing battle for all the humans left on Earth. All I can say is I don't want to be that... man. I don't want to look at the world like that. I don't want to do the things he's able to do."

"So, he was more powerful than you are?"

He winces, like he didn't really mean to let that slip. "He has to be. I mean, I'm young; I know I'm improving all the time."

"Then you weren't always able to do what you do now?"

"I'm pretty sure I wasn't even born the way I am now."

"What do you mean?"

"GenEx got me really young. They did a lot of experimenting on me. I think they... enhanced me, somehow."

I frown and look at Julie. She's glaring out the window. I don't know if she just doesn't like to hear about it, or if it's something they did to her too. Reggie goes on with his questions, ever the journalist, insensitive to the fact that Tom might need a break.

"So what will your powers consist of, in the future?"

Tom sighs. "I don't exactly know. I don't want to know, either. Oh, look, we're here."

324

He looks at me, and points to a house, so I lean and tell the driver to pull over. As we all get out of the mini-van cab, I watch Tom and can't help but wonder how he's doing with discovering his new skills. The man in Africa said he had to master new things... what if he's too paralyzed by his fear of becoming his future self to practice?

As the taxi pulls away, he glares at me, and then glances at the cameras before talking. "I know what I have to do, ok?"

I shrug, trying to look confident. "If you say so."

He nods and motions to a small house. We're on a cobblestone street, wide enough for two cars to fit comfortably. It looks pretty busy. There're a few market booths on the other side of the street, with crates of fruits and vegetables, and merchants behind them tending to women carrying reusable bags and baskets. The houses and shops are all stuck to each other, without even so much as an alley to reach the back of the buildings, though their height and the kind of bricks they're made of varies a lot from one to the other. The building we're headed to has yellowish white bricks and a bright orange wooden door. I look at Tom, raising an eyebrow, because he stops to inspect the house as if he suddenly doubts that this was the right place.

"You sure this is it?"

He thinks for a while, and then nods. "Yeah, I'm sure. Go ahead."

As the designated guy who speaks Italian, I go up to the door and knock, hoping he's right. If this isn't it, then we don't know how to find Marcello, and we're screwed. It takes a few moments, and then a scrawny old woman shows up. Her face is a mess of wrinkles and her hair is completely white, contrasting with the black dress and black scarf she wears. She looks me up and down, and though I swear I've not been afraid of a lot of people in my life, but I sure wouldn't want to cross her. She speaks to me in Italian so coarse that I barely understand it.

"What do you want?"

"Um... miss, we are here to see Marcello. Is he here?"

I shift on my feet, almost wondering what I should do to show more respect. I look at the others. Julie seems amused, though she's struggling hard to contain it. The guys are still filming, and when I turn back to the old lady, I see she's spotted that and is squinting with a mean look at them. She waves a hand towards the film crew, and though it's simple, it's done with so much attitude it's almost a rude gesture in and of itself.

"What is this?"

"Oh! Uh... guys, can we lose the cameras for now? We can ask Marcello if it's ok once we meet with him, all right?"

Reggie looks disappointed, but nods, and Dave turns off the camera and lowers it. I turn back to the old lady.

"We're sorry about that. Is Marcello here?"

She folds her arms, looks me up and down again, and then just turns around and slams the door in my face. I stand there, dumbfounded, for at least a minute before turning back to look at Tom. Dow all but glares at me.

"What did you do? Did you insult her?"

"No, I just asked if Marcello was here!"

"Great! Just great! What the hell do we do now?"

Tom rolls his eyes. "Stop arguing. It's going to be all right. Alex, mind the door."

I turn towards the door again, and just as I do, it opens to reveal Marcello. I'm so relieved I could hug him, but from the expression on his face, it would be very poorly received.

"You again. What are you doing here?"

"Mister Marcello, sir, we really need your help."

"How did you find me here?"

"It's a long story. May we step inside?"

He frowns at the film crew.

"What's this?"

"They're with us. Please, we won't take much of your time, we won't intrude, and we won't do anything you don't want us to do. May we come in?"

He sniffs unhappily and walks back inside, leaving the door open for us. I sigh in relief and step in after him, waving for everyone else to follow me.

He leads us through a cramped living room, in which are sitting four women. His wife is with them, and she seems to be the only one who's happy to see us. She waves at us and I wave back, awkwardly. We go through the empty kitchen all the way to the back door, which opens up to an alley. Marcello sits at one of the only two seats around a small wrought-iron table and looks at the camera crew like they're oozing green pus, and then back at me.

"Why are there cameras?"

I sit on the other chair without waiting for his invitation. "We met them in Africa, and they helped us a lot. In exchange, we agreed to let them film our story. They are wondering if they can film you using your talent."

He snorts. "Certainly not! I have no wish to become a tourist attraction!"

I sigh, and look at Reggie. "He doesn't want you to film him."

"Tell him we can fuzz out his face, so that no one will recognize him."

I turn to Marcello again, trying to stay calm. This is wasting so much time.

"He says he can make it so no one will recognize you. Hide your face."

328

"What about my voice?"

I don't even take the time to ask Reggie. I can deal with this later. After he's found Mister Lupino.

"Yes, yes, your voice as well. Can he film you?"

Marcello sighs, considering it, and I resist the urge to smack him and shake him and yell at him to just get on with it already. At long last, he raises his face and nods, looking like we're asking to pull out all his teeth with our pocket knives. I look at Reggie, but he already got the cue. He's signaling Dave to get recording again and prepping his sound machine, so I just get out my cell phone and turn to Marcello as I look for a picture of Lupino to show him while I explain the situation.

"The people we are fighting, who came to your house to attack us, you remember them?"

"Yes, of course. They are the reason why I am imposing on my sister."

"Well, they're still after us. They're trying to make us do something that will permit them to get on with their plan. And to make us do it, they have kidnapped my father, and my friend's mother."

Marcello frowns, nodding. He doesn't seem like he's going to need that much convincing, this time around.

"I understand. You wish for me to see if they are still alive, and where they are being held."

"Please."

I find a picture of Lupino. It's an old one where he's holding Nicolas, who was only a couple weeks old. I stare at it for a little while, then hand Marcello the phone. He looks at me, seriously.

"I will do it, because you helped me defend my home, and you have trouble because of it. But I am not someone you can just come to every time you need to find something."

"I know! And believe me, we wouldn't have come all the way to Italy if it wasn't really, really important."

He nods, making sure I understood his point, before looking down at the picture.

"Tell my wife to bring me the atlas."

I nod, and while he's concentrating, I hurry back inside to go fetch his wife. She meets me in the kitchen, and she's already holding the atlas. I blink, surprised, and take it.

"Uh... thank you, miss!"

She smiles, and pats my cheek affectionately. "Thank you for everything you did for us."

I nod, feeling really awkward, and wait for her to turn away before I feel I can run back to the yard. Marcello is coming out of his trance, so I rush over to him holding the atlas. He grabs it out of my hand and starts leafing through it. A huge knot seems to loosen in my chest. I hadn't even notice was there, like my heart hasn't been working for a while, and then it suddenly was again. If he found him, it means Lupino isn't dead, right?

He opens a map of the East coast of the States, and points to a place just outside of New Cambridge. Back home? Could it be that easy?

"This is where he is. In a cell, in a large facility."

I nod, memorizing the location. "Is he all right?"

"He seems well."

Dow puts a picture he pulled from his wallet in front of Marcello. "All right, now ask him about my mother!"

Marcello picks up the picture, and shakes his head, putting it back down.

"I do not need to look for this woman. She is in the same place as the man you had me look for."

I sigh with relief, but Dow doesn't understand, of course.

"Is he saying he won't do it? Why the hell not?"

"Because she's with Lupino. Relax, will you? She's safe, it's just he's already found her."

Dow sighs in relief, picking up the picture and putting it back in his wallet. He looks at me. "So, we know where they are for sure?"

331

I nod. I would light a cigarette right now. Why did Julie have to make me quit, dammit? Dow looks at Marcello, and then at me.

"What if they move them, though? Or they're killed?"

I frown at him. "Huh? What are you talking about?"

"What if they change locations? How will we know?"

I scratch my head. He's got a good point. I hadn't really thought about that. What can we do? I look at Marcello.

"It is really important to us that we find our parents. May we ask one more favor of you?"

He purses his lips. "Ask, and we shall see."

"Would it be possible for you to give us a number you can be reached at? We would call you once we are back in America to ask if they have been moved."

He raises his eyebrows like he's considering it. After a little while, nods.

"I believe it would be possible. Where can I write my number?"

"Just tell me what it is."

I take out my phone, and punch down the number in my contacts as he dictates it.

"Do we need to leave you a picture of them?"

He shakes his head. "No. I will remember. Once I have seen a face I seldom forget."

I stand up and shake his hand, probably with more enthusiasm than I've ever had shaking someone's hand.

"Thank you, sir. Thank you so, so much."

MAY 30TH, 11:14 PM

I'm not happy. I know they're right, but it doesn't mean I have to like it. When we get to the hotel, I spot a guy smoking, and I head over to him as the others are walking inside. Julie frowns, stopping, and calls out to me.

"Hey! What are you doing?"

"I want to have one cigarette. Just one. Is that too much to ask? I haven't bought a pack. I haven't smoked one in weeks!"

"Three days."

"Whatever! You guys didn't want to go tonight, you made me wait and go to a hotel and get some sleep, so I'm having a cigarette. All right?"

She frowns, looking like she's thinking about it, and then shrugs. "Whatever. I'll be in the lobby."

I sigh with relief, and go to the guy. He agrees readily enough to give me a cigarette and some fire, and it feels so amazing to be smoking again that he's not even done the one he was halfway through before I'm finished with mine. He raises an eyebrow, says nothing, and gives me another one. I consider refusing, but only for half a second, and I just take it and try to smoke a little slower than the first one. By the time I'm done this one, I can see Jimmy, carrying a duffel bag, making his way towards me from the parking lot.

"Hey man!"

He reaches me, and too manly to give me a hug, claps me on the upper arm hard enough that it hurts. I grin. "Hey, Jimmy. Glad to see you."

"You too. Shit, I don't think I've ever seen you look this rough."

I look down at myself. I still have my shirt that I didn't change the whole time I was in Africa. I guess I didn't really notice how much dirt there was there; it's turning a weird brownish orange. My pants are no better. It's a good thing I still have a clean suit in my bag. I know I've got stubble, too, even though I'm not that hairy. I hope I can find a razor; I didn't really think to pack one. I motion towards the hotel with my head.

"Come on, let's go inside."

I glance at the duffel. It looks full enough, but I have to wonder if he was able to find all the stuff Julie needed on such short notice. He only had a couple hours to do it, and that's some massively illegal shit.

Julie's sitting at the bar, and downs her drink when she sees us, hurrying over to us.

"Hey, Jimmy. You made it. You got everything?"

He rolls his eyes. "What am I, incompetent? Of course I got everything. I wouldn't have showed up if I didn't."

"Fine. Let's go. The others are waiting."

She takes us to our room on the fifth floor. To my intense relief, only Dow and Tom are there. The film crew is nowhere to be seen. Dow is pacing, but Tom is sitting on the bed, half asleep. I sit on the couch, Jimmy dumps his bag with a certain modicum of care on the small table in front of it, and Julie stands, looking around.

"Where are Reggie and the guys?"

Dow sits too, in the only chair, folding his arms. "They're in their own room. Asleep. I told them that's what we'd be doing. I figured you wouldn't want them to film this part."

Jimmy looks at me, incredulous. "Film? What the hell? And who's Reggie?"

I sigh. "He's the documentary film guy I told you about. He's been following us around and filming everything that we do."

He raises an eyebrow. "What, you're like, on a reality TV show?"

"Something like that."

He shakes his head. "Well, whatever. I ain't being in no movie, and you're not gonna want them filming the next couple days."

He unzips his bag. It's all there; a few handguns, magazines, and a bunch of grenades. Julie sits down and starts going through the duffel, picking what she likes, discarding the rest on the table. Dow's jaw drops.

"What? You're going to go in there guns blazing? Do you have any idea how much trouble we could get into?"

I stare at him. "What do you suggest? That we ask nicely?"

"Well..." He just stares at the arsenal, eyes wide, rubbing his chin, and shaking his head. "I just... I can't believe this."

Julie shakes her head, stuffing a couple cf guns and clips in the inner pockets of her stupid ugly trench coat.

"Look, Dow, like or not, we're going in. If they have enough nulls, which they will, we might not have powers to defend ourselves with. Now, since it's also for your mother, shut up and help us come up with a plan."

MAY 31ST, 5:45 AM

I stare at the building, stifling a yawn. Julie turns to glare at me from the driver's seat.

"See? You're tired too. We should have waited until tonight."

I return the glare with as much bile as I can summon this early in the morning.

"No way. First of all, I'm not going to let Mister Lupino rot in that place for another minute if I can help it. Second of all, leaving before they got up was the only way to ditch the cameramen."

She shrugs. "Yeah, well, if we fail due to drowsiness, it's your fault."

"Just drink your Red Bull."

She chugs it, and turns to the back seat. "You ready?"

Jimmy frowns seriously at the building, and then takes a gulp of whatever liquor he has in the metal flask in his coat pocket before nodding.

"Yeah. Let's go."

We all get out of Jimmy's car, Tom and Dow get out of the rental, and we make our way to the building. As we reach the part of the fence where we can hide from the cameras behind the dumpster, I see Julie concentrate and then disappear. She reappears right away, and nods at us.

"No EM field on this end. The whole floor they're in is protected, though. Too bad, I could have been in and out. I can teleport all of you in one at a time, at least on this floor. Once you're inside, wait for the rest."

She starts with Tom, then Jimmy, then Dow, and finally, when she's alone with me, she looks at me. "No heroics, all right? We get in, we do what we have to, we get out. That perfectly clear?"

"Yeah! What do you think I'm gonna do, run around shooting at the walls?"

"Just... we gotta survive. You remember what that guy said. We have to make it."

"We'll be fine."

She nods, and then kisses me, and the world rips away from me and is suddenly yanked back. I take deep breaths, dispelling the nausea that comes with her teleportation.

Something smells foul, and I have the small satisfaction of seeing that someone threw up, and I'm not the only one that feels sick when she does that.

As usual, she's completely unaffected, so while we're getting our stomachs under control, she gets her bearings. She disappears, and by the time she reappears a few seconds later, all of us seem ready to go.

"Ok, I disabled the cameras down the hall and in the stairs. We should get a move on. We won't have more than a few minutes."

I look at the others and Jimmy gives me a nod, gripping his baseball bat. We follow her down the hall and to the emergency stairs. The building seems pretty deserted, and I guess we're not even in the part of it where the offices are because it's bare, and beige, and everything that made it so unpleasant the first time I was trapped by GenEx. We go down two flights of stairs, and as we pass it, I notice that the security camera's cables have just been ripped completely out. I wonder how long we have before someone notices.

Eventually we reach the bottom, and she disappears before reappearing right away.

"All right, the coast is clear, and I took out that camera too. Let's go!"

She pushes the door, and we follow her out. This time the hallways are gray, and I recognize them. This might not be the same building, but it sure is decorated the same way; maybe they color-code it or something. We're definitely in the same kind of area I was in when I woke up after they took me, a year and a half ago. I'm starting to think this is too easy when, as we round the corner of a hall, we come face to face with three armed guards making their rounds.

For a fraction of a second that feels like minutes, we just stare at each other. I get ready to attack them before they raise their gun, but I can feel Julie's hand squeeze my forearm. I look at her and she motions to Tom, who's concentrating pretty hard. Eventually, the guards relax, turn around, and start heading the other way, talking about their day. Tom stays concentrated until they're out of sight, and then breathes a sigh of relief.

"I hope that doesn't happen again. I was almost too late."

Julie nods, and takes the lead to go to peer down the other hall. She leans over the corner, discreet and careful, and stares way too long for it to be a good sign. She finally slinks back towards us, grim look on her face, and whispers.

"Ok, so there are two of them guarding the entrance to the cells. I can't see the EM field generator, but I'm betting it's right past that door. The best thing would be for Antoine to become invisible, get inside, and turn it off. Then, I'd be able to teleport, I'd get them out, and we're done. What do you say?"

I frown. "It sounds too simple, but I don't have a better idea."

Jimmy raises an eyebrow at me. "I do. Get in there, kick their asses, take down that whatever-it-is, and get out of here."

I sigh. "How about we make it plan B?"

He shrugs. "As long as it's some kind of a plan. I don't want to get out of here without some kind of ass-kicking."

I smile despite myself. I missed Jimmy. And I'm going to miss him more, when I'm no longer working with him. I take a deep breath, squashing the anxiety that's rising in me, and nod to Dow.

"You feel up to it?"

He shrugs. "Just describe what it is I'm looking for, and we should be in business."

"It's a kind of big black box. It's got a dial. You gotta turn it to off. That's it."

He nods, concentrates, and disappears. I'm listening so much for his footsteps that the silence becomes audible, and oppressive, like something that's pressing down inside my ears and into my head. It lasts forever. Eventually, when I think he must have made it, my heart sinks when I hear a voice I don't recognize.

"What the hell?"

Julie peeks around the corner again, swears, and disappears. Jimmy grins at me.

"Plan B, boss!"

He starts running merrily towards danger, and as I follow after him, gunshots start ringing all around. I press myself against the wall, looking at Tom. He's pale, and looks terrified, but he nods at me. He's ready to do what he can to help, so I open my hand and try to make a flame. Nothing comes. I close my eyes, sighing. I'm worthless with a gun, but here goes.

I grab the gun I took from Jimmy last night, take the safety off, and crouch. I take a look around the corner, trying to get a good view. Some of the fighting is going on in the hallway that Dow was supposed to infiltrate, but closer to me, Julie is struggling with the second guard, who is holding her away from him by the wrists. She keeps trying to kick him in the balls, but he manages to move away at the last moment. I think at this moment how hot the way she fights is, and I give myself a shake. She needs help.

I take a look at the guard. He doesn't have a weapon in his hand, and I see it on the ground next to him, so I aim at him. I take my time, because Julie's in no immediate danger of death and I don't want to accidentally shoot her. After a second or two, something weird happens: Julie just stops moving, starts looking confused, and raises the gun to her own head. The guy is not moving either, and I don't know what's happening but it scares the hell out of me, so I shoot and hit him right in the side of the chest. He cries out and gasps, eyes wide. Julie frowns at him and watches him fall to the floor, then blinks at me, confused. I grin at her as I stand. I hear Tom shout a warning, but it's too late; by the time I turn around, there's a gunshot, and a sharp pain in my side.

It's a good thing I stood at that moment, I strangely reflect, because a second ago that would have been my head. I look up and see the two guards Tom turned away earlier, running towards us. Obviously, they were drawn by the gunfire. I raise my hand to use my power, but that's still not working. By the time I even think of the gun in my hand, one of them raises his arm, and the lower half of my body is suddenly encased in ice. I think to myself how unfair it is that they get to use their powers but I don't, and then the pain hits me.

I thought I was immune to temperature change, but I guess either I was wrong, or it has its limits when it comes to cold, or the fact that my power's been taken away also affects that. The ice is so cold it feels like my hands are burning, and no matter how much I struggle, I can't move an inch.

The guards reach me. The ice guy goes right past me while the other guy stops and grins at me. I frown, and though it's getting hard to see because of how much my teeth are chattering, I think I recognize him. That's the guy who almost killed me, back at the beginning of all this. The guy who was meant to kill me. I glare at him, but I'm immobilized and there's nothing I can do about it. He raises his fist, and all I can do is speak.

"What, you gonna beat up a guy stuck in ice?"

It doesn't faze him. He hits me full force, in the face, probably breaking my jaw. The pain is so intense that I can't see for a moment, and when I finally can, I notice that I'm on the ground, the mound of ice surrounding my lower half making me bend at an odd angle. I'm alone, I don't know where Tom is, and I'm completely helpless. I fucking hate myself. How could I have gotten beaten like this?

As my anger rises, I notice something: I'm not cold anymore. In fact, the ice that surrounds my hands is actually turning to water. I concentrate. Could my power be coming back? The ice all around me melts, and before long I can kick it, and it falls apart like nothing. My jaw hurts like a bitch, but I can open my mouth, so it's not broken; at least there's that. I'm dripping wet from the melting ice, but I'm so pissed off that by the time I make it to the hall where the others are fighting, it s coming off me in steam.

I can't see Dow or Julie, but Jimmy is fighting super-strength guy who kicked my ass, and apparently, losing, though he's putting up a good fight; I can see his base-ball bat lying in two pieces on the ground next to him. Tom is hiding behind the desk where it seems the two guards were playing cards; I can't tell what he's doing.

I crack my knuckles, thinking about how that fucker hit me when I was down, and concentrate. The fire forms all around him, on his clothes, on his skin. I could have made it a little quicker, I guess, but I feel like he definitely deserves it. He starts screaming, and by the time I'm done setting him on fire, he's running down the hall. He trips before he makes it to the end. Once he's on the floor, he rolls, attempting to put out the flames, but that's just tough.

Jimmy looks at me, grinning. Is he missing one of his teeth? It's hard to tell through all the blood. One thing's for sure, he doesn't look too good. He tries to get up, but his eyes roll in his head and he passes out. I make my way towards him, but I have to lean on the wall halfway there because I'm getting dizzy myself. I'm still bleeding from the gunshot on my side, and my face is starting to swell. The guy Julie was fighting, the one I shot, twitches on the floor. Tom gets up from behind the desk to jog towards me.

"Alex! Are you ok?"

"I'll be fine." I flex my jaw before I go on. I wasn't really prepared for how much it hurts to talk. "Where are the others?"

"They're in the hall over there, I think. They were still fighting, but I think they're winning."

He reaches to support me, but my body goes rigid. I don't understand what's happening for a second, and then I notice the guy on the floor that I thought was dying, staring at me with eyes wide and teeth gritted, like he's doing something incredibly difficult. Tom frowns at me.

"Alex? What's happening?"

I feel myself reaching for the second gun in my coat pocket. I want to tell Tom to get away from me, but it's getting confusing, like I'm not sure who he is. Who is he, anyway? Is he one of the guards? I raise my hand, and it feels like the most natural thing to do. Of course I'm gonna shoot him. He's a guard. He's the man my mother made me with. I feel myself pull the trigger, and I see him take a step back, his eyes wide, staring at my gun. He's a bastard. Why isn't he defending himself? As the shot rings, he raises his hands, eyes squeezed shut, and I hear the bullet ping off something invisible in front of him. He opens his eyes, one at a time, realizes he's unhurt. Oh. He's going to hurt me now. As I get ready for another shot, I see him turn to someone on the floor, someone shot and bleeding, and his eyes go wide.

My mind suddenly feels like a fog is lifting, like I was drunk, but now I'm suddenly sober, and I start to understand what I just did.

"Holy shit! Tom, are you all right?"

He nods, running his hand through his hair, and as I lower my gun to kill the guy on the floor, I see that the mind-controlling bastard's eyes, nose and ears are all bleeding; he looks definitely dead. Tom blinks rapidly at me. Shit, is he crying? He glares at me.

"Shut up. I am not."

I want to make a face at him, but I'm feeling dizzier and dizzier, and I have to lean on the desk. I do, but it's weird, the desk seems to zip away from under my hands. I'm suddenly sitting, and I realize that it was just my arms, not strong enough to hold me up anymore. Tom frowns at me.

"Alex, are you ok?"

I find the strength to nod. I open my mouth to talk, but I just don't have the energy. I know he can hear me think, so I think of Julie, and Mister Lupino, and hurry up, they need help. He seems to hesitate, like it's some kind of agonizing choice, but then he sighs and runs off.

I look at Jimmy. He's still passed out. Is that blood under him? I don't know. Everything is getting darker. I close my eyes. Just for a minute. I swear.

MAY 31ˢᵀ, 6:11 AM

Someone is slapping me on the cheek.

"Wake up! Wake up!"

I blink, and I feel my eyes roll around in my head like they're trying to find the hole they're supposed to be staring out of. I'm sitting somewhere comfortable. I think it's a car seat. Yeah, it's a car seat. Julie's face is right over mine, a worried expression on it. I try to talk, but she jams something in my mouth. Liquid pours in, and I swallow. She takes it away just as I realize how disgusting it tastes, and spit out what I hadn't swallowed.

"Ugh! You're making me drink that shit again!!"

"It's not shit, it's piss. Now stay here, I gotta get your friend."

She just disappears. I lick the back of my hand, like that's going to make the fact that I just drank piss a lot better, and look around. I'm alone in Jimmy's car. The rental is gone. Does that mean that the others made it out ok? As anxiety starts to squeeze my chest, Julie reappears with Jimmy, who seems to also be coming around. She hands me the keys.

"Start the car!"

I stare at the keys, and then look at her, as she's making Jimmy drink from the small bottle she just gave me. I want to tell her I don't drive, I don't even properly have my license yet, but it's not the time to be finicky. I start the damn car. At least, this time, it's automatic.

I'm getting on the freeway by the time Jimmy wakes up fully, coughing and spitting.

"Holy shit! What the hell is that crap?"

Julie puts away the flask.

"You don't wanna know. Let's leave it at that. All right?"

Jimmy frowns at her, and then at me. "Shit, you made him drive?"

She frowns, looking at me in utter confusion. "Well... yeah, why?"

"He's gonna make the car explode by the sheer power of his crappiness."

Julie looks at me, sees I'm not protesting, and starts laughing. I'm not in a laughing mood, though. I'm not even in a don't-piss-me-off-while-I'm-driving mood.

"Are they ok?"

She calms her laughter, smiling at me through the rear-view mirror. "What?"

"Lupino. The others. Are they safe? Are they ok?"

Her smile makes that subtle change from derisive to kind, and understanding.

"They're all fine. They're in a car with Antoine. He's taking them to the hotel. Don't worry. He even found Naomi, and Russell."

I let myself breathe, finally, and I drive the rest of the way in silence. I have to admit, it's exactly like Jimmy says. It's a lot easier to do this when I'm feeling relaxed. That, and the automatic transmission helps.

MAY 31ˢᵀ, 6:57 AM

I finally manage to park the car after three tries. I guess that's one of my weak points in driving, too. As soon as I yank the keys out of the ignition, I toss them at Julie, and practically run to the hotel. I don't really notice whether or not Dow's rental is back. I just go as fast as I can, heading for Dow and Tom's room.

I make it before Julie and Jimmy to the elevator. As I'm riding it up, Julie just appears next to me, grinning.

"Not trying to escape, are you?"

"What? No. I just... well, I wanna see for myself how he... how everyone is."

She smiles, looking at the doors, but I can feel her fingers entwining with mine. When the doors open, I don't let go of her hand, but drag her along with me to their room. It occurs to me then that she could probably have teleported, but it doesn't matter by then. I knock on the door.

"Dow? Tom? It's Alex! Open up!"

The door opens, and it's not Dow or Tom, but Mister Lupino. He's looking well, if a little tired, and wearing a radiant smile. For a moment, I just stare at him, like I can't believe we made it; he's safe, and then I just wrap my arms around him and hug him so tight I practically lift him up off the floor. He laughs, and then pats my arm.

"You are a very strong young man, son. I am not as robust as I once was. Be mindful of that."

I let go of him. My hands are trembling, and my throat feels tight. I'm glad Jimmy isn't here to see this, or he would be making fun of me. Mister Lupino grips both my forearms in his, his eyes twinkling with pride and shining with tears. He doesn't say anything for a long time, at the end of which he just gives me a small nod, which tells me everything. He's happy. He's proud. We saved him.

Julie clears her throat, and I suddenly realize we've been standing in the threshold of the door, blocking it. Lupino chuckles, and we just walk into the room. Dow is sitting on the couch with an old woman I've never seen before. Tom is curled up on his bed, apparently asleep. Lupino goes to sit on a chair, which he pulled up next to the couch. The old lady smiles at me, and strangely, I detect a hint of pride and approval in her expression.

"And this is the son I have heard so much about, Domenic?"

She has an almost undetectable accent. French, I think, or maybe German. Lupino nods to her. "This is my son Alex. Alex, this is Jeanine. She is your friend Antoine's mother."

I nod. I look for a place to sit down, find none that's practical, and just stand.

"Pleased to meet you."

She smiles. I turn back to Mister Lupino. "Would you like me to get you a room? I'm sure they have something comfortable here. I can..."

He raises a hand to stop me, and I wait to hear what he's going to say. He stands.

"It is not necessary. I will get a room myself. For now, I am famished. We had not had breakfast yet. Jeanine?"

He holds out his arm. She smiles, stands, and wraps her arm around his, putting her hand in the crook of his elbow. I look at Julie, and then at Lupino again.

"Would you like us to come with you?"

He shakes his head. "I think not. I believe your lady friend is very much looking forward to seeing you alone."

I turn to Julie and she grins at me, wiggling her eyebrows. I nod a bit at Mister Lupino. "All right. Please be in touch."

He shakes his head and puts his free hand on my forearm.

"I am sorry about what happened. It shall not happen again. You should not be the one to worry about me. Besides, I have called some people. I will not be alone, like I was in Italy."

I nod, feeling relieved. I know what that means, and he'll be in good hands. I watch him walk out, and it occurs to me that he seems pretty cozy with Dow's mom. Before I have time to say anything to Dow about it, Julie grabs my arm and I'm suddenly in my room. I groan at the sudden feeling, and sit on the bed. She stands in front of me, waiting for me to feel better, but when the nausea is gone, the tight feeling in my throat just gets worse and worse. I stand, going to the window.

This stupid hotel doesn't have a balcony, so I don't have the option of going anywhere to have true privacy. I can't control it; it must be the fatigue. After all, I didn't sleep much last night, and before that I'd been on airplanes for two days, changing time zones and everything. I take deep breaths, but it doesn't help. Damn it, I'm relieved. Lupino's ok. He's safe. Everyone's safe. Things are back on track. Why am I fucking crying?

Just as I'm telling myself that this is possibly the least sexy thing I could be doing, and that I gotta find some way to hide it, Julie comes right up behind me, wraps her arms around my waist, and rests her cheek on my back. I lean my forehead against the glass of the window and close my eyes. I slowly start feeling better, and I turn around to wrap my arms around her too.

I want to lean my chin on her head like I used to do with Lori, but she's too tall, so I just press my forehead

355

against hers. She's smiling at me. I think she's going to say something, but she just kisses me. It's different from all the other times she's done that; before, it had always felt urgent, needy, like it had to lead straight to sex. Now it feels soft, and calm, like all that exists right now is our mouths, and the rest of our bodies are simply a support for them.

When it's done, she leans her head on my chest, saying nothing. I watch her, and then bury my face in her hair. There is nothing else in the world right now than her, the feel of her body, the smell of her hair.

"Alex?"

"Hmm?"

"Would you have come for me like that?"

I blink, and it takes me a few seconds to answer, because my mind was turned off and I really didn't expect anything like that.

"Of course I would. I would have come for you with no guns, and no backup."

Her grip gets tighter, and she sighs contentedly. "Good."

She lifts her face so she can kiss me, but this time the kiss has a lot more passion behind it, and she presses herself against me. I feel myself get hard, and as I start responding to her touch, a knock comes at the door. She groans, and then turns toward it, annoyed.

"What is it?"

"It's Reggie! We've been looking for you all morning!"

"Go away! We're not here!"

"But..."

"Go film Dow and Tom. We're having sex!"

There is a silence on the other side of the door, and then I can hear steps leaving. I chuckle, quietly, so they don't hear me if they're not far. She grins.

"What?"

"Liar."

She raises an eyebrow at me, her grin widening. "Wanna bet?"

JUNE 2ᴺᴰ, 11:17 AM

I look at the glaring red digits on the hotel alarm clock. Today's the day. Just thinking about it fills me with dread. We had a long talk about it yesterday and designated Dow the official speaker, because he's older and does that kind of stuff for a living, but that doesn't make it any easier. I'm still going to be standing there, in front of all these people, and showing them what I can do. Julie stretches next to me and then cuddles up, kissing my shoulder.

"Stop agonizing about it. It's going to be fine. I mean, we've survived like, three certain death situations this month already. We can do this."

"Doesn't it scare you?"

She shrugs. "Shitless. But it's happening, whether I want to or not, so we have to make the best out of it."

"It's in less than an hour."

She smiles at me, then sits up and stretches again. I watch the way it makes her back arch and her breasts perk up. She turns to me.

"Hey, you just said it, it's in less than an hour. Which means we have to get dressed, eat, and get going. No sex!"

I have to smile, and I watch her as she gets out of bed and gets dressed.

"Besides, haven't you had enough? It's practically all that we've been doing for the past two days. Sure, we got out and had dinner with your new dad, but that's like the only occasion we even stepped out of here."

I shrug. "Can you complain? It's kept the film crew off our back."

She laughs. "Come on, get dressed. We can't be late."

I sit up, find my pants, and pull them on. It's a good thing hotels have a cleaning and ironing service; I couldn't have stood it if my suit wasn't in perfect condition for this.

"We can't be too early, either. We'll be sitting ducks. We have to time our arrival just right."

She nods, and when we're dressed, we walk out. As soon as we're in the hall, we're assaulted by Reggie and Dave, and we have to literally dodge the camera to make it to the elevator. Reggie sticks the microphone in my face, riding downstairs with me.

"So how does it feel, now that the big day has arrived?"

I shrug, trying to act cool. "I guess we'll see how we should feel about it when it's done. No use worrying about it now."

Julie gives me a sly smile, but says nothing. Reggie doesn't notice, but goes on.

"Do you think you're sufficiently prepared?"

"Of course. We worked on this like crazy people. We're too prepared."

The elevator reaches the ground floor. Dow is there, with Tom, Lupino and Jeanine; they're eating muffins from a box that Tom is holding. He presents it to me when we reach him, and I grab one.

"Thanks."

Julie does too, and then Tom offers it to Reggie and Dave. I look at Dow. "Got everything down?"

"Oh yes. This is going to be one of the defining moments of my life. I have to do this right! Besides, my mother is watching."

He smiles at Jeanine, who laughs softly, then he turns back to me. "Seriously, though, I'm a bit nervous. I've never spoken in front of so many before. They're expecting thousands of people!"

I frown. I was actually afraid that no one would come. "How do you know?"

"It was all over the news last night. They've scheduled more cops just to work the site. It's going to be huge."

I chew on my muffin, concentrating on not letting panic show on my face. Thousands of people? How could this have happened? Dow goes on, answering my question before I have time to ask it.

"Evidently, they've started a whole Facebook page dedicated to the conference. They're calling it 'SuperDay'. Isn't that cool?"

"Yeah. It's awesome."

Dow looks at me and chuckles. "Hey, don't worry, it'll go fine. After all, I'm the one who has to do the speech, so what are you worried about?"

JUNE 2ND, 12:02 PM

The van stops on the other side of the street, and I'm frozen in my seat. There has to be at least ten thousand people out there. There are crews from at least seven... no, eight different news stations, and at least a hundred cops doing crowd control. We chose the steps of the courthouse, partly because Dow is pretty familiar with it, but partly because we could stand on top of them and be heard well below. I'm not sure that this is going to be the case anymore, but I can see that there's a podium there with what seems to be microphones and speakers. Someone went through the trouble of organizing all this? What the hell?

Reggie and Dave get out quick, filming us exiting the van. It takes a few seconds, but as soon as the first person spots us, the buzz spreads through the entire crowd like electricity. By the time we've even reached the edge of it, there's so much agitation that the few cops are easily overtaken, and we have to back up towards the van. I look at Julie, but she's nodding at Tom. She lays a hand on his shoulder and disappears with him, reappearing at the podium. The effect is incredible and instantaneous. The crowd starts shouting, screaming, and trying to get to the podium, though fences have been erected. I notice that three men are approaching Tom, when Julie appears, grabs me, and suddenly I'm standing next to them. She disappears again.

I shouldn't have had that muffin; I'm fighting the urge to throw up. The men approaching Tom blink at me, then look at each other and keep walking towards us. I feel myself panicking, and I look at the crowd. The last thing I want to do is fight someone in front of all these people. I mean, we're trying to get them to be on our side, it's not time to show them how deadly we can be. But the oldest of the men, a guy with a nice, dark-blue suit and white hair smiles at me, extending a hand. I frown at him, hesitating, and then I hear Tom's voice in my head telling me to go ahead. I glance at him, and lean forward to shake the man's hand. He shakes it vigorously, clasping it in both of his, grinning.

"I am very pleased to meet you, Mister...?"

He hesitates, and I guess it's his way of asking me for my name. "Alex W... I mean Lupino. Alex Lupino."

It's the first time I say it, and it sounds so good it gives me the little boost of confidence I needed to be back on top of the situation. The man nods.

"I am Senator Robert Lafayette. This is my assistant, Matthew McDonald, and my friend, Daniel Thompson."

I shake hands with them both. A senator? And who are these people? What's going on here? Dow joins us, and as they introduce themselves, I spy Reggie and the film crew arguing with some cops at the bottom of the stairs. I nudge Tom He looks at the cops, and all of a sudden, the crew is allowed through. They look a bit confused, but seize the opportunity.

"Mister Lupino?"

I look around, but then realize it's me being addressed like that. This is going to take some getting used to. The man called Daniel Thornton is smiling at me. The senator and Dow are talking.

"Uh, yeah?"

"I was just saying that I took the liberty of contacting the senator."

"You did?"

I frown. I should be thanking the guy, he's probably the one that organized all this, but I know GenEx is pretty connected; I can't help but be suspicious. He nods.

"My daughter insisted. She speaks very highly of you. As I hear it, you have been of great help to her."

I frown, not understanding. Who the hell do I even know that still has her parents? He turns, motioning to a couple of women standing off to the side, and the young one waves at me with a happy smile. For a second, I'm stunned, because she really reminds me of Lori, all frail, and skinny, with her hair bleached blonde, but then I recognize her.

"Jill? You're Jill's father?"

He nods. "And I can't thank you enough for returning her to us. We had no idea what was going on there until we had her back. We have been trying to do something to put an end to the organization since then, and you have just provided us with the opportunity."

I shake my head, incredulous, and smile at him. "Well, uh, really, you've helped a lot too. We really didn't know what we were doing, here."

He chuckles, and is about to say more, when the senator steps up to the podium and gestures for us to come closer. Everyone does, so I do too, and the senator raises his hands to quiet the crowd. Surprisingly enough, it works, and everyone just stares at us in rapt attention.

"My friends, I am glad to see you in such great numbers on this auspicious day. Today, a large part of what we know to be true will change. The very way we see the world will never be the same, after what you are about to hear and see. You will discover with me a new group of people, who have actually been present among us for a very, very long time. Today, they come out of the shadows." He smiles at the crowd and glances at us before turning back to them. "But I know you have not come here to hear me talk. So, without further ado, let me present Antoine Dow."

He backs away from the podium, gesturing to Dow, who nods at him and steps up to the microphone. He takes out a folded piece of paper from his pocket, and smoothes it out on the podium. He leans forward, opening his mouth to speak, and suddenly Tom pushes him out of the way, then does something with his hands. There is a gunshot, and I can hear the bullet ping off of Tom's shield. He points to the fifth story of a building across the street, turning to Julie and shouting.

"Up there!"

"I see him!"

She vanishes. The people are screaming, and they're starting to panic. The senator is being surrounded by bodyguards, and Dow is staring at the crowd, stricken, completely frozen in place. Something needs to be done, or this will be a disaster. I step up, and lean toward the microphones.

"Nobody panic! Stay where you are!"

My voice comes out of the speakers about ten times louder than I intended it too, and it even causes a little bit of feedback, but to my intense relief, it has the desired effect. Everyone stops, and they stare at me with wide eyes, though some are looking around to locate the shooter. It helps that Julie reappears at this moment holding a guy dressed all in black in a headlock, and a sniper rifle in her other hand. A murmur goes through the crowd, but before it gets loud enough, she uses the hand that is holding the gun to put two fingers in her mouth and whistle loudly at the closest cops.

"Hey! You law enforcement guys! How about enforcing some law, here?"

They look at each other, but rush to arrest the sniper. I watch them, and I feel the crowd starting to go wild again, so I raise my hand a bit like I saw the senator do. When that doesn't work, I yell.

"Hey! It's all right, we got the guy! Now since we almost got shot here, how about having the courtesy of staying five minutes to hear what we have to say?"

They start to settle down. I turn to Dow, who's white as a sheet, but looks ok otherwise. I use the excuse of clapping him on the shoulder to lean to him and whisper in his ear.

"Say what you gotta say, but make it short. I have a feeling we won't be able to hold them here for long."

He nods, licking his lips, and steps up to the podium again. He doesn't have his paper; I guess he lost it. Well, if he's tried cases in court, he's probably good at winging it, which means it's going to be fine. Hopefully.

He clears his throat. "I'll try to keep this brief. A week ago, most of you saw the YouTube videos of us claiming to have extraordinary abilities. Well, as you have just now seen through this unfortunate event, we really do have these abilities. But we are not alone. A lot of people around the world share these extraordinary talents. They are healers. Or psychics. People who can manipulate fire. Or become invisible. But, first and foremost, they are people. Just like you. Brothers, sisters, sons, mothers. And they need your help.

367

"For the past few weeks, my friends and I have been forced into hiding by an organization known as GenEx. We suspect they are the same people behind the little assassination attempt you have just witnessed. This organization takes people like us, without trial, without us having done anything wrong, and locks us up. Experiments on us. Attempts to control us. So we stand here, in front of you, begging for your help.

"We live in a free world. A world where no one should be imprisoned because of the circumstances of their birth, whether it is their gender, the color of their skin... or the abilities that set them aside from the norm.

"This is why we come to you today. We are reaching out to everyone, whether or not you have special abilities, to stand with us and demand that this government recognize our basic human rights. Because, while we may not be exactly the same as all of you, we are, first and foremost, human. Thank you."

He steps back, and there is silence for a few seconds, then the crowd erupts in a mess of questions, exclamations, and photo flashes. Dow looks at me; he seems exhausted. I sigh, step forward, and hold my hands up.

"All right, all right! One at a time, or we won't answer any questions at all!"

JUNE 2ⁿᵈ, 8:47 PM

I'm about to step out of the restaurant when I see Mister Lupino walk toward me from the bathroom. He's seen me, and I hope he doesn't draw me back to the table, but he just changes course and comes to meet me.

"Alex! Leaving? And without your lady friend?"

"Uh, no, Mister Lupino, I was just going to get some fresh air."

"Going to smoke?"

"No, I quit. Well, I'm trying to quit, anyway. Julie doesn't like it."

That seems to make him much happier than I'd want it to. "Good! Good. I am glad to hear it. It is a filthy habit." I try to smile, and he just laughs and claps me on the upper arm. "Alex, you have made me very, very proud today."

That changes my forced smile into something I couldn't have repressed if I wanted to. I don't know if he means the fact that I've started using his name as my own, or the way I handled the press conference, or whatever, but any of it would make me happy.

"Thank you, Mister Lupino. I do my best."

He shakes his head. "When will you learn? Will it not be strange to call me Mister Lupino, when that is also your name?"

I smile. I guess he's got a point. "I'll try."

He nods happily, and starts to walk away. I catch him, putting my hand on his forearm. This is as good a time as any, I guess.

"Mis... I mean... papa." He looks at me, waiting for me to formulate what I have in mind. I don't know if I'm going to be able to. "I just want to say... thank you."

He raises his eyebrows. "Alex, my boy, I should be the one thanking you for all you have done for me. You have given me back a chance at having a family. You have saved my life, once again. What could you have to be thankful for?"

I look at him. It's hard to say, because nothing feels adequate. "Well... you."

He looks serious, and we stare at each other for a long time before he pulls me into his arms, hugging me tight-ly. Strangely enough, it doesn't make me feel awkward or weird. It feels like I've found some bit of me somewhere that was missing. This feels like I'm finally home, even though I've never really known such a place.

After a while, he lets go of me and smiles. "Do you still wish to go for some air?"

I lean over, and see that the others are still in heated debate, and sigh. "Yeah... I won't be long."

He nods and walks away, smiling. "We will be waiting for you for dessert."

I walk out and go lean on the wall, sighing. I hear laughter beside me and I jump, but it's only Jimmy, smoking a cigarette.

"Jimmy! What are you... gimme one of those."

He grins and hands me a cigarette. "Never figured you'd quit, man. Especially not for a woman."

"Shut up."

I light up, breathe in the smoke, and release it slowly. Once I'm a bit more relaxed, I raise an eyebrow at him.

"So what are you doing here? This is so not your neighborhood."

He grins. "Been following you. Waiting for an opportunity to talk. You're turning into an important dude."

I raise my eyebrows. "You've been following me? Since when?"

He shrugs. "The conference. Good job on crowd control, by the way. Didn't think you had it in you."

I shake my head. "You've been following me all day? Shit."

I think for a bit. That means he watched for the nearly three hours of questions from the press after the conference. And he sat outside through the meeting in the senator's office that took all afternoon. And the meal with Mister Lupino that took all night.

"Yup. So what'd you talk about with the senator, anyway?"

I grin. I got out of that one easy. "He wants to center his new campaign around us. You know, have our rights become sort of the cause he embraces. So I made him understand that I was probably not a good choice. When he saw who my father was, he understood."

Jimmy makes a face at me. "Your father?"

"Oh. Yeah. I forgot. Mister Lupino made me his son."

"Shit."

He shakes his head in disapproval. "Well, I guess I don't have to worry so much about him putting a bullet in your brain for walking out on him, then."

I stare at him in utter shock. "You were actually worried?"

He blinks at me, and then shakes his head. "No. That's not what I meant."

I take another drag from the cigarette, hiding my smile behind my hand. He sighs, and looks at me again.

"So it's all done. You're leaving."

"I'm not going anywhere. I'm staying right here. Just, I won't be doing the same work, is all."

He shakes his head. "What the hell are you gonna do?"

"Actually, we've had kind of an idea."

"We? Who the hell is we?"

"Dow, Julie, Tom, me."

"Yeah. Your new best friends."

"Jimmy, you're my best friend. That doesn't change just because I won't be working with you."

He snorts, but I can see in his eyes he feels a lot less sour about it.

"So... what's your idea?"

I smile. "We're starting a foundation. A place where people like us can turn to for legal aid, education, protection, all sorts of help."

He takes out a couple smokes, handing me one. I look over my shoulder to see if Julie is watching me, and since I don't see her, I take the cigarette. In for a penny, in for a dime.

I light both of our smokes and Jimmy squints at me, then rolls his eyes.

"I guess it's not completely stupid."

"Glad you approve."

He snorts again. "So... do I tell the guys I'm in charge, now?"

"Yeah." We stay quiet for a while, and then I smile at him. "You know, I'd like to come over for a beer next week, when things have quieted down a little."

He raises an eyebrow at me. "You drink beer now?"

I shrug. "Julie insisted. It's not so bad."

He laughs. "Hah! Well, if she can make you drink, I don't care if you quit smoking. She's got my vote."

"Let's say Thursday?"

"Yeah, I guess. But let's not go to my place."

"Why not?"

He gives me a sidelong glance, and then looks away and clears his throat. "I moved."

"Oh? Where?"

He frowns at the ground, and takes a long time to answer. He thinks he's tough, and he is tough, but sometimes he's kind of funny. By the time he's decided, I know exactly what he's going to tell me.

"With Erik. Ok? I moved to Erik's place. He has this big house, and rent is expensive when you drink whiskey. Ok?"

He's all aggressive and staring me down, like I'm gonna say something, so I just smile.

"Ok, Jimmy. It's really, really ok."

He frowns at me, then looks away. "Fine. I guess I'll see you Thursday, then."

AUGUST 28TH, 5:47 AM

Julie stirs in her sleep next to me, and I sigh. If I could only have a cigarette, maybe I'd be able to sleep like she does. It doesn't seem to be getting any easier, though it's been months now. I guess it shows me how stupid and judgmental I was towards Lori, when I was younger. It really is hard to quit something you're that addicted to. She's been on my mind a lot, lately, and not just because I've finally moved back into the large room I used to share with her.

I look around at the boxes. We just finished moving Julie in, and already, the curtains are changed on the windows and everything looks different. After the repairs from the explosion and fire, I had everything repainted different colors. The room is littered with the Chinese we ate in bed. The sheets don't smell like Lori anymore, either. But then again, Tom had been sleeping here for almost two years, so I didn't really think they would. Maybe Lori really isn't my problem.

I step out of bed, and walk quietly to the hallway. I stand there, staring at the door I've opened exactly once in the past two years. I promised Julie I would start getting rid of that stuff. And I really should. But I don't know when.

I walk to the door, and put my hand on the handle. I hesitate before turning it. It creaks a little bit from lack of use, and I'm standing in his room again. I can't believe the bulb on his nightlight is still working; I should have turned that off, or unplugged it. But after I gave him away, I just couldn't; it feels like it's still preventing him from being afraid of the dark, wherever he is.

I walk to the crib, and remember the nights when I would sneak in when I got back too late to see him before Lori put him to bed. He's not there, of course, but I have this perfect picture of him in my mind. It feels like it's not just the crib that's empty, but I am. Like a dark, black void that's making my chest cave in from the inside. I close my eyes and take a deep breath.

It was a mistake to give him up. I didn't know it then, but I do now. I thought I was going to be dead by now. But I just turned nineteen, and with my change of careers, there's a good chance I'll live to turn twenty, and twenty-five, and maybe even thirty. I could have been a father to him. I won't make that kind of mistake again.

"What are you doing?"

I start at the sound of Julie's voice, and turn to see her standing in the doorway, wearing one of my white t-shirts. Her hair is messy, and her eyes are heavy with sleep. I look back at the crib, and sigh.

"Moving on, I guess."

She presses her lips together in a sad expression, and walks toward me to hug me from behind, leaning her head on my back.

"I'm sorry."

I sigh, and cover her hands with mine. "It's all right. I had to do this sooner or later."

"We'll do it together in the morning, all right? After the sun gets up. And we don't have to throw or give anything away. We can always just store it."

"What for?"

I turn towards her and she shrugs, smiling up at me. "Who knows? We're young, and life is full of second chances. Don't you think?"

I look at her, focusing on her face, her smile, her twinkling green eyes.

"Yeah. It really is."

She grins, and lets go of my waist, taking my hand. "Now, come on. We gotta get some sleep. We're getting up in a couple hours, and we have a big day ahead of us."

She leads me out of the room, and I follow her. I leave the door open behind me this time. There's no real reason to be closing doors anymore.

PREVIEW: *COMING HOME*

I rub my eyes with my palms. My head hurts so much. I feel like I work so hard, but I can't keep up with the number of files that come through here. I'm ridiculously slow to read, and to write; I'm such a dumb-ass, I should have never been stuck with a desk job.

I look at the clock and sigh in relief. At least, it's lunch time. I can drop this for a little while. I put down the file, and as soon as it touches the desk, the phone rings. I drop my head and bang my forehead on the desk. I'm cursed; I can never get any rest. I consider ignoring it since it's technically lunchtime, but I can see that it's Dow calling, so he probably has something urgent. I reach to pick up the phone, and I swear I'm going to rip his head off if he's just forgotten to look at the time again.

"Yeah?"

"Alex? There's a situation."

I groan and lean my head in my hands. Now I wish he had just forgotten to look at the time and had a simple question for me. Whatever this is, I don't have time to deal with it today.

"Is it an emergency?"

"Kind of, yeah."

"What is it? Can't it wait? We have the meeting with the Secretary of Defense later."

"I know. I can take care of that. This really can't wait, and it's more up your alley."

This could be good news. There are very few things in this world I want to do less than that meeting. If it saves me from that, I don't care what the emergency is; I'll take it.

"Fine. What is it?"

"It's a school. Tesla Elementary. There's been an accident."

"I'm guessing if you're calling me about it, it doesn't involve a broken arm and a jungle gym."

"No. It was two little boys, having a fight. Six years old. One of them electrocuted the other. With his hands."

That makes me regret the breakfast I had, and change my mind about wanting lunch. Six... that's about the age my son is, right about now. I haven't seen him in over five years. Kids that young shouldn't have to worry about getting into deadly fights.

"Shit. Is he... I mean... did he...?"

"No. The victim is still alive. He's in hospital with serious injuries, but his life isn't in jeopardy. It's the boy with the powers we need to take care of. The school wants him removed right away, the parents don't want to take him, and the victim's family is threatening to sue."

"What do you mean his parents don't want him?"

"I'm not sure. It's complicated. The secretary at the school just told me they're refusing to pick him up. She couldn't say any more, she really needed for us to come as soon as possible so I said I was sending someone right away."

"Fine. So what do I do with him? Do I just pick him up and bring him to the center?"

"That's the idea. But talk to the secretary and call the parents first. You need their permission to take the child from the school, or else we could be accused of kidnapping."

"All right. I'm on my way."

ACKNOWLEDGEMENTS

As usual, I find myself indebted to so many people who had a profound impact on the writing of this book, my life, and my career as a writer.

First of all, as always, a huge thank-you to those of you who read it first, and who helped give it birth. Manon, Marie-Claude, Marjolaine, you are the best critique group anyone could ask for. I am grateful to have you in my life. Thank you for the corrections, thank you for the encouragements, thank you for driving me on, whether or not you realized you were doing it.

A very special thank-you to Wakhanu and Stefano, who helped me with the authenticity for Kenya and Italy, two places I have never visited personally.

Also, in particular, I owe a huge debt of gratitude to Franck, who made the wonderful illustrations for all the books in the series so far. Thank you for your wonderful art, for taking the time to read the books, and your amazing friendship.

It seems appropriate that I should thank my family, whether by blood or by choice, since it's such an important theme of this book and series. So in that spirit, thank you to Phil, Émilie, Annie, mom, Loulou, Sandrine, Suzanne, Cédric, Maxime, Amélie, Véro, Gaetan, Bernard, Françoise, Félix, and my grandparents. Your encouragements, interest, and occasional hard truths keep me going.

A big thank you to my amazing colleagues from the Vanier and Rideau branches of the Ottawa Public Library.

As always, to Joelle, my partner in all things, thank you for being my creative sounding board, and the person that weathers all my dark moments. To you, and to Manue; you have a lot of responsibility to claim in the making of this particular story.

Last, but certainly not least, to the extraordinary team at Renaissance Press, thank you for pouring your hearts and souls into projects like these.

ABOUT THE AUTHOR

Caroline Fréchette is a sequential artist and author. She has published several short stories, both sequential and traditional, as well as two graphic novels, all on the French Canadian and European markets. She was the editor and director for the French Canadian literary magazine *Histoires à boire debout,* and works in a library. She has been teaching creative writing since 2005, and manages the writing page *Ice Cream for Zombies. Kindred Spirits* is the third book in the *Family by Choice* series. For more information, you can visit her website at carolinefrechette.com.

www.ingramcontent.com/pod-product-compliance
Lightning Source LLC
Chambersburg PA
CBHW060147260626
47160CB00001B/163